MARYSUE
RUCCI
BOOKS
SCRIBNER

Also by Suzanne Berne

The Dogs of Littlefield

A Crime in the Neighborhood

The Ghost at the Table

A Perfect Arrangement

Missing Lucile

The BLUE WINDOW

—A Novel—

SUZANNE BERNE

MARYSUE RUCCI BOOKS
SCRIBNER

New York London Toronto Sydney New Delhi

MARYSUE
RUCCI
BOOKS
SCRIBNER

An Imprint of Simon & Schuster, Inc.
1230 Avenue of the Americas
New York, NY 10020

First Marysue Rucci Books/Scribner hardcover edition January 2023

Interior design by Laura Levatino

Manufactured in the United States of America

1 3 5 7 9 10 8 6 4 2

Library of Congress Cataloging-in-Publication Data has been applied for.

ISBN 978-1-4767-9426-6
ISBN 978-1-4767-9428-0 (ebook)

For Evie

THE BLUE WINDOW

1

You could *assume* A stood for Adam. That's what the mother assumed if she found a note in the kitchen that said something like "Going out. A."

You could also assume A stood for the first letter of the alphabet, or A for anonymous. Or if you chose to get philosophical, you could posit that A meant "against" and that A was making a political statement by becoming A. If you were into physics, A might stand for something extra negative, like A for Anti-Matter.

Or if you had been on campus three weeks ago, A probably stood for Asshole.

Whatever it meant, A was not I. That was the point.

A did away with I.

I = Death.

You might *assume* the above statement was related to what happened during finals, on the lawn in front of the college library. But, A would suggest, obvious causal reasoning was as bad as complicated causal reasoning. Neither proved anything.

Plus, explanations turn into excuses.

Though if A were ever called upon to argue the case for rejecting "I" (while testifying before the student judiciary council, or say, Congress), this might be A's response: Erasing the first person is the only responsible moral position to take in a world full of moral positions, most of them absurd and all of them dangerous.

To wit: the enraged Twitter lava flow accompanying news coverage of any march, speech, parade, Sunday school Easter egg hunt.

Thus: It is profoundly unsafe to attach to anything, to identify as anything. Ergo: Show no concern. Have no opinion. The world is full of fake news, so don't make any. Hence: Eliminate "I"—the raised hand. The flag of existence.

Solution: A = Absent.

Actually, it had been easier than expected to shed the first-person pronoun and most possessive word forms, once A discovered that anything could be said in the passive voice. For instance, when the mother asked if A had walked Freddy while she was at work, A could answer, "It seems so" or "It seems not."

If she said, "What have you been doing all day?" A might say, "Naps occurred" or "Videos were watched." Added value of the passive voice—no definitely positive or negative statements. Although sometimes affirmation was necessary, like when the mother said, "Should I buy more avocados when I go to the grocery?" For those occasions, A used "Perchance," a word so affected it could only mean "Yes."

It hadn't even been that hard to give up self-related urges, i.e., fapping. Passivity breeds passivity.

This afternoon, when the mother arrived home from her office and opened the bedroom door to begin her usual interrogation, A reported: Lunch had been eaten. The trash had not been taken out. Freddy had not been walked. Job applications to Starbucks and Wegmans had yet to be emailed.

"Bad choices were made," she said, and came into the room to sit on the edge of the bed. She looked at T-shirts, dirty underwear on the floor, sighed, and said she'd had a long day. "I won't bore you with the details." But then, as usual, she did.

The men in her divorce therapy group couldn't understand why "mansplaining" was a problem (Why not explain things that need explaining?); a client arrived forty-five minutes late for a session and then wondered if he still had to pay for it; another client spilled coffee on the office rug and went on talking as if nothing had happened. And then, as the mother was getting into her car to drive home, a huge SUV pulled in right behind her, forcing her to inch out of her parking spot while the driver stood on the sidewalk to make sure she didn't scratch his bumper. Have a good day! she called out as she drove away.

A watched her mouth open and close with the familiar feeling of being made of the thinnest, clearest crystal and every word spoken within hearing being a small jagged rock. Important to remember that she was not trying to be brutal, or even tedious. She was modeling forbearance. The key to survival, she liked to say, is accommodation (though she also said she loved her work and loved her clients). But in her determination to be understanding no matter what the circumstances, she sometimes gave an impression of deficiency, as if she had forgotten how to behave otherwise. Automatic goodness was not really goodness. But what was it?

Oppression. That's what it was.

She'd smiled, shook her head. Said she was looking forward to a quiet evening, to having a glass of wine. Maybe after dinner the two of them could watch something? How about an old movie? There was a stealthy drift of her lemony perfume as she leaned forward and reached for A's hand, which A slid under the sheet before she could reach it.

"Sorry if I'm being intrusive, sweetheart." She sat back, still smiling, though her eyes looked unsteady. "But I miss talking with you."

These types of assaults were increasing and growing more cunning. Fatigue setting in. Every morning the same routine: wait for the mother to leave for work, then cereal in bed, videos, lunch in bed, videos, followed by her return and the afternoon offensive ("Going for a walk, want to come?"), a short reprieve, and then more attacks, like the one tonight at dinner ("So I've got some ideas of what might be fun for us to do together"). Until windows finally went black. End of Day 18 in Year 2019 of the Battle Against the Self, beset on all sides by demoralizing reminders of familial attachment.

Exile: the only remedy.

Meanwhile, until such plan could be formed, filial relationship must be abbreviated further. Ditto with the father. Designate by glyphs? Math coordinates? Chromosomal contribution? Yes. The ultimate reduction: X = Mother. Y = Father. For other human associates use first initials, especially for former friends (FF), especially from college.

Except one, for whom there could be no letter, no referent. Only a blank, a gap, the nausea of nothing. . . .

Time to abbreviate even thought.

LATER THAT NIGHT, while padding barefoot down the upstairs hall on the way to take a leak, A was halted by the unmistakable sounds of Being Under Discussion.

"Let's not pressure him." X was talking to Y in her bedroom on speakerphone.

"He's going through something."

"You keep saying that, Lorna." Y's speakerphone voice was both remote and too loud, like someone calling from a space module. "He's been home since the end of May."

Y himself was back in Seattle after two weeks in Japan, spent at a medical conference in Tokyo and then sightseeing with his research assistant/girlfriend, Angelica. "I've tried calling and texting. But I never hear anything. What's he do all day?"

X said that as far as she knew he stayed in his room watching videos on his laptop. Hadn't been seeing friends. Would hardly step outside. His acne had also gotten worse.

"I don't know what's going on," she said, lowering her voice so that A had to lean against the door panel, "but he seems incredibly unhappy. I suggested going back to Dr. Melman, but he refuses to see anybody."

"We've been through this kind of thing before," said Y. "Remember when those kids quit his band?"

A grimaced, but stayed pressed against the door.

"This is different," said X. "He doesn't even sound like himself."

"How do you mean?"

"Almost like he's not the one who's speaking."

"I could try to find him some kind of internship out here." Y sounded doubtful.

"If I can barely get him out of his room for dinner, Roger, I don't think I can get him on a plane to Seattle. Maybe you could come for a visit?"

A brief exchange concerning logistics: flights, car rentals, the difficulties Y faced taking time off from the lab after having been away. What's today, Friday? Next week might work, no, the week after would be better. This was so similar to phone negotiations overheard during the past five years that A stopped listening and began contemplating a foray to the kitchen for a banana. Self-erasure required constant scourges, hence yesterday's decision to become vegan. Hunger, however, now constant. Good. Hunger focuses the mind. When one is starving, all other thoughts seem immaterial.

Conversation shift: X now reporting a phone call from someone named Dennis, a Vermont neighbor of her mother's; apparently she'd tried to rehang a bird feeder blown down from a tree branch and had fallen off a ladder. Possible sprained ankle.

Questions from Y: Doctor consulted? Have you spoken with her?

X: Won't answer the phone. You know how she is.

New Problem: Grandmother. How to designate? From forty-four autosomal chromosomes, what contribution from her? What region of genome? Scandinavian. X's father Anglo something. Y's parents: Polish Russian Jewish Who Knows. No straightforward input from any quarter, instead must consider genetic recombination, chromosomal exchange segments, hybrids . . . i.e., a complicated inheritance.

On the other side of the door, the conversation had shifted once again. Y was speaking: "Is it a girlfriend, you think?"

A's head filled with static, at leaf-blower volume. Barely clearing in time to hear X say she didn't know.

"Any sign he's *had* a girlfriend?"

"Not that I know of."

"Do you think he could be gay?" Y was proceeding in his usual systematic way. "When did your brother decide he was gay?"

"He didn't decide he was gay," said X. "Anyway, I don't think that's it."

A stepped back from the door but continued to hover in the hallway, face itching, slightly frightened by such parental ignorance and bafflement.

"I think he's depressed," X said.

"Depressed? Like *depressed*?"

"Well, not clinically, I'd say it's situational. But something's wrong. The other day when we were driving home from the dermatologist's? I asked if he wanted to stop somewhere for lunch. He didn't answer, so I said, 'Do you care about stopping or not?' And he said he didn't care about anything."

"Kids his age always say stuff like that," interrupted Y.

"Wait. So I tried to make a joke of it. I said, 'Not even onion rings?' And *he* said, 'The only way to live in this crap world is to care about nothing.'"

Silence.

"Roger? I'm worried something happened at school. Something he feels he can't talk about. Maybe he needs—"

"He needs a job and a girlfriend," said Y. "That's what he needs."

A made an involuntary, throttled noise. From the other side of the door came a sudden hush. X must have detected eavesdropping, lifting her chin to listen, like when Freddy whined at the back door to come in. But after a moment she began speaking softly once more. "That's not very helpful. I'm really worried about him."

"Sorry," said Y, "but he's nineteen. He can't hide in his room all summer."

She must be glad about the eavesdropping. Maybe she hoped Y would now offer some actual advice that A would overhear and then follow while pretending not to. Like when Y recommended pre-med courses first semester, and instead A registered for Interpretative Dance, Ceramics, and something called Ecology of the Mind. Then dropped everything but Freshman Writing and French to sign up for Chem and Bio, plus labs, but not before sending Y that original course list.

X said, "I've been trying every way I can think of to get him to talk to me."

"So what if you forget about talking and just try to distract him?" Y was the one who sounded distracted. From the background came the clatter of someone noisily clearing plates. "Stop worrying about him and maybe he'll start thinking he's actually okay."

X gave a frustrated sigh. "That is not how it works."

"Then act like you're worried about something else. Say you have to go up to Vermont to check on your mother. See if he'll go with you. Get him out in the fresh air."

A snorted quietly. As if. Meanwhile, solution: G = both genome and grandmother. G could also stand for her nickname, Grootie. Short for *Grootmoeder*. Dutch for "old lady from whom one received DNA."

"How am I supposed to convince him to come with me?" said X. "And I certainly can't leave him here on his own."

More plate-clearing on Y's end of the line. "Tell him you can't go alone."

"What?"

"You still haven't told him, have you? What she did? Well, maybe now's the time. Tell him you need the moral support."

X said she would think about it.

More discussion of travel logistics and why traveling from Seattle this week was impossible. Several references to "we" that did not include X. No further mention of G, or what she'd done, or why X might need "moral support."

But G had now lumbered into A's mind and refused to leave it. Stooped, squarish, broad-faced, in brown wool pants and a brown cardigan that smelled of mothballs, with scuffed leather buttons dangling loose from black threads. Short gray hair that looked like she cut it herself. Pink-rimmed oversized glasses with smudgy lenses. Arriving every year on Thanksgiving Day in an ancient tank-like Volvo with splits in the upholstery patched with duct tape. Sitting silently among whatever other guests had been invited for dinner, a Kleenex tucked into one sleeve, extracted at intervals to wipe her nose. If a question was directed toward her she pretended not to hear it or answered in monosyllables. The next morning she'd be gone, rarely mentioned until next Thanksgiving.

Though following A's seventh-grade visit to Washington, DC, and the Holocaust Museum, X revealed that G's older sister had been a nurse in the Resistance. The sister typed coded messages onto medicine jar labels and gave the jars to G to deliver by bicycle across Amsterdam; they'd also sometimes hidden children in a kitchen cabinet. When soldiers came to arrest her sister and father, G escaped down the back stairs and bicycled out of the city to a convent school, where nuns took her in. Under intense questioning, X insisted she knew nothing else. G had related these events when X was a little girl, but if you asked G about it now she'd say she didn't remember. This turned out to be true. The next Thanksgiving, when asked how old she was when the war began, G stared through her smudgy glasses from across the table and continued forking up brussels sprouts. A spent the rest of the meal trying to imagine her as a girl on a bicycle.

Was this what Y was referring to, by "what she did"? Had they forgotten that A already knew? Shared senior moment.

Conversation between X and Y seemed to be winding down and A was moving off down the hall when Y said abruptly, "So how are *you* feeling."

"How am *I* feeling?" echoed X, sounding startled.

A hesitated beside the framed charcoal sketch hanging near the bathroom, drawn by X as a girl of the farm in Virginia where she'd grown up. Four chimneys rose above a scribble of trees and a smear of pasture, with a wavy stroke to indicate the Blue Ridge Mountains.

"Yes," said Y. "How are you feeling?"

Two potato-shaped clouds floated above the mountains. Strange question. Was Y asking how X felt about Angelica, his now live-in research assistant/girlfriend, the one making all that plate-clearing racket to show she was pissed about Dinner Interruptus?

"I feel fine," X said.

Or was Y literally asking how X was feeling? Like whether she had a cold? Epidemiologists were always thinking about people getting sick.

"I'm fine," X repeated. "How are you feeling?"

Downstairs on reconnaissance, gathered supplies for the night: a banana, a jar of peanut butter, and two apples. Stuck to the counter by the fruit bowl was one of X's "To Do" lists, jotted neatly on a yellow Post-it: *Call plumber for dishwasher, order mulch, dentist appt, call Roger, call Dr. Melman (?).* With a tremor of contempt, picked up the Post-it by one corner and dropped it in the trash.

Back to bed to resume watching an episode of *Cupcake Wars*. Self-erasure required watching only videos of absolutely no interest, viz yesterday's scourge had included *Slow TV: Salmon Fishing* and a YouTube video about how to rescue an earring lost down a drain. The problem was how to avoid getting caught up in them.

While waiting to find out whose Swedish Princess Cupcake would come out on top, A's phone dinged. No one but X and Y texted anymore. Not since the immediate aftermath of That Night, when phone had to be buried at the bottom of the laundry hamper. All messages deleted.

Going to VT tomrow to see Grootie.

A peered at the screen, awaiting another text. Rarely could X limit herself to just one.

Sprained ankle. May stay a few days.

How much food was in the house?

New air bubble: *I'd like you to come along.*

A sat for several minutes without responding. Because here, at last, was a true scourge, a scourge of the hair shirt variety, instead of fake ones like watching golf tournaments. It didn't matter that X had probably decided to go to Vermont because she thought it would be "helpful," "a chance to do something together"—it was still a scourge. In fact, more of a scourge. The logic was plain: If the self was outraged at the prospect of spending five or six hours in the car with X, driving to Vermont to visit an old woman in a house full of mothballs and used Kleenex, if the self could conceive of nothing more hideous, then to be vanquished, the self must submit to this ordeal.

Indifference was the goal. If A could be said to have a goal. Herein lay the premise of self-denial: If death of I equals death of hope, then death of hope equals death of shame, and thus death of shame equals freedom of soul.

Maybe. Maybe it worked like that.

Another ding.

I could use the company.

2

Though it was not yet nine, Lorna had already walked and fed Freddy, watered the garden, run to the supermarket, and texted her Monday and Tuesday clients about canceling or rescheduling their appointments. Now she was kneeling before the open refrigerator, adding peppers, celery, carrots to the shopping bag beside her, thinking over the two dinners she planned to make in Vermont, at the same time consulting the list in her hand and wondering whether she should have bought a second bottle of wine. She couldn't remember how far Marika lived from the nearest town. As she closed the produce drawer, she sank backward onto the wooden floor and for a few moments sat cross-legged in a square of sunlight, staring at the quiet, reasonable kitchen around her. Its counters of green stone and white cabinets made the kitchen feel cool despite the warmth of the day, and familiarly soothing, with its accumulated smells of toast and coffee.

She'd slept badly the night before, lying awake thinking about the drive ahead, trying to reconcile her reluctance at the idea of going to Vermont with a conflicted sense of duty toward Marika—who had not herself called to ask for help, who probably did not want it—mixed with gratitude for Roger's suggestion that she seize this opportunity to get Adam out of the house. Mixed also with uneasy amazement that Adam had agreed to come. His statement about caring about nothing turned her stomach to ice whenever she thought of it, which was all the time.

Why do you think you feel that way? she'd asked on the way back from the dermatologist's. No answer. She'd wanted to stop the car and shake him, and then pull him into her arms. She'd wanted to say: You have to care about *something*. Instead she'd said, probably too evenly, or as Adam would say, too "therapist-y": It must be painful to feel you care about nothing.

If he can say it aloud, she told herself, he trusts you can hear it. Just keep supporting him. A change of scene will make a difference. A chance to get him out of his own head.

She stood up and shut the refrigerator door, glancing at the rest of her list: *Leash, water bowl, dog food, mail/newspaper. Empty trash. Pack. Set alarm.* All taken care of except for packing and the alarm.

"Let's go," she said aloud. From his dog bed by the back door, Freddy stood up arthritically and gave her a hopeful look.

As for Marika, she thought, heading upstairs, tending to an ailing elderly person was of course the right thing to do. Children first depend on parents and then, often quite suddenly, parents have to turn to children for help, even parents like Marika, who had done very little parenting. All of that was clear enough. Even clear was Lorna's guilt for feeling obligated to make this trip, rather than willing, and her awareness that she probably would not be going if visiting Marika had not proved unexpectedly convenient.

Naming your emotions, she often told clients, makes them easier to govern. And yet words like *guilt*, *obligation* seemed to have no relationship to the heavy, dark refusal that reared inside her at the thought of spending hours with Marika, asking questions that would go unanswered, fetching things that would prove to be unwanted, fixing dinner that would go unremarked upon, cleaning up afterward.

"But we'll make the best of it," she said to Freddy, who had followed her up the stairs and stood in the bedroom doorway slowly waving his tail.

He was a large golden retriever with a mild white face, an obliging, unobtrusive, even somehow tactful dog; he rarely barked and did not beg, and spent much of his time lying on the front hall carpet into which, despite his size, he often seemed to disappear. Though he was now anxiously eyeing her overnight bag, lying open on the unmade bed.

"Don't worry," Lorna paused to scratch his head, "you're coming with us."

Her feelings about this visit, she decided, opening her top dresser drawer to pull out her nightgown, were understandably irrational. So little was being asked—a few days of helping an old woman with a sprained ankle—and yet the prospect was exhausting, and seemed to raise the possibility of something unmanageable. She had enough to take care of with her clients, and with Adam.

We've been through this before, Roger said last night. He's being dramatic. Kids always say stuff like that. Get him some fresh air.

Well, there would be plenty of fresh air up in Vermont on a lake.

"And we can always turn around, if it doesn't work out," she said, once again addressing Freddy, still hovering apprehensively in the doorway. It wouldn't be the first time.

She returned to packing her overnight bag. Sandals, swimsuit. June in northern Vermont can be cold. Socks, sweater. It might rain. Raincoat. She'd tried twice yesterday evening to call Marika, unsuccessfully. Probably for the best. Marika would have tried to discourage her from visiting and now that Adam had agreed to come along, Lorna was set on going. Though Adam's sudden compliance remained puzzling. After two and a half weeks of hardly speaking to her, he'd said yes as soon as she'd asked. Why? He must realize this visit to Vermont meant hours in the car with her, each way, and sharing a motel room. The answer could be simply boredom; after nearly three weeks at home he'd finally had enough of watching YouTube videos and eating Cheerios in bed. But intuition suggested a strategy on his part, a further evasion.

Fine, Lorna thought, adding her sun hat to the bag and a pair of sneakers. Evade away, you're still coming with me. And in any case, when it comes to evasions, I know all about them. She looked at her closet. They might decide to go out to dinner somewhere, although this possibility was hard to imagine with Marika's sprained ankle. But she took out a blazer and a pair of flats. It had been clear for some time that her overnight bag was not going to fit everything she needed, but for several minutes she tried to close it, anyway.

IN A CORNER OF THE BASEMENT, behind Adam's drum kit and Roger's old fishing rods, was wedged her large black suitcase, four or five cardboard boxes stacked on top of it. Lorna had forgotten about the boxes, brought down from the attic when the roof started leaking last fall, along with all sorts of junk, some of which had been up there since they moved in two decades ago. Cleaning out the basement was a chore she'd tried to assign Adam his first week at home, thinking it might be a distraction. In response he'd gazed at her as if she had not spoken, as if he himself were not there, as if "basement" were a concept that did not exist.

The boxes were closed, but not sealed. She examined them with weary mistrust. The top one was full of old shoes, which should be thrown away; the next two, old books. Another box held folded sweaters and a small round hatbox. She held the sweaters up one at a time, pretending to look for moth holes, trying to ignore the hatbox.

It had a black lacquered lid, and had once belonged to her grandmother, offered to Lorna for "keepsakes." Inside was a welter of faded birthday cards and foxed snapshots of school friends. Postcards. A mimeographed graduation program. Girl Scout badges. An old key ring with a green plastic horseshoe: WELCOME TO PONY

CLUB. You do not have time for this, Lorna told herself, looking at the creased yellow cover of the spiral memo pad in her hand, already opening it.

Lists of girls she'd wanted to have as friends. Boys in third grade she'd liked. Names she would give a dog, when she got to have one. Jokes to tell at sleepovers. Fitness exercises.

On the last page, in rounded ink letters, a little smeared, one more list: "How to Be a Better Girl":

close mouth while chewing
say please and thank you
keep hair out of face
change underwear every day
do not slurp soup
do not ask for seconds while others are eating firsts

Lorna flipped the memo pad closed, briefly shutting her eyes. Several of these reminders had come by way of dinners at friends' houses and gently mortifying comments from their mothers, who were, of course, only trying to be helpful. She knew she should feel moved by this list, by the image of that little girl gripping a pen and getting ink on her fingers, trying to be "better" in a world she believed was ready to reject her for not being clean enough, neat enough, polite enough, for having lost her own mother because she had been, in some unfathomable but cataclysmic way, inconsiderate. But its earnest pathos only made her more tired.

She was about to drop the pad back into the hatbox, when it occurred to her that Adam might think the list was funny. After another hesitation she slipped the pad into her pocket, closed the hatbox, and stacked it with the rest of the boxes back in the corner behind Adam's drums. He used to like stories about when she was a girl, especially the embarrassing ones.

Roger's methodical voice followed her as she carried the suitcase upstairs into the bedroom. You still haven't told him, have you? Tell him you need the moral support.

Easy for you to say, she thought grimly. Every time I open my mouth, I can see him stop listening. Whatever I do will be wrong.

In that case, Roger responded. You can't lose.

She dragged the big suitcase onto the bed, unzipped it, and then stood gazing into its black interior.

THE WATER WENT SUDDENLY COLD as Lorna was rinsing shampoo out of her hair. Adam must have flushed the toilet. At least he was awake, although probably he'd done nothing about packing.

While she dried her hair she thought about what to say in the car on the way to Vermont. Adam, I can tell you're upset about something. Adam, whatever it is that's making you unhappy—even if you think it's the worst thing in the world—I'm here to tell you it won't last. Believe me, I've been there. Adam, are you listening?

Most likely he would find the timing suspicious. He'd think that by revealing something unfortunate about herself, she was hoping he'd talk about whatever had happened to him. Which was the truth. He might get angry. He might feel sorry for her. Probably he'd demand to know why she hadn't told him before.

Did you like just forget *that your mother deserted you?*

The old Adam, anyway, might say something sarcastic like that.

No, I didn't forget. But there are things you can decide not to think about.

Disappearance, not desertion, was how Lorna had thought of it as a child. One day Marika was there, the next she had vanished. Leaving behind a strangeness so profound that for several days no one spoke of it. She was simply gone. No place laid for her at breakfast. No sound of her voice on the stairs. No smell of her cigarettes or lipstick prints on coffee cups. No sunglasses on the hall table or hairbrush on her dresser. Although the longer she was missing the more she was everywhere.

On the third night, Lorna and Wade were called into the den after dinner and their father told them to sit down on the old plaid sofa between his bookcases, filled with biographies of generals and accounts of Virginia battles. He sat in his matching plaid chair by the fireplace and lit his pipe, making his usual show of puffing to get it going, holding the match flame above the pipe's bowl. On the mantel, a glass case held his Purple Heart and Bronze Star, awarded to him as a captain in the 28th Infantry Division after he'd been shot in the Ardennes. Because he was deaf, for a long time Lorna had believed the Ardennes was part of the inner ear.

Well, he said finally, pulling on his pipe. He puffed out a cloud of sweet tobacco smoke. Your mother might be gone for a while.

Pinkish summer twilight pressed against the window screens. Beside her on the sofa, Wade picked at a scab on his lower lip. He had just turned thirteen, but his big head and black horn-rimmed glasses made him look older, except for the babyish folds under his chin.

Fact is, their father added mildly, puffing out another fragrant blue cloud. Don't think she'll be back.

That was all the information ever offered. *Water under the bridge*, their grandmother might say, if the subject came up.

Lorna leaned toward the indistinct face in the steamy bathroom mirror. Another reason she had kept this story mostly to herself was that it was so hard to explain. Usually people can account for their life-altering events. She hung up her towel and got dressed; a few minutes later she examined herself again in the bathroom mirror, now clear, as she put on a small pair of silver hoop earrings. She bent closer to apply eyeliner, and then blush to her cheeks.

It wasn't that she'd kept Marika's disappearance a secret from Adam, so much as waited for the right time to tell him. That was also the truth. If he accused her of keeping secrets, she could remind him of his childhood separation anxieties. Do you remember those bedtime debates we used to have, about whether I'd still be there in the morning? *But a burglar could crawl through your window and stab you. An asteroid could crash into your bed.* And I would tell you: Those are fears, not facts. I am not going anywhere.

Night after night he'd made her promise to be there when he woke up. She was almost forty when he was born; her age relative to his friends' parents may have been worrying. In any case, stories about vanishing mothers would have frightened him, and he'd never seemed curious about his grandmother, aside from the story Lorna told him of Marika's experience during the war. Also, children take parental deprivation to heart and she hadn't wanted him to feel guilty for having a mother when she hadn't had one. Then after Roger moved to Seattle, she hadn't wanted to raise the specter of abandonment.

On the other hand, she thought, smoothing concealer over the bluish shadows under her eyes, if she'd told Adam years ago about Marika's disappearance, he would have found it disturbing, but he would have let her reassure him, and gradually that story would have become simply a story. Now, because it had been withheld, it would be invested with too much significance—seen to be essential, as explaining "everything." Especially her attachment to him, her willingness to drop whatever she was doing the moment he called her, her habit of taking him too seriously, as he liked to complain.

But you didn't take him seriously enough, Lorna thought, stepping back to regard the pale, dark-eyed woman in the mirror. That's the problem. You pretended you'd always be there to reassure him, instead of helping him reassure himself. That was your mistake.

In the front hall by the newel post, she encountered Adam's open backpack. Twice that morning she had sent texts reminding him to get his things together, and surprisingly he had done so. It was not prying, she reasoned, if she looked into an open backpack. Inside were a black T-shirt that didn't look clean, a laptop charger, and a pair of underwear. Missing from his backpack were a toothbrush, a sweatshirt, socks, pajamas, and also his laptop, to which he must be socketed this minute.

"Is this all you're bringing with you?" she called up the stairs.

THEY WERE IN THE CAR by ten, Freddy snoring in the backseat. Fortunately, the motel Lorna had booked allowed dogs. During the day, they could keep Freddy leashed outside Marika's house. She explained this plan to Adam as they drove toward Route 128, mostly for the illusion of chatting. But after a few minutes he put in his earbuds and closed his eyes.

Adam kept his eyes shut for the next two hours. Lorna listened to the news on the radio and tried to think of how to bring up the subject of his grandmother. At some point she drifted into thinking of when Wade had been sent away to school, at the end of the summer after Marika left. An awful scene: Wade lying on the floor in the front hall, dressed in a gray cadet uniform, screaming that he was going to be eaten by cannibals. Granny standing over him in her housecoat and sneakers, repeating, *Look on the bright side.* Their father holding his pipe, looking relieved that he couldn't hear anything. *Save me!* Wade had shrieked, turning to Lorna hiding behind the newel post at the bottom of the stairs.

A few miles after they crossed into New Hampshire, Lorna stopped at a convenience store next to the gas station outside of Lebanon and bought sandwiches and two plastic bottles of water. Adam stared at the bottled water and when she handed him his sandwich, he said tonelessly, "Ham and cheese."

"I thought you liked ham and cheese." Then remembered that two days ago he'd mumbled he was going vegan. She gave him her turkey with lettuce and tomato, first subtracting the turkey.

"But there's mayo on it," she warned.

Vacant gaze.

"Mayonnaise? If you're vegan you don't eat mayonnaise because there are eggs in it. I'm sorry I forgot. But maybe," she continued carefully, "because you just became vegan, we could negotiate a few non-vegan foods, for now?" Thinking that if she could win some flexibility from him on this issue it might lead to other unbendings. "I bought a coconut custard pie for dessert tonight," she added. "Would that be okay?" A possible twitch of assent.

They sat eating in the car.

"Seems hot for June," she remarked.

"Climate change," he muttered, with another pointed look at the water bottles.

"I thought it was because we were in *Lebanon*," she smiled. "Get it?"

He narrowed his eyes, emanating disgust. Which was preferable to emanating blankness and answering like a zombie whenever she asked a question. The only way to provoke a reaction from him these days was by trying to be funny, though the reaction was a wince. It reminded her of when she was pregnant and drank orange juice if she hadn't felt the baby move in a while because it made him kick.

As they finished their sandwiches, she asked, "Have you been using that cream Dr. Knapp prescribed? Because I think it's helping."

Misstep. Any overt encouragement caused immediate shutdown. He was back to that vacant gaze. Gathering up their sandwich wrappers and napkins into a bag, Lorna again found herself wondering why he had agreed to come with her.

She got out of the car to throw the bag in a trash can at the gas station, glad for a few moments away from Adam's repressive muteness. It was clear he was suffering and that he was punishing himself as a way to address his suffering; also clear that he was unaware that self-flagellation usually ends up flagellating those nearby.

Or maybe he did know? Maybe his idea of self-punishment required him to continually reject help, which required help to be continually offered.

She had, of course, conjectures about the source of his unhappiness. Humiliating sexual experience; ostracism following a public fight with his roommate, Dan, a skinny, puritanically progressive boy with a lot of sheep-colored hair, whom Adam had sometimes referred to as Q-tip; failed exams; reported for drinking by his RA. But in either of the last two cases, she would hear about it, so why hide what happened. He'd always confided in her about fights with friends, so most likely it wasn't that. As for sexual rejection, he'd probably at least hint, in the form of a question ("Why do some girls . . . ?"). And whatever Roger thought, if Adam were gay, she believed he would have told her. They had always been close, and coming out was nothing like what Wade must have experienced at that age. In college nowadays, at least according to Adam, it was considered weird to be straight.

Was it possible he was unhappy about Roger's decision to move in with Angelica? Grieving the loss of a lingering fantasy that his parents might get back together someday?

Whatever the reason, he was depressed and she didn't know why, which was frightening. Yet, showing that she was frightened would make him think she couldn't handle whatever it was he was feeling.

So act like you're worried about something else, Roger had said.

"How about driving the rest of the way?" she asked from outside the car, leaning down to Adam's window. He shrugged. "You could use some highway practice." Though he didn't like driving her car, a VW wagon with manual transmission, which she loved for its boxy solidity, and because a stick shift gave you more control. But he had taken his driver's ed lessons on an automatic, and still had trouble shifting gears and remembering to release the clutch.

Probably to avoid more discussion about driving, he opened his backpack.

"Crap," he muttered, as they pulled out of the parking lot. "Laptop not here." The charger's white cord was still entangled with his underwear, but no laptop. He had forgotten it.

"Well, if you left it at home, maybe that's not such a bad thing." Lorna checked the rearview mirror, trying to mask her enthusiasm for this mishap. "It might be nice for you to get outside more. The lake is supposed to be good for fishing. Weren't you watching a fishing show the other day?"

She thought of Roger's tangle of fishing tackle in the basement. "We should have brought along your father's fishing rods. He used to love fly-fishing." Momentarily encouraged by the idea of Adam fishing, she added, "Did you know there's supposed to be a monster in the middle of Lake Champlain?" She smiled again. "You could try catching it."

Then saw by his drawn expression that her efforts to be funny were beginning to cause actual pain.

Sorry, she thought, staring back at the road. Sorry, sorry.

3

X was making some joke about fishing for monsters as A tried to absorb the blow of no laptop for the next few days. It was X who put the backpack in the car. Into which the laptop had, almost definitely, been placed that morning. Fine. Whatever. Phone still in possession. Better for watching videos, anyway. The smaller the people, the less it seemed to matter what happened to them.

"Speaking of your father," X said, once they were back on the highway. (Had they been speaking of him?) "I guess you know about Angelica?"

Obviously. Scowled at the good-luck charm swinging from the rearview mirror, a jade owl with a red-thread tail. *She's a lot of fun*, Y kept saying on the way from the airport at spring break, as if Angelica were a new edition of Monopoly. Tall, taller than Y, thirtyish, with disturbingly white teeth, lots of shiny black hair, and clanky silver bracelets that slid up and down her arms. One night they went for dinner at a Chinese restaurant and Angelica insisted on everyone reading aloud their fortune cookie fortunes. Hers was: *You will soon get a big surprise*. Wow! clanked Angelica. Wonder what *that* will be? A month later, a text from Y saying he and Angelica were moving in together.

"I think your father is pretty serious about her." X raised her voice as a truck roared by, passing so close that it shook the car. "I just wondered if you have any feelings about it."

Pause. "Okay. Just asking." Quietly Concerned Smile.

Shut eyes, best defense.

But after half an hour of listening to a TED Talk on lice ("It is thought lice would be among the only survivors of a nuclear winter") and looking out the window at nothing but trees and an occasional moose-crossing sign, A was bored enough to sit up when X asked, "So perchance could we talk for a few minutes?

"You're probably wondering," she said, "why we don't see Grootie more often."

Had not been wondering. If considered the matter at all, assumed they saw G only once a year because she didn't like driving from Vermont to Massachusetts in her prehistoric Volvo. As to why they never visited her, figured they hadn't been invited.

"There's something I haven't told you." X was staring at the road, a pair of black sunglasses on top of her head, short brown hair blowing around her face from her half-open window. What would Dr. Knapp see if presented with X as a dermatology patient? Moth-colored freckles dappling her cheeks (sun damage). Mole above right eyebrow (suspicious?).

"And since we're spending a few days with her," X went on, "and something might come up, I should probably let you know."

Fan of creases at the eyes, skin faintly pleated around the mouth. Prescription: Moisturizer. Palliative care.

"Basically, it's that your grandmother left us when we were children. I was seven. Wade was thirteen. We woke up one morning and she was gone."

For a moment, A was too stunned to hide it.

"Why?"

"That's a good question. And the truth is, I don't really know." X shook her head regretfully. "It wasn't something anyone ever talked about."

Mouth hanging open. Close it, you idiot.

"How could you not have talked about it?"

"I know it seems strange," X said matter-of-factly, as if it wasn't strange at all. "My father was hard of hearing, as you know, which made it difficult to ask him anything. And back then people didn't explain things to children the way they would now.

"Also," she went on, still in that matter-of-fact voice, "I didn't see her again for a long time. More than thirty years."

What explanation could there have been? A thought wildly, staring out the window at a stockade of pine trees. Mothers didn't leave children and not see them again for more than thirty years. Fathers, yes, maybe, but not mothers. Wasn't it against the law? As annoying as X could be, it was impossible to imagine doing without her; even now, the thought that she would some day die produced an instant labyrinth of grief.

"She went to California, apparently." Squinting into the sun, X lowered her sunglasses over her eyes. "I think she taught French at a school out there. But when you were about a year old, I got a postcard saying she'd moved to Vermont, with an address and phone number, and I decided to bring you up to meet her. It didn't go very well, but after that she started coming for Thanksgiving."

A pressed back against the seat, overwhelmed by a sickening wave of rage, pity, and helplessness, subverting any attempt at disinterest. What to object to more: this outrageous information, or just hearing it now?

Not prepared, not prepared at all for this one.

Though, on second thought, why such a shock? There had been signs: the once-a-year Thanksgiving visits that barely lasted a day. And that G was hardly mentioned the rest of the time. Perfect example: that charcoal sketch in the upstairs hall, with its scribbled rooftop and wavy mountains. X used to point out invisible things in the dark blurry lines. Pastures and a creek, a spring-fed pool, the stables, an old family graveyard. Described jokes she and her brother played on their father, who tried to hide he was deaf by nodding to anything said to him. *Dad, we're going to set the barn on fire, okay?* Told stories about how she and Wade would hide in the hayloft to spy on the stable hands, who Wade insisted were Russian agents. They would drop straw on their heads and jump across stacked hay bales pretending to escape from the KGB. Once, Wade tricked her into leaping off the hayloft ladder into a pile of fresh "horse apples," ruining her new saddle shoes. Otherwise, she hardly mentioned Wade, either. But not a single story, ever, about her mother.

"So why didn't you say anything before?"

"I wanted you to have a grandmother," said X reasonably behind her sunglasses. "And I guess I wanted you to like her."

The weird thing was, *had* always kind of liked her. Partly because of that story about her as a girl in Amsterdam, which had made A feel secretly related to Anne Frank, but mostly because she hardly said anything. At some point during Thanksgiving she'd crank herself up to mutter, How's school? A would say, Meh, and that would be the end of it.

Though one year her visit had coincided with the French Phase of tenth grade, following the Drummer Phase and the brief life of the Perps. Not a bad band. They had a lot of sound, someone said. And they were getting better, until the other kids accused A of being too bossy and not being able to keep a beat. Refusal to speak English for two weeks afterward, to discourage advice from X on dealing with disappointment. A resistance tactic G seemed to support. During dinner she'd come out with the useful remark, *Il pleut comme vache qui pisse*. It's raining like a pissing cow.

"Did *you* like her," A asked, reluctantly, "when you were a kid?"

X frowned. "I don't really remember. I did think she was beautiful. She had long blond hair back then and she used to wear pink lipstick."

Beautiful? Unsuccessful attempt to superimpose long blond hair and pink lipstick on the broad gloomy old face behind the Thanksgiving turkey.

"Of course I've tried to talk to her," said X, as if in response to a question she'd hoped to be asked. "Over the years. But whenever I've tried to ask her anything, she says she doesn't remember. Which may, actually, be true." She began explaining recent neuroscientific discoveries about the effect of stress on memory.

Involuntary interruption: "So why do you *think* she left?"

"Well, Wade used to insist she was a spy." X turned to give a too-encouraging smile. "He thought everyone was a spy in those days. It was the Cold War. We lived in northern Virginia. Some of our neighbors probably were spies." Another smile. "But most likely it was because she met somebody. The usual story."

Where they had been in the woods before, they plunged now into a true forest. The trees were mostly pine, densely needled. Sunlight shafted down greenly, as if they were driving underwater.

"It was hardest on Wade," X went on, peering at the road as if she were having trouble seeing in the shade. "I think he was afraid she left because of him."

She stopped for a moment, and then said, "He was always in trouble for getting into people's things, especially hers. Going through her dresser drawers, pretending he was looking for clues. If she caught him at it she'd go after him with a hairbrush."

Time to end this conversation, which was threatening all resolution to stay detached from everything, and would soon lead to corrupting questions like, How do *you* feel about hearing all this, sweetheart? Also, the TED Talk about lice had incited scalp-itch.

X paused to remove a strand of hair from the corner of her mouth. It was loud in the car from wind rushing through the open windows. Ask to turn on the air conditioner instead? Probably the car would feel even more claustrophobic.

"Children usually act out in some way in a family crisis," she said. "Wade certainly did. It got so bad my father sent him away to military school, although I think it was more because he was worried Wade was gay."

Outside the window, a clearing in the pines, a meadow with a stream. It was obvious what she was doing: Another calculated assault, an attempt to extract "talk."

Now she was on to psychological theories: Trauma repeats itself. Because G had still been a child when she lost her family, she'd reenacted that trauma by abandoning her own children. It was difficult to care for others when you hadn't been cared for yourself, etc., etc. As for not talking about what happened to her during the war, probably she had blocked those memories. It was also true that people who suffered a trauma often felt that if it went unmentioned it was containable, which led to intimacy issues.

At least all this analysis was only irritating; still it must be derailed.

"Sounds like a bunch of excuses."

"I'm just trying to explain," X said, sounding hurt, "what might have happened."

In an instant, the windshield was replaced by the dark lawn of the college library. Arms, legs, a muddle of bodies. A cry. Phone lights flashing. And those terrible words: *What* are *you, anyway—*

No. Stop. Press hands to eyes. Press harder. Harder. Until everything goes red.

Nobody would ever understand what had happened. No one. Not even neuroscientists. *Let's take a look at this kid's brain. Hey, it's full of spikes, like a medieval mace.* Every thought excruciating, and dreams were worse. Last night a nightmare about a mob of gigantic lobsters surrounding the bed, clicking their claws.

No escape. No excuse. Each hour a nuclear winter.

X was still talking. "Though to be honest, for a long time I just tried not to think about her. You can get through all kinds of things by not thinking about them."

Was that another joke? So extra. Took hands from eyes, letting the red sparks fade, blinking at the sunny windshield. Braced sneakers against the dashboard. Sometimes X made cracks like this with her shrink friends who came over to drink wine on the patio. Or maybe this was why shrinks became shrinks, so they could spend all their time thinking about other people's problems and pretend they didn't have any themselves.

The air lost the hygienic scent of pine and filled with the smell of manure; they'd left the forest and were driving into farmland, dotted with barns.

Then without warning, X said, "Listen," and reached out and touched A's shoulder before instant flinch-reflex could be activated. "I just want you to remember that things change. You can't control other people's behavior, but you're in charge of your own."

No more questions. Cease all communication.

Earbuds back in place, some measure of security restored. Also totally clear now that X had told this story to show what a good mother *she* had been, how wise and understanding. How lucky A was, by comparison.

It was almost sad, to be so obvious.

4

Marika lived on the northeastern shore of Lake Champlain five miles from the Canadian border, six miles from the nearest town, on a tapering stretch of land called the Neck. Most cottages along the Neck were invisible from the road, announced by names painted on gray boards or canoe paddles nailed to tree trunks. Names that grew fewer as the pine, spruce, and oak trees grew denser. Lorna didn't recall this part of the lake as being so heavily forested or as feeling so remote, and began to think they were lost.

But just as she decided they should turn around, she spotted a boulder on the left side of the road painted in flaking white paint with the number she was searching for. At the end of a narrow rutted driveway was a one-story, brown-shingled cottage with green trim, deeply shaded by trees.

It was more or less the cottage she remembered from her visit years before, though more weathered, the shingles speckled with lichen and the roof so thickly carpeted with dry pine needles that it looked almost thatched. They parked beside a pile of stacked wood and got out of the car. Except for the creak of branches and the intermittent calls of small birds from somewhere high above, it seemed extraordinarily quiet; the air was clear, and there was a feeling that comes sometimes with being on a northern lake, that it looked the same as it had fifty, even a hundred years ago.

Leaving Adam to give Freddy a walk, Lorna made her way to the back door. Through the baggy screen the kitchen was dark and empty. "Hello?" she called. After knocking twice, she tried the door handle and found it unlocked. "Hello?" she repeated, stepping inside. "Anybody home?"

It took a moment for her eyes to adjust to the dim kitchen, which smelled sharply of mildew. A linoleum counter materialized, knotty pine cabinets. Dripping faucet. And then she made out a closed second door, next to the refrigerator, glowing around the edges and leading to the rest of the house.

"Hello?" Lorna had a hand on the latch of that second door, already preparing herself for Marika's protests: Shouldn't have come all this way. A lot of fuss over nothing. And to say in return: Oh, no, it was no trouble. Glad to give you a hand, glad to get Adam out of the house. But even as she lifted the latch, it was impossible to ignore that what she really wanted to do was turn around while there was still time and head back out to her car.

"Hello?" she called again, opening the door.

A flood of late afternoon sunlight struck her full in the face, pouring through a picture window overlooking the lake, shining off the water and into the house, reflecting off the ceiling, walls, floor-boards. All the windows were closed and in that brilliant, shut room the mildew smell from the kitchen mingled with woodsmoke and something faintly sulphurous. Lorna put up a hand to shield her eyes. Only then could she see an armchair, positioned to face the lake, and in it a dark motionless figure.

How long did she stand in the doorway before saying, "Marika"?

Slowly the old woman in the chair stirred and sat up, struggling a little. But she didn't turn around, only crossed her arms and stared at the blazing window in front of her.

"It's just me," Lorna said, her pulse quieting. "I just got here. How are you feeling?"

No response.

"Your neighbor Dennis told you he called me, didn't he? I tried you a couple times yesterday, but then figured your ankle might make it hard for you to get to the phone." Lorna moved to stand by the armchair, putting her back to the window in order to see into the room. Rebuff was expected. Don't make too much out of it.

"Dennis said you needed some help."

Marika did look up then. From behind the lenses of her glasses, her pale blue eyes were huge and watery.

"I don't need any help. I can take care of myself."

She was dressed in baggy knit slacks and a long-sleeved navy shirt, a white tissue tucked in at one wrist. Her short gray hair appeared to be unwashed and more unevenly cut than usual, and she looked thinner since last Thanksgiving, more shrunken, her head sunk between her shoulders, her long fingers swollen, knuckly and purplish. A pair of needles and a length of knitting lay in her lap.

"Well, your friend Dennis was worried about your ankle." Lorna eyed a stick leaning against one of the armchair's faded-chintz armrests. Not a cane, but a stick. Covered in pine bark, a twig sprouting near the top.

"He's not my friend," said Marika.

A black fly bumped against a side window. Lorna watched it fumble at the pane as she sat down on the brown corduroy sofa opposite Marika's chair. The room was stifling. "I'm sorry to hear that. In any case," she said, once more shielding her eyes from the sun. "Here I am. And guess who's with me?"

Marika picked up her needles, silhouetted against the bright window. "Your grandson," said Lorna more loudly. "He's out walking Freddy. He can stay outside if you don't want him in the house. Freddy, I mean."

Again no response. Marika began working her needles.

By now the trepidation Lorna had felt in the kitchen, her brief panic after opening the door and confronting that still figure in the armchair, had given way to exasperation. So far this encounter was becoming just another version of Marika's Thanksgiving visits, full of exaggerated consideration on Lorna's part and exaggerated refusal on Marika's, when it was hard to offer her so much as a cup of coffee without Marika insisting she didn't need anything. A standoff that was grueling for them both.

One that had begun eighteen years earlier, almost to the day, when Lorna had carried Adam into this same room, had sat with him on this same sofa. Nothing had changed. The intense light from the window. The silence. The constriction in her chest, the breathless unreality of regarding this frowning woman who was her mother. Although back then there had also been the dislocating shock of how old Marika was, how pale and shapeless and gray, that she wore glasses, and was dressed in an oversized yellow T-shirt with a brown stain near the collar and faded dungarees. No resemblance to the glamorous, aloof figure of memory, with her long blond hair, lipstick, and cigarettes. Followed by the realization that not only had Marika taken no pains with her appearance for this reunion—unlike Lorna, in a new blouse and skirt—but had made no offer of anything to eat or drink, had uttered no welcoming pleasantries. This is your grandson, Lorna had said as soon as she sat down. But how could Adam's small bare feet, waving as he wriggled in her lap, how could his tiny fat hand, reaching for a stuffed blue rabbit held out for him, bear any relation to that indifferent, slack creature in the armchair?

The room had been hot and close then, too, as Lorna made nervous small talk about the drive, Adam's teething, Roger who was at a medical conference in Detroit, their wedding in Wellfleet two years before, and asked polite questions that went mostly unanswered. The old woman listened, or appeared to listen, but said nothing. In response to Lorna's letter asking if she could visit and bring Adam, Marika had written, *I look forward to seeing you both.* Yet presented with Lorna and a baby in the flesh, she seemed to have no interest in either; in fact, she seemed almost offended by their presence. After half an hour, she announced she was tired and said they should go to their motel. Could we meet later for dinner? Lorna had asked. Marika said, Let's not make a fuss. Maybe I will see you tomorrow. Fine, said Lorna, shocked all over again by this dismissal. Fine, I understand.

But as she stood to leave, hugging Adam so tightly he started to cry, she'd turned to the old woman and said fiercely: I came up here because I want him to know he has a grandmother. And then she drove home. What a waste, she told Roger that night on the phone, reaching him at his hotel. I will never do that again. Yet that fall she had written once more to Marika, this time to invite her to Thanksgiving, "just for the day." And Marika had responded by appearing annually at Thanksgiving from then on, so that she could be seen to exist.

Hard to make less of a fuss than that.

Still, you couldn't deny that those Thanksgiving visits had created at least the semblance of a relationship. During dinner, for instance, when everyone was eating and talking, it was possible to imagine that Marika was glad to be included, even if she wasn't joining the conversation; she always ate heartily and after dinner sat in the living room watching the football game with Roger while Lorna did the washing up. It had been worth it, these arduous holiday performances. Roger was an only child and his parents had both died when he was in medical school, leaving Marika as the only surviving grandparent. Lorna had wanted to give Adam the feeling of being part of an extended family. Appearances did matter. Showing up mattered, even if done perversely, belatedly. Something even Marika recognized. Why else send that postcard of the lake from Vermont, all those years ago?

As for Marika's current rudeness, she must be frightened by her fall, by the prospect of having to depend on other people. Which must be why she hadn't answered when Lorna called out and knocked a few minutes ago, and why the door from the kitchen was closed, and why she was treating this visit as an invasion.

"I've gotten us a motel room," Lorna said. "We can go there whenever you want, but I'd like to unpack the groceries I brought along." She focused again on the fly's gyrations. "And I'd like to take a look at your ankle."

Marika shifted one foot. "You're looking at it."

"Does it hurt?"

A shrug.

Lorna settled back against the sofa. Early in their marriage, she'd sometimes tried to describe her work to Roger, and he would tease her by pretending not to understand the point of it. Screwed-up people are like everyone else, he'd say, only more screwed up. What's the big deal?

Okay, she thought. Try it that way.

"I can see that you're not in the mood for conversation right now." This was a tactic that often worked with uncommunicative clients. "That's fine. We don't have to talk. It was a long drive. I'm fine just sitting here with you."

The silence that followed held a note of surprise. Lorna sensed some sort of recalculation taking place within the old woman opposite her, an impression reinforced by the way she shifted in her armchair, moving her hips from side to side, as if suddenly finding her seat cushion uncomfortable.

A cloud had drifted over the sun; the lake was now clearly visible through the picture window, a wide shining expanse interrupted here and there by forested points and small islands, shading from green to pale blue as they receded toward paler-blue mountains. An astonishingly beautiful view that filled the entire room, which Lorna either had not noticed on that first visit or had forgotten. Below the house was a short wooden dock, and to the left of it, wedged into the rocks, was a cement urn planted with a lavender bush, in full bloom.

The room itself had the stark look of something unchanged but also provisional. Beside Marika's armchair was an upended wooden crate and on it a small lamp with a dusty glass base. Knotty pine walls, rusty electric baseboards. An oval braided rag rug in dingy shades of brown and beige ran half the length of the room, halting at a squat black woodstove. The only other furniture was a picnic table, covered with a red-checked oilcloth, two wooden benches pushed underneath. A yellowed map of the lake was thumbtacked near the door to the kitchen.

Several times in the past few years, concerned about Marika's old Volvo, Lorna had tried to inquire into her financial situation and had always received the same answer: *I keep to my budget*. Perhaps she should have kept asking, although the pine stick and the Spartan furnishings suggested something beyond thrift. A kind of frankness. A facing of facts.

"By the way, where's your car?" Lorna asked. "I didn't see it parked outside."

The fly had returned to circle Marika's head. She put down her needles and made a brisk movement with one hand, batting it away. Then she dragged the tissue from her sleeve and blotted her nose with an expression that was, if not welcoming, at least not a frown.

"So," she said hoarsely after another moment, "what's for dinner?"

5

As she listened to the kitchen cabinets opening and closing, Marika glared at her stick. She was hungry. If she'd been alone she would have heated a can of soup and been done with it. Also she'd had to put on a sweater because Lorna insisted on opening all the windows, saying it would be good to get some fresh air in here. Making a fuss over a little gas. This visit was a stupid mistake. Said so to Dennis yesterday, before she hung up on him. Never needed help before, didn't want it now.

Except lately she'd been having some sort of spells.

A breathlessness. A feeling like just before you fell down the stairs. Followed every so often by something else, a flabby blundering in her chest, as if her heart were trying to turn over. Afterward she'd find herself slumped in her chair or leaning against a wall, the lamp or a pot staring back at her, as if to say: What do you expect *us* to do for you, old woman?

Two days ago, Dennis stopped by to say he'd made up his mind about Florida, reaching under his beard as if he'd been keeping Florida there all along. He was leaving at the end of next week. Next *week*? And when were you going to tell me? I'm telling you now. As she began pointing out what a stupid idea it was, going to Florida in the summer—you'll boil your brains down there, you'll get malaria—

he reminded her that he'd wanted to leave last December, but stayed on after her accident.

Not really an accident. A lot of fuss over nothing. She'd been driving along and one minute the road was there and the next she was sitting in her car in somebody's potato field. I got you through the winter, Dennis said from the deck. Wouldn't step inside, wouldn't even look at her. My son's been asking me to come. Needs help with the business. He's got the twins now. Don't be stupid, she said. He just wants free babysitting.

Enough, said Dennis. I've had enough of that.

After he left, one of the spells came on while she was in the kitchen. That night she lay awake, gripping the edge of the bedspread. If she told Dennis about her spells, he'd call the hospital. Next thing she'd be in a wheelchair in front of a TV set with a bunch of old people who couldn't stand up if you set a match to them. But if she said nothing, he'd leave for Florida and never come back. That's when the sprained ankle came to her.

She *could* have sprained her ankle while dragging the ladder out from under the deck after the bird feeder blew down. No reason why she couldn't have sprained it. Climbing a ladder at her age. Dennis wouldn't leave her with a sprained ankle. And by the time it was better she would have gotten him to change his mind.

But then that fool had called Lorna. And now here was Lorna, with her nursey voice: How are you feeling? Let me take a look at your ankle. She'd had to stop herself from saying: Not even twisted. Go home.

Maybe she'd say that after dinner.

AS ALWAYS SHE ATE SLOWLY, deliberately. Lorna and the boy faced her across the table, Lorna with a glass of white wine, talking ever since she sat down, pushing salad leaves around with her fork. Jibber-jabber. News she'd heard on the radio on the way up in the car. Refugees. Detention centers. Marika concentrated on her roast chicken, cutting all the meat from the bones and saving the skin for last. A store-bought chicken, one of those dried-up ones you could watch turning on a spit. Then it was Russian interference. Cyberattacks. Bread not bad. The boy was eating a peanut butter sandwich. He'd said almost nothing since walking into the house except, What's your code? Code? He means the internet, Lorna had said. He's asking if there's access up here. What kind of access?

The breeze from earlier had stopped, the lake had gone flat. Now the Middle East was exploding. Marika moved the chicken bones to the side of her plate and buttered another slice of bread, thinking about breakfast, wondering how much of the bread would be left over. It would make good toast.

"Just one disaster after another," Lorna was saying. "You have to wonder what's going to happen next?"

Over the lake came an evening pause. Marika laid a hand on her chest and closed her eyes. But nothing happened, only that falling-down-the-stairs feeling. When she opened her eyes, the boy was goggling at her.

Lorna had set down her wineglass. "Are you okay?"

"Fine," she coughed. "Chicken's dry. Got stuck in my throat." A buzzing. Same old horsefly was back, zigzagging above the table.

"I wonder if this is a good time to talk about your ankle?" Lorna's voice seemed to come from behind the woodstove.

"What about it."

"How about seeing a doctor tomorrow, to make sure it's not broken?"

"No," Marika said, refusing to look at her. "It's not broken."

For dessert Lorna had brought along a coconut custard pie. Marika ate her slice more slowly even than usual, savoring its gluey sweetness. The sun began to set, gleaming along silverware handles on the table and suffusing the windowpanes with golden dust. The boy asked for a second slice of pie. Lorna was talking about the

Affordable Care Act. From out on the lake came the steady *grit, grit* of a duck.

Lorna cleared the plates. A few minutes later, she was back with mugs of straw-colored tea that smelled like grass clippings. "I'd like to take you to a doctor. Is there someone in town you see?"

The boy was goggling at her again. Still had barely opened his mouth, sounded like a caveman when he did. Reminded her of someone. Who was it?

"We'll call in the morning, to make an appointment."

"I don't need a doctor," said Marika.

BY THE TIME she was in her armchair, knitting in her lap, the big window was full of blue dusk and the moon was rising. You could see the moon twice, above and on the water.

Hushed voices from the kitchen. "In the morning," she heard, and then, "I'll take care of it." Lorna was washing glasses and dishes in the plastic dish tub, as Marika had instructed; now came the chink of each thing set in the drying rack.

She picked up her needles. She'd learned to knit as a girl and had taken it up again in the last few years. One day at the library she'd sat down with the paper and saw that someone had left a plastic bag of knitting under the table. When no one claimed the bag, she took it home and began knitting the half-finished scarf she found inside. Around the same time her bowel movements became more regular. She knitted only scarves. Every Christmas she gave one to Dennis; mostly she unraveled them as soon as they were done and knitted them again.

Sometimes she fell asleep while knitting and woke up not knowing where she was, drifting between her chair and a place she couldn't recall but where she'd just been. If it happened to be an evening like this one, with the moon making a bright path on the water, she found herself thinking about all the things that must be in the lake.

Things dropped from boats, lost or cast off: oarlocks, bottle caps; wristwatches, eyeglasses, wedding rings; green with algae, silted over, unseen and forgotten, yet still there.

The screen door twanged open. The boy must be going out with that dog.

"Chicken bones," she barked, "go in the can under the sink."

"Are you saving them for something?" called Lorna.

She didn't answer. The screen door opened and shut again. Lorna would be carrying the dish tub outside to toss the dishwater onto the ground.

You don't have a dishwasher? she'd asked earlier. What about a disposal? No, Marika had said, and don't let anything go down the drain. The pipes were old and easily clogged. You could really use a disposal, said Lorna.

As Marika waited for the door springs to sound again, there was a flicker outside, something flashing, weaving like a bicycle light through the trees.

6

The evening air had turned more humid, carrying the strong mineral scent of fresh water. Lorna emptied the dish tub at the edge of the driveway and then walked around the side of the cottage, where the chorus of frogs and crickets was joined intermittently by the banjo strum of a bullfrog. She climbed onto the deck. Through the lit windows, she could see the old woman asleep in her chair.

So far everything had gone pretty well, better than predicted. In fact, she could say she was cautiously optimistic. That initial scene in the living room had been awkward, but once Lorna had started making dinner, Marika seemed to grow resigned to this visit, even, in her own way, appreciative. And getting Adam out of his bedroom and off his laptop was turning out to be a minor miracle. He was on another walk with Freddy, using his phone as a flashlight.

She sat down in a weathered Adirondack chair. A bottle brush of pine needles was inked against the paling sky, and through the trees the lake glowed milk-blue. Fireflies glinted from clefts of darkness. Something was making her uneasy. What was it? At dinner she'd caught Marika staring across the table at Adam as if trying to remember his name, and he'd blanched when he realized she was looking at him. Maybe she should have mentioned something to Marika about his skin, explaining he was sensitive about it, that he was having an allergic reaction to hormonal changes. On the other hand, Marika had a mordant sense of humor that flashed out disconcertingly every so often; she might make a comment like: So, allergic to yourself, eh?

Lorna lay back in the Adirondack chair and looked up at the night sky, alive with stars. Dinner had actually been fine. Adam had apparently accepted her suggestion to be a flexible vegan, at least for now; he had eaten the pie, for instance. When asked if he wanted another slice he had not answered "Perchance" or "It seems so," but nodded politely. Aside from that odd moment at the table, when Marika put a hand to her chest and closed her eyes—"Did she stop breathing?" Adam had asked in the kitchen, and surprised he'd noticed, Lorna said it seemed like indigestion—Marika had eaten with good appetite. And she'd finally explained what happened to her car: Engine died. Not worth fixing. But how do you get to town? Oh, I have a ride when I need it. She'd even asked after Roger. How's Dr. Wiseberg? Still fussing with germs out there in Seattle? Viruses. He's an epidemiologist. Well, said Marika. Hope nothing catches *him*.

It was the drive up with Adam that was bothering her. She hadn't handled the revelation about Marika well; she'd meant to work up to it, but then she'd blurted everything out, unsettled by that long silence in the car. An old device, using her own difficulties to help Adam articulate his. Though was that what she had been hoping to do? It seemed to her now that she'd been trying to protect him from something.

Adam hadn't seemed particularly disturbed, apart from his first startled questions; probably she had been too worried about his reaction. She and Roger could discuss all this when she called him later to say that she'd taken his advice and they were in Vermont. When it came to Adam, they could talk for hours. She was always frank with Roger. She tried to be honest when she thought she had failed Adam in some way, or when Roger said something insensitive, or obtuse, as he had the other night. *He needs a job and a girlfriend, that's what he needs.* And Roger was frank with her; though he'd be the first to admit that "touchy-feely" language, as he still insisted on calling it, did not come to him naturally. Dr. Robot, Adam used to call him when they argued over homework.

So why had he asked how she was feeling?

Their marriage had ended as thoughtfully and generously as was possible. At the time, people probably blamed Roger. He could have stayed where he was, while for her a move would have meant surrendering her practice, which had taken decades to build, and uprooting Adam, who'd finally made some friends. Yet she had encouraged him to go; lately she'd sometimes wondered if, in some suppressed way, she had wanted him to go. They had come late into each other's lives, and then Adam had been born so soon afterward. It was something she'd avoided examining too closely, yet the question had long been there, how they would have managed, if they hadn't had Adam to talk about all the time. What would they have talked about instead? They might have traveled. Or taken up hiking, or maybe learned how to do something together, like woodworking, which two of her clients in couples' therapy decided to try; they built a shed, and it had seemed to solve a problem for them, how to frame their relationship: sometimes their marriage was a house, sometimes a shed. But most likely, Lorna thought, shifting her gaze from the lake to the dish tub at her feet, she and Roger would have ended up as they had, apart, because the truth was they'd lived their own lives from the beginning. In some essential way, they'd kept to themselves.

Which didn't mean they didn't care about each other. She had been genuinely glad to see Roger receive the sort of recognition he'd been afraid would never come. His own lab. A team of researchers. They might be divorced, but they were still allied. No one had left anyone.

Something jumped in the lake with a silvery plunk.

Lorna looked up. She had planned to sit outside a little longer, enjoying the warm evening, but the press of dark trees around her, the small, absorbed rustling noises in the underbrush suddenly brought to mind a few tasks to finish before she and Adam could leave for the motel. With a sense of being tracked by many bright, unseen eyes, she picked up the dish tub and made her way back into the house.

A PAIR OF WHITE MOTHS stuttered around the overhead light in the kitchen as Lorna put away the last of the dishes. She hesitated for a moment, and then switched on the transistor radio set on the windowsill above the sink. A voice announced that the temperature was currently sixty-five degrees, with winds out of the southeast.

"What are you doing?" came Marika's voice from the other room.

Lorna switched off the radio. "Just taking care of a few things."

Hanging by the old-fashioned Frigidaire was one of those free calendars on thin paper that insurance agents send out at Christmas. E. G. Morse & Co. in Burlington had provided this one for 2019, a different bird for each month. June was a mockingbird, *Mimus polyglottos*. The entire month was empty. She lifted down the calendar to look at past months. Nothing scheduled on any of them.

Beside the black push-button telephone on the counter, and underneath a phone book, lay a yellow legal pad. The pad's first twenty pages or so were folded back, each page divided into three columns, "Chores," "Weather," "Visitors," and filled with line after line of cursive handwriting. Marika once said nuns at her convent school rapped girls' knuckles with a ruler if they did not properly loop their *l*'s or finish their *f*'s. The letters had grown larger in the past years; *l*'s and *f*'s sprawled across each page.

Each entry was dated. Chores ranged from "housework" to sweeping pine needles off the deck. On Tuesdays Marika did her grocery shopping. Every Friday she listed the same errands: "CVS, library, P.O." This past week the weather had been logged as "fair" and "warm" with temperatures noted. Under "Visitors" over the past two months were different birds at the bird feeder, a raccoon that got into the trash cans, a meter reader, and Dennis, recorded every Tuesday and Friday. Here, it seemed, was Marika's ride. Dennis was also listed several times next to notations like "deck stain" and "grout."

"What are you doing in there?" Marika called from the living room.

Lorna slid the legal pad under the phone book. "Almost done."

Snooping. That's what she was doing. Like Wade when they were children, going through dresser drawers and poking into closets, snitching a handkerchief, a matchbook, hunting for "clues." Sometimes they would go on missions through the house together, pretending to find cameras in light switches and microphones in toothpaste caps.

In the living room every light was off but the lamp by Marika's armchair, which flickered every so often as if the bulb was going out. Lorna set the bottle of Hennessy, brought as a gift, and two glasses on the picnic table, poured cognac into each glass, handed one to Marika, and sat down on the sofa.

"Proost," said Marika, raising her glass. She took a sip and went back to knitting. Within the warm sphere of lamplight, she looked almost benign, only the small garnet earrings she always wore burning a little.

"So how have you been up here?" asked Lorna.

"Well, we're desperate for rain."

"It hasn't rained? It rained at home last night. The weather app on my phone said it rained here, too."

"Hasn't rained in weeks," said Marika positively.

The moths had followed Lorna into the room and were batting against the lampshade. She looked at the dark window and then glanced at her watch, tired after the drive, and ready to head to the motel. But Adam was still on a walk with Freddy; so in an effort to find something to talk about, aside from the weather, she asked how deep the lake was. Marika said she didn't know, that nobody knew.

"Someone must know." Lorna yawned. "Isn't there something

that's supposed to live at the bottom of it? Like the Loch Ness Monster?"

Marika didn't answer and continued knitting, pausing every so often for a sip of cognac. Lorna forgot to drink hers, listening to the ticking needles and watching the loose blue weave purl between them.

"I bet it's cold up here in the winter," she said eventually.

"Not too bad," said Marika.

"But most of your neighbors must head south." Lorna saw Marika make a face. "It must get pretty quiet," she continued, picturing the empty kitchen calendar, the birds and the raccoon under "Visitors."

"No," said Marika.

Lorna took a sip of cognac. Her statement to Adam earlier in the car came back to her: *You can get through all kinds of things by not thinking about them.* There must be a whole lake's worth of things that Marika did not think about. She drank the rest of her cognac and set the glass on the floor.

"I guess my question is whether you ever feel lonely?"

"Lonely?" Marika stopped knitting.

"Well, you're pretty hidden away up here."

The lamp flickered and for an instant Marika seemed to disappear. Just then Lorna heard Adam out in the driveway, telling Freddy to get in the car. The car door slammed and a few moments later the kitchen door opened. "Freddy just puked," he called.

Lorna cast a quick look at Marika and got up from the sofa. In the kitchen Adam was standing by the screen door, drinking a glass of water.

"He ate something," Adam said. "A stick or something."

"Well, he does that sometimes." Glancing again at her watch, Lorna said, "It's getting late. Let's go say good night to your grandmother."

7

Marika didn't look up from her needles as Lorna told her that they were heading to the motel and would be back in the morning.

"Okay," she said. "Goodbye."

"Do you need anything before we go?" Lorna was gathering up their glasses. "By the way, I think the bulb in that lamp might need replacing."

Marika said the bulb was fine.

"Sure I can't get you anything? Need any help getting ready for bed?"

"No." Marika shrank back in her chair. "I take care of myself."

"Well, I guess that's it then. We'll see you tomorrow."

Marika continued knitting, listening to the screen door bang shut and then, a few minutes later, to their car backing slowly down the driveway, the engine accelerating as the car turned onto the road. Listening until its light roar was replaced by a groan from the roof, a whisper of pine needles, and a faint scratching from somewhere in the kitchen.

When she was sure they were gone, she slipped the ball of yarn into the bag by her chair and switched off the lamp. Propping her stick against the armrest, she stood up in the darkness and shuffled to the bedroom to turn on the lamp by the bed. Then stood blinking at the room before slowly removing her cardigan and shirt. She sat down on the bed to tug off her slacks and shoes and unpeel her socks. All of this activity proved exhausting, and for a few minutes she rested on the edge of the bed in her bra and underpants, staring at the closet door, listening to that distant scratching.

At last she pulled her flannel nightgown from under the pillow, trying to move quickly now, and dragged it over her head, enduring the nightly panic when she couldn't find the neck opening. Into the bathroom to wash her face and brush her teeth. Then into the kitchen to switch off the light.

Where, in the moonlight, she leaned against the sink, breathing in a lemony trace of Lorna's perfume, and put a hand once more to her chest.

8

"Of course I never would have brought him along if I'd thought something like this would happen."

Under the white light of the neon RECEPTION sign in the parking lot, X was smiling in the patient way that signaled Difficult Accommodation in Progress.

"The woman at the front desk said they don't even accept service dogs." She rested one finger on the steering wheel. "Which I think is illegal, by the way. But she said if they found a single dog hair in the room they'd charge us a three-hundred-dollar cleaning fee."

Grumble sounds from the phone.

Two fingers. "Yes, I know it's ridiculous. I've tried calling every other motel in town, but everything's booked."

More grumble noise. Yes, acknowledged X. She'd made a mistake: she'd *thought* the motel website said dogs were allowed, but apparently that had been a different motel's website. She'd looked up several motels last night. Yes, it was very inconvenient. Clenching the steering wheel now. But here they were, with Freddy and nowhere for him to go.

Dilemma: G said yes to Freddy staying with her, but no to having him in the cottage. X said that Freddy, who'd puked again in the car, shouldn't be left out alone. Someone needed to keep an eye on him.

Which was when A said, "Agree to embed with Grootie."

X raised her eyebrows and shook her head, just as G said brusquely, "All right, I'll have the boy here."

LIT UP BY HEADLIGHTS, the cottage looked larger, taller, as if it had acquired a second story since they'd left it an hour ago. Though as soon as X killed the engine, the cottage immediately plunged back into darkness. Darker than regular darkness. Bears-skunk-snake darkness. Frogs were making a weird creaky ruckus, like hundreds of them stepped on at the same time. Wasn't it supposed to be quiet in nature? Wasn't that why people came to places like this?

A light snapped on in the kitchen. Nine twelve on phone screen, but felt like midnight. Battery at twenty-three percent. And then as the car door slammed, realized with the exact same metallic thunk that the charger inside the backpack that morning was the laptop charger. To go with the laptop that wasn't there. Phone charger at home. X would have to loan hers. Which she'd say she couldn't do because clients were always calling her and her phone needed to stay charged. From somewhere out on the lake came a long quavering shriek, creating a sudden stillness in the air as it died away.

Within a few minutes Freddy was leashed to a post on the deck with an old towel to sleep on and X had driven away in a flurry of apologies and promises to be back early in the morning. Leaving A alone with G in the living room, lit only by the lamp by her armchair.

"Sit." She pointed to the sofa.

It had seemed like another convenient scourge, to volunteer to sleep on the sofa here instead of at the motel, where, but for Freddy, would have had to bunk with X. But now major misgivings. Bordering on freak-out.

The room was stuffy, chicken from dinner still hanging in the air along with a strange smell reminiscent of AP Bio labs during the weeks spent on frog dissection, a smell that might be coming from G. The pine knots on the wood paneling each resembled a dark unblinking eye.

"Sit," she repeated. Clutching her stick, she sank into her armchair.

Sofa both squashy and hard, as if stuffed with balled gym socks. A blanket was folded at one end, under a flat pillow in a whitish pillowcase.

She was watching. Seemed to expect something. Thanks for the warm welcome? Pretend to check phone. Buy time.

With both hands on the armrests, she looked kind of like Abraham Lincoln seated in the Lincoln Memorial. Similar gaunt heaviness. Big cheekbones, too much forehead. Stony penitential set to the mouth. No trace of the beauty X claimed she'd once had. Except maybe for her eyes, an unusual light blue behind the smudgy lenses of her glasses. Try not to look at her nightgown, or imagine primordial breasts underneath.

"Do you want someting?" she said. On the crate next to her stood a bottle and two glasses. "Cognac. Or some other ting?"

Taken aback by this offer, said, "Cognac would be an okay ting," accidentally echoing her slightly mechanical accent. But her face remained expressionless as she poured amber liquid into one of the glasses and handed it over. Hope cognac tastes more or less like beer.

G lifted her glass and muttered something that sounded like "Proust."

Cognac lit up throat, resulting in a brief, hard coughing fit.

G drained her glass and lifted the bottle with a questioning glance. "So," she said, setting the bottle back down. "What shall we talk about?"

Talk? Somehow had not foreseen. New scourge. Already woozy from the cognac, uttered the first thing that came to mind.

"You don't have a TV."

She gave a snort. "Don't have time for that foolishness."

"Or a dishwasher." Approvingly. "You have a very small carbon footprint."

She made no response and they sat staring mutely at the picture window. The lamplight made their reflections look ghostly in the dark glass, but also strangely similar.

Minutes passed. Decades.

Finally, unable to think of anything else, mumbled, "So, was wondering. About your, like, life?"

She didn't move, and her eyes were half closed, but a muscle contracted at the corner of her mouth.

"Like, what you did? In the war?"

Still nothing. Maybe she'd fallen asleep. Some animals never fully closed their eyes, always alert to predators. Or maybe some animals didn't have eyelids? Possibly snakes did not have eyelids. Tried to recall whether the frog dissected in AP Bio had had eyelids. The fetal pig in Anatomy and Physiology last fall had definitely had eyelids, also eyelashes. Girlish eyelashes. Ugh. Think of something else.

"It must have been really scary."

Almost immediately G frowned. But instead of ignoring this moronic comment, as she did whenever anyone spoke to her at Thanksgiving, she looked into her glass and said, "We all had our facts."

In the kitchen, the old refrigerator hummed. There was a scraping sound from somewhere, like fingernails against a wall.

"What do you mean by facts?"

She leaned back in her chair, long veiny hands folded on her belly. The lamplight was now strong on one side of her face, leaving the other in shadow. "You did what you did," she said, widening one blue eye. Then she said, "Why do you care about that old stuff?"

"Everyone cares." Like, practically every movie was about it.

"Where *you* live, maybe," she said. "Most people don't think of it."

"That's not true."

Although it could be true. Anyway, what did she mean by "where *you* live"? Because Y was Jewish? Was she being anti-Semitic or just random? Something descended from the ceiling and paused in midair, seemingly attached to nothing. A green inchworm.

Despite feeling queasy, A took another sip of cognac. "Anyway, maybe people care because they still don't understand it?" This idea seemed possibly intelligent. "Like people know *what* happened, but they still don't get *why*. So they can't let it go."

G lifted one foot and gave a kind of grimace. The inchworm completed its descent and disappeared. Outside on the deck, Freddy gave a short whine.

The lamp by her armchair had begun flickering again. "So," she said, with either a burp or a grunt, "what about you?"

Me? almost said. Instead shrugged.

"You tell me a fact."

A fact? You want a fact? Well, okay, how about this: All human interaction is self-regarding, self-serving, and self-delusional. No one really listens to anybody else, i.e., we aren't having a *conversation* right now, we are monologuing in tandem. But could not say any of that without sounding like a pompous douche, and also at this moment, head full of cognac, maybe didn't believe it. Had, actually, been listening to her.

After a further pause that hopefully seemed thoughtful, switched to French, where the impersonal could rescue one more naturally from oneself.

"On ne comprend pas."

Rather than looking more annoyed, for the first time that evening she smiled. "I forgot you speak French."

"Un peu."

Another dry smile. To be a citizen of the world, she declared, a person must speak more than one language. She herself spoke four. A flare of ancient vanity ignited her face. "Your mother is not good at languages."

"*C'est vrai.*" X couldn't sing on key, either. They sipped their cognac in the unsteady light, fellow citizens of the world.

Then G said, "*Quels sont tes faits?*"

Face heated up and started to itch. "*Pas de faits.*"

A long look from G. "No facts, eh?"

Here it was again: the lawn by the college library. Shouts, sobs, face pressed into the grass. The perpetual throat ache. But after a moment of staring fixedly at the dark window, realized with a kind of amazement that for once something else was creating that throat ache.

It was G. In that shabby old armchair and smelly nightgown, all alone, night after night, a woman who had looked upon death, destruction, madness, and refused to talk about it. Who knew you couldn't understand if you hadn't been there, that even if you had been there it couldn't be described, because to describe it would be to accept it. Who knew that people were full of ugly facts and, unlike X, didn't believe in explanations and excuses.

You did what you did. End of story. What a fucking relief.

"Facts," speaking thickly, "don't matter. Nobody cares about them. Nobody even knows what they are."

The shriek from earlier sounded again out on the lake. A moment later a huge black bug banged against the dark windowpane like an insect meteor.

From the armchair came a long, submerged rumble, like the digestive noises that Freddy made in his sleep.

"Tomorrow," G said, and made a series of crab-like movements to rise from the chair. "Tomorrow," she said, leaning on her stick, "my bird feeder needs hanging up."

"Sure."

"Don't do it if it's too much trouble."

"It's not too much trouble."

"Some other tings need doing. Chores. How long will you be here?"

"Couple days?"

"There are some tings to take care of."

No idea what she said next, but it sounded like she'd gone back to French. She stumped across the room with her stick. At the door to her bedroom, she turned around and said to shut off the lamp, no use flushing money down the toilet, and then closed the door behind her, leaving A to get ready for bed in the dark.

9

It was a magnificent summer morning, the sky a faultless blue, interrupted here and there by a few tall white cloud banks, flattened at the bottoms like layer cakes. As Lorna drove along the Neck toward Marika's cottage, she caught glimpses of water between the trees, sunshine pouring into the lake as if it were an enormous bowl of light.

She turned into Marika's bumpy driveway and parked once more by the woodpile, where she sat for a moment in the car, searching her purse for a packet of aspirin, finding only an old cough drop. She'd had another mostly sleepless night, unused to being in a motel room, which smelled like the insecticide she sprayed on her roses. People in the next room had watched television loudly until late and then had some sort of argument, ending in raw sounds that could have been weeping, or something else. The too-bright lamps in the parking lot had stayed on all night, casting bluish shadows into her room. After trying to call Roger and getting his voicemail, she'd spent hours listening to the ice maker across the hall dislodge regular small avalanches.

In the living room, Marika was in the same outfit as yesterday, sitting in her armchair with her stick by her side, facing the picture window. She sat at that window most of the time, judging by the rounded ends of the armchair's arms, shiny and grayish with a shell-like tarnish from where she must rest her palms. Lorna was about to comment on the view, the way the lake was framed by those distant mountains, but something obdurate in Marika's expression made it seem as if she wasn't actually gazing at the lake; she looked like someone staring at a brick wall.

"Good morning," Lorna said instead, setting the box of doughnuts she'd bought onto the picnic table. "How did you sleep?"

"Bad," said Marika energetically.

"Sorry to hear it."

"Kept getting up to pee. Usually don't have dinner so late."

"Well, I didn't sleep well, either," said Lorna, gazing at the doughnut box. "So I guess that makes two of us."

It had been a calculated risk to buy doughnuts, which Adam loved and would find hard to resist. A little pleasure would be good for him. But she also knew that it might look as if she'd again forgotten he was now vegan, or was trying to tempt him, or was discounting his resolve. Or that she was being passive-aggressive?

A mosquito whined around her head. Outside on the deck, Adam was sitting cross-legged beside Freddy, peeling the bark off a twig, also in the same clothes he'd been wearing the day before. Since arriving home he'd worn the same two faded black T-shirts—one with a picture of Earth inside rifle crosshairs—and either a pair of moldy-looking black jeans or a pair of torn cargo shorts, which went unwashed unless she raided his room to carry them off. She'd begun to suspect this dreary outfit was a protest. Not only against whatever had happened to him and, of course, the planet, but against her own ironed blouses and clean pants, her "To Do" lists. A protest against getting on with things.

"At least it's a beautiful morning," she said, over the low thunder of her headache.

"Yes," said Marika, without interest.

"Look at the sun on your lavender bush." Lorna stepped over to the picture window. "What a bright purple."

"Apple cores."

"Is that what you feed it?"

"Ash. Bonemeal."

"Well, it seems very healthy." Lorna waved at the mosquito. "How's your ankle?"

Marika grimaced and shifted in her armchair.

"I wish you'd let me take you to a doctor."

Marika shook her head. There were things she needed to do. Errands. She hadn't done them on Friday, her usual day, because of her ankle. From glancing through that legal pad in the kitchen the night before, Lorna figured that "errands" meant visiting CVS, the post office, and the library, and unwisely said as much.

"How do you know that?" Marika demanded.

"I saw your list in the kitchen. Of chores and things. By the way"—Lorna tried to clap the mosquito between her palms—"your neighbor Dennis seems to come over a lot for someone who's not a friend."

Marika frowned. "My landlord."

This was a surprise. Lorna had been under the impression that Marika owned the cottage. But before she could pursue the subject further, Marika declared that she was tired of waiting and was ready to leave.

"It's not even nine o'clock," objected Lorna. "Let's have some coffee first."

"I've had coffee."

"Well, I haven't," said Lorna. Untrue, if you counted the watery stuff she'd brewed in the little plastic contraption in her motel room. But she'd been looking forward to sitting quietly by the lake for a little while, and it was never a good idea to let people bully you, especially insecure people; it only frightened them further.

"Fine," Marika said grudgingly.

"I'll make some coffee for us both." Lorna redoubled her efforts to be cheerful. "I'd also like to say hello to Adam. I hope you don't mind if he and Freddy come along on the errands?"

"Doesn't want to." Marika peered over the tops of her glasses at the doughnut box. "He and that dog are going to stay here."

On the deck, Adam was sitting in a blade of hot sunlight, his back against the bottom of the Adirondack chair, staring at the lake as if hypnotized. He didn't look up from the twig he was peeling when Lorna bent down to give him a kiss, though Freddy lifted his head and thumped his tail. When Lorna asked if Freddy had been walked and fed, and if he had enough water, Adam pointed to Freddy's water bowl by the side door, which was full.

It turned out that Marika was right; he did want to stay. His grandmother had asked him to do some chores.

"What kind of chores?" Lorna knelt on the deck to pick burrs from Freddy's ruff, feeling a faint flush of irritation, although helping his grandmother was exactly what she'd hoped he might do, despite steadfastly refusing to do any chores at home.

"Hang up her bird feeder. Nail down some loose boards on the dock." He ticked off items on his fingers. "Clean the gutters."

Lorna fanned herself with one hand. "And you agreed to all this?"

Adam shot her an affronted look. "She needs help. She's like *old*."

And what about me? Lorna felt another flush of irritation. Don't I need help? From a pine tree overhead came a high-pitched scolding. A squirrel stared beadily down at her. No, she thought, that's not my question. Don't you wish you had stayed with me at the motel? That's what I'm really asking. That was the source of her annoyance. Adam had survived his night on Marika's lumpy sofa with so far no complaints. In fact, he seemed almost gratified by the discomfort.

Here was another consequence of not telling him about Marika long ago: In his present mood, Adam probably blamed Lorna for surviving her traumatic childhood, viewing it as shallowness. Instead of suffering irreparable damage, which would show depth of soul, she had ended up in the suburbs with a successful practice, a golden retriever, and a three-bedroom house with an attached garage. She had not been sufficiently miserable. The real damsel in distress was clearly his bad-tempered grandmother in her bleak cottage.

Though she had to admit that he looked better this morning. Eyes brighter, more color in his cheeks, and the blemishes on his chin and forehead seemed to be fading.

"Okay." Resisting the urge to reach out and smooth his hair. Instead she folded back one of Freddy's silken ears. "If you decide it's too much, let me know. The landlord should take care of the gutters. So did you two have a chat last night, before you went to bed?"

Adam gave a fractional nod.

"Well, good. So were you okay on the sofa?" A shrug. "So nothing else happened?" Another pause. It was clear by Adam's set face that he was willing her to stop talking. "Nothing like last night at dinner? Grootie's bout of indigestion, or whatever it was? That was a little surprising."

Finally he said, "Why?"

"Why what?"

He shrugged again and snapped the twig between his fingers.

Did he mean how could she be surprised that Marika would suffer from indigestion, among other ailments, given her age? If so, fair enough. He was calling her bluff. For years she had been expecting to be summoned to Vermont. Someone would call to report that Marika was in the hospital. A bad case of the flu, a broken hip. Please come as soon as possible. Though she'd never imagined anything past the summons itself.

To Adam she said, "If you mean have I been worried that one day something would happen to Grootie up here on her own, the answer is yes. Which is why I'm glad we're here now." Neither spoke for several minutes, staring with equal concentration at the lake, where two small boats with striped sails cut back and forth across a bright span of water, narrowly avoiding each other. Lorna smoothed Freddy's ear back down.

"All right," she sighed at last, getting up off her knees. "How about some breakfast? Avocado toast?" She kept her voice casual. "I also brought doughnuts."

Adam said he'd already had breakfast. An apple.

An old percolator sat by the stove, the basket inside black and greasy. Lorna dumped the coffee grounds into the covered galvanized steel bucket just outside the kitchen door. When full, Marika had said, the bucket was toted to the compost heap by the woodpile. Probably chicken bones attracted animals—that must be why they stayed in a can under the sink. Or possibly, unpleasantly, Marika ground her own bonemeal. Lorna pictured Marika in winter, bent against the cold, trudging with her bucket through the snow.

From the doorway, Lorna asked where she might find the toaster.

"Don't have one," Marika said from her chair.

"You don't have a toaster?"

"Use the stove."

The mosquito was still orbiting the living room. Lorna slapped at it with the dish towel. "You know," she said, unable to keep the exasperation from her voice, "there's nothing wrong with a few conveniences to make life more comfortable. A toaster is not a luxury. It's an amenity." She slapped again at the mosquito. "And being comfortable," she added, "is not a crime."

When she glanced around, Marika was staring at the window, where beyond waited the lake, wide and shimmering.

10

After X and G drove off on their errands, A continued to doze on the deck in the sun, registering eyelid warmth, breeze against forehead, the pencil-box smell of the lake. Breathing deeply in what felt like the first time in months.

At last, thinking maybe it was time for a swim, stood up, stretched, and yawned, gazing unseeingly at the stone tub of purple flowers by the steps to the dock. Last night stayed up watching a downloaded episode of *Celebrity Rehab*, hoping to drown out the frogs. Phone now dead and X had left her charger at the motel. Weird, being so cut off. Even though the thought of following anybody's Instagram or looking at Facebook was intolerable. Anyway, had probably been unfriended by everyone back to pre-K.

A woodpecker drummed nearby, as precise and reverberant as a toothache.

Actually, it was kind of *great*, to be in the woods, by a lake. Could post photos, too, if phone weren't dead (and if posting wasn't such despicable self-referential crap). Treetops. Sun on the water. A single pebble at the shoreline. The suggestion of being alone and glad of it. Kind of like *Walden*, assigned in Lit Core, but not read, though managed a fairly decent five-page essay on it, anyway. "Thoreau: In Silence, Redemption." Stuck in some Thoreau-blather from Wikipedia and something about "modern consumerist competitive chaos" and "soul-sucking social media" and gotten a B+. "Intriguing," the professor had commented, i.e., Total bullshit but grammatically more or less correct.

With a vague idea of testing the water and seeing which loose boards G wanted hammered, went with Freddy down the stone steps to the dock and examined the fraying rope bumpers and a pair of rusted cleats. The breeze was stronger on the dock, waves splashing rhythmically against the iron pilings with a hollow ringing sound. A gull skimmed by, wings flashing. Far out in the water, something moved. A heave. A splash. Maybe the monster that X said was supposed to live at the bottom of the lake. Haha. Obviously a fake. In the blurry black-and-white photo that came up on Google yesterday, the monster looked like a couple of old car tires and an umbrella handle.

Figures now appeared on a neighboring dock, a man and woman carrying canvas tote bags toward a bobbing motorboat, a little boy trailing after them, hugging an inflated pink elephant. Suddenly the boy tripped, fell, began to wail. No response from the father, loading the boat, but the mother hurried back to lift the kid to his feet and take his elephant. He kept crying as he followed her, pulling on the back of her sundress.

In the other direction, several more docks jutted below cabins and cottages built onto the rocks. Two had flags on flagpoles. The American flag: blech. Stripes rigid, stars boring. Symbols of allegiance to anything were noxious, especially if revered by large numbers of people and considered sacrosanct. And yet, somehow this morning, surrounded by shining water under a clear blue sky, the sight of those rippling flags was almost moving. They looked affirmative, muscular, sort of glorious, and just for a moment, wondered what it would be like, to sacrifice one's self for something.

IN THE YARD, the fallen bird feeder lay at the bottom of a pine tree, next to a ladder. Dragged the ladder past the deck and propped it against the cottage to make an inspection of the gutters, or to look as if one had been made. While standing by the ladder and squinting at the roof, heard a car drive up, twigs and pebbles popping under the tires. Annoyed that X and G had returned so much earlier than expected, did not move, but pretended to be absorbed in studying the gutters.

A voice called out, "Hey."

Whirling around, was confronted by a tall man in a black T-shirt, jeans, and work boots standing beside a white pickup truck. Big gut hanging over his belt buckle. Wild-ass gray beard covering most of his face. A Red Sox cap covered the rest of it.

"Who're you?" demanded the man.

Hesitation. "Grandson."

The beard gave an impression of being startled. After a moment, he pointed to his chest, said, "Dennis," and crossed a hairy pair of arms. "Friend of your grandma's."

Freaky voice: high and a little gaspy, like someone after a tracheotomy. Accent sounded southernish. *Grand maw.*

"So, she got you doing her chores now?"

"Guess so." Why sudden shifty feeling, as if caught trying to steal something? (Like—the bird feeder?) Who was this old dude, anyway? Handyman? "She has a few things that need doing."

"Your mom here?"

"They've gone to town."

Staring contest, during which the need for small talk became increasingly acute. Small talk: noun: the phenomenon of asking questions you have no interest in asking, and the other person has no interest in answering, yet an exchange considered necessary to establish basic human connection. However, no topic seemed basic enough to connect with this dick with a truck in the driveway. Gnats danced in the air. D = Dick = Dennis. Tiny smirk.

"So, do you, like, live here?"

"Off and on." D uncrossed his ham-sized arms. "Last few years mostly on." Leaned against the hood of his truck. "Wife's family used to have a place up here." And went on to reveal, in about thirty-two words, that he'd moved to Boston after law school and started coming to the lake to fish. Bought a bunch of camps as investments. Got divorced. Retired.

"Camps?" said A politely, relieved to find that D was a lawyer and not a handyman, which seemed to balance things out between them somehow.

"Cottages."

"Do you own this one?" When D nodded, A said, "Wow." Then cringed, afraid of sounding snide. Implying the cottage was a measly thing to own.

Just then, Freddy could be heard making heaving noises from somewhere near the woodpile. Must have been eating sticks again.

"Well, anyway, thanks for, you know, stopping by."

"Like to keep an eye on my properties," said D, glancing toward the woodpile.

"How many do you have?" At the same time thinking that D didn't keep enough of an eye on his properties, if they all looked like this one, which *was* measly. Gutters clogged. Rotting shingles. Leaky faucet.

"Six," said D. "Had to start naming them to keep them straight. Loon. Squirrel."

Interesting. Kind of. A's cabin for two summers at camp had been the Kingfishers, at perpetual war with the Blue Jays on the other side of the showers. The origins of this rivalry were obscure, yet it remained intense, conducted mostly through archery and canoe races, but also through nighttime raids, short-sheeting, and the occasional kidnapping.

"This one here was Bear," continued D, "but your grandma didn't like it, so I took the sign down." He fell silent for a moment. "Your grandma and I," and then stopped again as if reconsidering something he'd been about to say.

Finally, in his soft, gaspy voice, "We used to play chess."

"Chess?" repeated A in astonishment.

The beard moved ruminatively. "Anyhow, getting out of here soon. Moving south. Son's in Florida." He looked at his truck. "Time for a change, while I still got most of my parts."

A nodded in a guys-discussing-vehicles sort of way. Probably the son had a truck, too. Imagined two men standing under a palm tree, each holding a wrench.

A pair of geese flew overhead, honking back and forth with a sound like *rawf, rawf* that could be heard long after they disappeared over the lake. As if summoned by the geese, Freddy now plodded into the driveway, tail wagging. He halted beside D, his big golden head hanging.

"Nice dog." D bent down to give Freddy a pat. Then he drew back his arm and pretended to toss a football. Freddy gazed at him tiredly.

"Yeah, well, he keeps throwing up," said A. "He's like allergic to something." More staring. "So," giving up on small talk, "did you come by for something?"

"Wanted to see if your grandma's ankle's any better. Usually she takes a walk around now." D gave Freddy a final pat and then straightened up and stroked his big beard. "Sometimes I go along. Make sure she stays on the road."

Image of G plunging off the road into a bank of blueberry bushes. Lying crumpled on the ground, one hand outstretched, palm sprinkled with pine needles.

"She seemed better this morning," absently scratched a bug bite. The bugs had gotten bad. You could get eaten alive in a place like this. "But this weird thing happened last night at dinner where she, like, seemed to stop breathing."

D quit stroking his beard. "Stopped breathing?"

"Yeah. It was weird. But then she was fine."

Neither of them seemed able to think of anything else to say.

With another sigh, D reached out a large hairy hand. "Well, time for me to get moving. Nice meeting you, Adam."

A shook his hand, startled to be called by name. For some reason, never imagined G would mention to anybody that she had a grandson.

The older man climbed into his truck, limping noticeably. But then instead of starting the engine, he stuck an elbow out the window. "Hey, Adam," he called. "Want to see the lake while you're up here? Get the lay of the land? Got a boat." Adding, with false-sounding heartiness, "Got a six of beer."

"Sure," simultaneously thinking: Do *not* want to go out on a boat with this sad old beard, or drink beers, and have to talk about law school, or football or baseball, or trucks. Going out in a boat with D was, in fact, a completely undesirable activity, which therefore meant it qualified as a scourge.

"Sure. That would be fun."

D lifted his hand and started the engine. "Later," he called, and backed expertly out of the driveway with impressive speed, fishtailing as he reached the road.

11

Marika refused to visit the urgent care clinic. It would take too long to see a doctor. When Lorna pointed out that she could get all of Marika's errands done while Marika waited for an appointment, Marika said she didn't want to sit for an hour in a waiting room full of crying children with bellyaches or fishhooks in their thumbs and that she was fine in the car. Despite the heat, she wouldn't let Lorna roll her window all the way down, either.

"I'm cold-blooded." Marika gazed out at the miniature suns flaring from a dozen windshields. "I like being hot."

She watched Lorna head toward the post office, and then folded her hands as she contemplated the village green across the street, an open rectangle of grass interrupted here and there by shade trees and wooden benches. To the left was a bridge with wrought-iron railings, leading across a narrow-channeled river to a long redbrick building, once a paper mill that now housed the post office, a hairdresser's, and a couple of shops selling knickknacks and T-shirts for tourists. A diner called the Millstone had opened there a few months ago, replacing a coffee shop that had been there for years. On the other side of the green were the library, Hannaford's supermarket, and the CVS. At the far end, on a rectangle of white gravel and surrounded by a low box hedge, was a modern three-story brick building with plate-glass windows on the first floor. A sign in front read SILVER SHORES SENIOR LIVING. Marika frowned at a strip of grass directly in front of the car, shrapneled with foil wrappers. The heat made her sleepy and within a few minutes she had dozed off.

She woke to a knocking on the window and to a pair of black sunglasses. It took her a moment to recognize Lorna, who opened the door and said she was done with all of Marika's errands. Marika looked groggily at her watch. Only thirty minutes had gone by. Her errands usually took her over an hour.

"Did you get my hand cream?"

Lorna held up a CVS bag. "For your scales."

"Hah," said Marika appreciatively.

Lorna suggested an early lunch at the diner. "It might be fun," she said. "My treat." She smiled coaxingly under her sunglasses.

Marika frowned. "What about the boy?"

"I'll call him," Lorna said. But the boy didn't answer his phone. Lorna said she thought there might be no cell service at Marika's part of the lake; but when she tried Marika's number he didn't answer that, either.

She looked worried as she put her phone back in her purse, but then smiled. "It's good that he's getting outside. The fresh air is good for him. He seems to like it up here."

THE MILLSTONE WAS DESIGNED to look like an old-fashioned railcar diner, with a chrome counter, a black-and-white checkerboard floor, and booths with red vinyl banquettes. Large sepia-tinted photographs of country railroad depots hung on the walls. Why try to make something new look old, Marika wondered testily, missing the former coffee shop, which had not tried to look like anything. Her pine stick attracted stares as the hostess led them to a booth, and Lorna made a fuss about helping her onto the banquette; but there was an agreeable smell of coffee and bacon, and soon they were safely seated.

Lorna's phone buzzed. She looked at it and said, "A client. Sorry. I need to take this." A few moments later she was standing in the parking lot in her sunglasses, one arm across her chest, talking on the phone. Marika turned away from the window to examine the railroad photograph hanging above their booth. It showed a ramshackle wooden structure in an empty, burnt-looking field with tracks running in either direction.

"Sorry," Lorna repeated when she came back and sat down again, pushing her sunglasses onto the top of her head. "A small emergency."

Marika nodded, thinking that people should keep their emergencies to themselves. Especially when other people were about to order lunch.

A pudgy teenager with a silver nose ring and unruly greenish hair appeared with menus and a pitcher of water. He reminded her of someone, with his big head and thick greasy-looking hair, and the way he shrank back when he noticed her examining his nose ring. They ordered sandwiches and Marika ordered coffee, still trying to figure out who this boy reminded her of. It was troublesome these days, how often she forgot things, but as soon as the waiter disappeared through the quilted metal doors leading to the kitchen, it came to her, and relieved at this discovery she leaned forward.

"You know who the boy looks like?"

"Which boy?" Lorna unfolded her napkin.

Marika had known which boy she'd meant when she started to ask her question, but now he'd run into a dark alleyway and she lost sight of him. In her confusion, she picked up her own napkin and said, "Your boy."

Lorna said, "Adam? Who does he look like?"

Still confused, Marika said a name she remembered: "Wade."

"What?" Lorna sounded shocked. "You think Adam looks like Wade?"

Marika pressed her lips together. That wasn't what she'd meant, only that the waiter had somehow reminded her of someone, a different boy, who'd made her think *Wade*, and then once again slipped into that alley out of sight. But she'd said, "Your boy," and now that it was said she didn't know how to correct herself.

"I don't see it," said Lorna, sitting back against the banquette.

But while they waited for their lunch, Lorna talked about Adam. She was worried something had happened to him last semester at college. Some sort of upset. She wished he'd tell her about it. Then she moved on to things Adam might do once he graduated from college. Roger wanted him to go to medical school, but Adam might want to be an activist. Last summer he'd worked for an environmental organization.

"All he talked about was saving the world."

"From what?" Marika was again looking at the photograph of the old railroad station. She felt she recognized it, too, but she couldn't think from where. Everything lately was reminding her of something else.

"Climate change, mostly," said Lorna, and began talking about sea-level rise, floods, and forest fires. "Anyway," she said finally, smoothing a wrinkled corner of her paper place mat, "he's taking some time this summer to find himself."

Marika snorted. "What's he need, a compass?"

"I suppose, in a way." Lorna smiled. "He's only nineteen."

"Seems younger." Marika glanced toward the kitchen. "Maybe it's the spots."

Lorna stopped smiling.

"There's something strange about the way he talks," said Marika, warming to the subject of Adam's faults. "Maybe he got hit on the head at college."

"No," said Lorna stiffly. "As I said, he's just a little lost at the moment."

"I have a very good sense of direction." Marika felt for a tissue. "I was a Girl Guide."

"Is that like a Girl Scout?" asked Lorna. "You mean when you were a child?"

"Learned how to tie knots and build a fire." Marika blew her nose, already wishing she had said nothing, given the alert way Lorna was looking at her. But now that she'd mentioned the Girl Guides, she found herself interested by what she recalled.

"Learned how to take bearings from the sun," she declared, surprised that this was true. Her troop had gone on a camping expedition and cycled to the Hilversum forests. The next instant she was lying on a blanket in a dark meadow surrounded by pines, breathing in campfire smoke and listening to the giggles of other girls while a calm voice began naming the constellations.

"I've never heard you talk about that before," said Lorna.

Their food arrived. As usual, Marika ate in silence. After finishing her tuna sandwich, potato chips, and the parsley garnish, she drank a second cup of coffee and then pulled the tissue from her sleeve to wipe her nose. Lorna got another call and excused herself from the table again to stand out in the parking lot. She hadn't eaten much of her chicken salad sandwich and when she came back she asked the green-haired waiter to wrap it up.

He returned with a white paper bag and the check. Lorna took out her wallet, handed him a twenty and a ten and said to keep the change. Marika remained silent, aghast that two sandwiches and coffee could come to thirty dollars.

When the waiter was gone, Lorna leaned forward. "I was wondering if you'd say a little more about when you were a girl? Like being in the Girl Guides? What else did they teach you?"

Marika considered not answering. Lorna's questions were never as simple as they sounded and often led to other questions. People these days thought that was good for you, jabbering on about yourself. That's how Lorna made a living, getting phone calls, listening to jibber-jabber. But Lorna had just paid thirty dollars for lunch, so Marika said she'd learned what berries you could eat and how to find north by the stars.

"Found my way across Europe," she said. "By myself."

"Did you go by bicycle?" Lorna asked.

"Train," said Marika vaguely.

"I thought you stayed at your convent school after the war?"

Marika returned her gaze to her empty cup and noted an ashy taste in her mouth. "Too much coffee," she muttered.

Grasping her pine stick and ignoring Lorna's offers to help, she hitched herself off the banquette and across the checkerboard floor to the restrooms. The stick had become so reliable, she almost needed it by now.

12

They drove once more into the spectacular day. The breeze washed through the car in bright waves, smelling of pine and warm granite, and despite objecting to having the windows open, Marika had tipped her head back against the seat, half closing her eyes, with an expression, it seemed to Lorna, almost of enjoyment.

"It's good to get you out of the house," Lorna observed after a little while.

"Blow the stink off me, you mean."

"No," said Lorna. "I mean good to get a change of scene."

She chose a dogleg route along the lakeshore that took them past a series of handsome white clapboard farmhouses set behind thick green lawns and pebbled driveways. The sort of houses described as "rambling." Slowing down to admire them, Lorna pictured large, multigenerational families gathered inside in the evenings, playing board games around a coffee table, or spending rainy afternoons reading novels and old issues of the *New Yorker* on a screened porch, the younger children playing hide-and-seek, calling for their parents to come find them.

A small black dog ran across one of the lawns and began barking. Marika had sat up and was now peering at the white houses, too.

"What a bunch of energy bills," she said.

Exactly like a remark Adam would make, Lorna thought, suppressing a shiver. Down to the flat tone, somehow more censorious for being uninflected. She'd tried to phone Adam again from the parking lot after lunch, but again got no answer, feeling almost guilty for having been so interested in Marika's disclosure about being a Girl Guide that she'd briefly forgotten the block of ice in her stomach. Why had Marika said Adam resembled Wade? They were exact opposites. Adam had a mother who had been there his entire life, for instance, and would do anything for him. They had not one thing in common. Except perhaps in being intelligent, and stubborn, and too unprotected, and exhibiting a kind of desperate bravado when frightened, putting on an elaborate show of caring about nothing.

"I still don't see," she said, "why you think Adam looks like Wade."

"I don't," said Marika.

"Then why did you say so?"

Marika didn't answer. She had her eyes closed.

"So," said Lorna, her voice softening, "you sometimes think about Wade?"

"No," said Marika.

They left behind the handsome farmhouses, the road narrowing to wind along a rocky escarpment. Below, the lake shone like a sheet of metal in the sun and from this vantage point looked almost limitless. Here and there were small islands, some occupied by a cabin or two; others hardly more than a tumble of boulders with a few pine trees.

As Lorna slowed down again, this time to navigate a sharp turn, Marika gave a little wheeze, going suddenly pale.

"Are you all right?" Lorna glanced at her.

"I'm fine," Marika said, pressing closer to her window.

"This road is kind of twisty." Lorna slowed the car further and raised her sunglasses to the top of her head to inspect Marika more closely. "Are you feeling sick?"

Marika's eyes stayed shut and there was a sheen of sweat on her forehead.

"Maybe the tuna."

"Do you want me to pull over?"

"No. Keep going."

They drove for five or ten minutes in silence, but when the road had turned inland and flattened out, and some color had strayed back into Marika's broad gaunt cheeks, Lorna said, "How are you feeling?"

"Fine," said Marika gruffly. "Don't make a fuss."

"Okay, but will you let me know if you want me to stop?"

"Stop," said Marika, still pressed against the window. In her fingers was a bit of white tissue, which she was spasmodically shredding.

"Stop? Do you mean pull over?" Lorna slowed the car again.

"Stop asking questions."

Lorna returned her gaze to the road. All right, she thought, with a small swell of pity. I get it. You don't feel well, but you don't want to admit it. Like a lot of things in your life. But some things have to be admitted. They were passing a long fence, behind which stood a herd of dirty black and white cows, followed by a barn that was not quaintly painted red, like most Vermont barns, but was instead gray and splintered-looking, half fallen down.

"I think," she said carefully, after ten more minutes had passed and Marika's color was normal, "that this might be a good time for us to talk."

Marika turned and gave her an unblinking stare.

"About you," Lorna went on, "living alone up here."

Marika sniffed. "My ankle feels better."

"I'm glad about that." Lorna settled her sunglasses back over her eyes. The sun had grown stronger over the past half an hour, blazing against the asphalt so that at moments it was hard to see what was ahead. "But I think we need to talk about getting you some help."

There. She'd said it. The rest of the list could wait till later: beginning with a doctor's appointment. These attacks of indigestion, if that's what they were, might indicate high blood pressure, or some sort of heart condition. Marika's hearing, too, should be checked.

Also her memory. That morning she'd had trouble recalling the combination to her post office box when Lorna asked for it, and had to go through the motions of turning the dial to retrieve the numbers. More concerning was when Lorna stopped in at the library to renew Marika's detective novel; the librarian reported that sometimes Marika checked out the same books she'd just returned, unable to recall whether or not she had read them.

She's *old*, Adam had said.

She was also alone. At least as far as Lorna could tell, judging from her calendar, with nothing on it, and that notepad with no one listed under "Visitors." Except, it seemed, for birds, and this Dennis.

"Your landlord has been good about giving you rides into town." Lorna glanced once more at Marika, who after that basilisk glare had given no further indication that she was listening. "But I'm sure he gets busy sometimes, with other commitments."

Marika made a small irritable gesture with her fingers. A drift of torn tissue floated to the floor of the car.

"So," Lorna continued, keeping her voice level and unalarmed, "I think it's time to consider some alternatives." She tightened her grip on the steering wheel. "As I'm sure you know, there are places, complexes, where you can live on your own, but also be around other people, and also get care, if you need it.

"There's a place not far from me, in fact," she heard herself add. "We could look into it, if you're interested."

This was unplanned, and as soon as she stopped speaking she felt almost light-headed. What had she just said? She'd been thinking of mentioning Silver Shores Senior Living, which she had noticed when she was heading back to the car from the CVS. Planning to ask if Marika knew anyone who lived there; perhaps they could arrange for a tour. But instead, out had come this extraordinary invitation.

And yet, was it so extraordinary? It was the sort of offer people made all the time to elderly parents. A transition that would be awkward, of course, no use pretending otherwise, and taxing for them both, especially at first, and might feel, probably would feel, like a mistake; but after a while it would begin to seem more natural, once Marika got acclimated, and once Lorna herself got used to the notion that Marika was living nearby. Avalon Towers was a nice place, according to a client whose father lived there. Near the park, with a view of the pond and the soccer fields from the upper floors. Lots of natural light. Clean and secure. Graduated care.

Marika dragged a tissue from the endless supply in her sleeve and blotted her nose.

"It could be nice. You could come over to dinner." Lorna tried to picture Marika at Avalon Towers, sitting in a lounge with fellow residents, watching a game show on television or listening to the middle school chorus sing Christmas carols. "I could pick you up on my way home from work." Her sense of panic remained, but at a lower ebb and accompanied now by a flicker of expectancy. *Things can change*, she'd said yesterday to Adam in the car. Something she believed, absolutely, or she wouldn't be a therapist; and yet it had been a while since she had thought about change for herself.

"Well, think about it," she said.

They drove on in silence for another ten minutes. Marika sat hunched in her seat, staring at the windshield with her lower lip pushed out, apparently deep in thought. Perhaps turning over Lorna's offer, examining its various angles and potential benefits; perhaps amazed at the idea that such a reversal could happen, that after so many years they might find themselves living in the same place, meeting regularly, and at least in the eyes of the world, behaving more or less like a normal elderly mother and middle-aged daughter. Not that they would see each other all the time. Marika was not a social person; she would want her privacy and independence, and so, of course, would Lorna. Still, proximity would lead to a certain understanding, a shared frame of reference. Outings to the mall, doctors' visits, sometimes lunch in town or a dinner out. Not closeness, but familiarity. Moments like the one after Lorna returned from buying Marika's skin cream, and Marika had guffawed at Lorna's comment about her scales. Perhaps, in the obscure way she considered things, Marika was thinking along those lines, too.

As they were approaching a boatyard, where canoes lay overturned on a gravel lot, Marika did seem to decide something. She sat all the way up in her seat and began massaging her knuckles.

"Did you remember that chicken sandwich?"

"Sorry?" Lorna said.

"That the strange boy wrapped up. Did you remember to take it?"

"He wasn't strange. And no. I forgot."

"Well, that was stupid," said Marika.

For a moment Lorna felt only a dull disbelief. Then her face went hot. Stupid, she thought, fingers trembling on the wheel. Stupid is right.

Directly ahead was a dip in the road, a trough caused by erosion or a hidden stream. Instead of slowing down, Lorna pressed on the accelerator so that when the car hit the dip, it gave a lurching bounce and for a fraction of an instant went airborne. Then with a hard jounce the tires returned to the pavement, jostling them both roughly in their seats.

Over the rushing air from the windows, Lorna raised her voice bitterly. "I'm not the only one who has made mistakes."

"What?" Marika lifted a hand to her ear.

"*Mistakes.* I'm not the only one who's made them."

Marika had been clutching the door handle with her other hand. Now with a pensive look, she released it and sank back against her seat.

"Well, I didn't forget half a chicken sandwich," she said, dabbing at her nose again. "If that's what you mean."

13

A was on a ladder propped against the side of the house, bare-chested, shoulders getting sunburned, wearing a pair of old canvas gloves, scooping fistfuls of pine needles and sodden black leaves out of the gutter. The morning's damp freshness had given way to sticky afternoon heat, but for the past forty-five minutes everything had been forgotten but the rich, musty smell of decayed vegetation and the satisfying physical rhythm of scooping leaves, dropping clumps of them to the ground, climbing down the ladder to shift it a few feet, and then climbing up again. The ladder made a precise shadow against the side of the house and from out on the lake came distant shouts and the drone of motorboats.

Halfway through the gutters, X's car came bumping down the rutted driveway. Had planned to be sulky, left so long without lunch; but instead greeted X and G good-humoredly as they emerged from the car, even pretending to drop pine needles onto X's head when she stood by the ladder.

"You had a visitor," called down to G. "That guy. Dennis."

G had been shuffling from the car toward the back steps with her stick. Now she stopped and craned her neck, turtlelike, to look upward. "What did *he* want?"

"Said he usually comes by to take a walk with you." Adding, with a shower of soggy black leaves, "Says you used to play chess with him."

"Chess?" said X as G began shuffling forward again, picking up her pace. The kitchen's screen door spronged open and then whacked shut.

Paused gutter work, waiting for a further remark from X, for whom this chess info should be surprising. But she was staring in the direction of the roof without seeming to be looking at anything, face white and tense-looking under her sunglasses.

"Forgot phone charger," A said at last. "Battery dead."

"Oh. Left mine," she echoed, in a pathetic attempt to be funny. "At motel."

Possible responses: (1) Vicious outburst. (2) Insist that X drive to the motel to get her charger. (3) Demand to go to the motel with her and use their Wi-Fi. Instead shrugged and went back to digging leaves out of the gutter.

"I should take a photo to send to your father," X said after a few more moments.

"Does he like even know where we are?"

"I tried calling him last night. You should put on some sunscreen. You're going to get burned."

No, *you* are, thought sullenly. She was the one who wore a sun hat the size of a manhole cover. A had inherited Y's swarthy complexion. Also Y's thick eyebrows, big chin. From X, nothing. Except G. And this stupid weekend in Vermont. In a burst of fury, climbed down from the ladder, moved it several feet to the left, climbed back up and attacked a new stretch of gutter, where a whiff of something putrid filtered up from the downspout.

"So what did you think of him?" X had pulled out her phone and raised her sunglasses to peer at it. "Dennis. The landlord. What's he like?"

Hesitation while picturing D by his truck in his baseball cap and bushy survivalist beard, arms folded above his beer belly. Mr. Toxic Masculinity. Although there had been something apologetic about his soft, gaspy voice, a kind of pleading. Like his offer to go out in his boat, to show "the lay of the land," tossing in that six-pack.

"Old. With a beard."

"Well, he's certainly been attentive to Grootie." X put her phone back in her shoulder bag. "Pretty interesting that they play chess."

Finally.

Worked on unclogging the downspout while X said her father and brother used to play chess after dinner. Mostly as a way to keep Wade calm and out of trouble. But on summer evenings, they'd sit in the den where the chessboard was set up, so absorbed by their game that it was sometimes midnight before they looked up from it.

No one cares, thought A. Then wondered why Y had never suggested playing chess. Sunlight sifted through feathery pine needles.

"Where's Freddy?" X asked, and then called, "Freddy? Where's my good boy?" After a moment, Freddy staggered into view from behind the woodpile. "Here, buddy." Freddy leaned against her knees, wagging his tail as she plucked a bramble from his ruff and scratched between his ears.

"Anyway," she said, still addressing Freddy, "I'm glad Grootie has a friend up here. Though she made a point of telling me yesterday he wasn't one."

"He's moving to Florida."

"What?" X stopped scratching Freddy's ears, squinting up into the sun. "When?"

"Soon. Said he needs his parts."

"His parts?"

"Son lives down there."

"Ah." X lowered her sunglasses. "Well, that's going to be hard on Grootie. It seems like she depends on this Dennis for just about everything."

A reached into the downspout again, discovering the remains of an old bird's nest, with bits of eggshell and a few pinfeathers, which broke apart as soon as it was extracted.

"I did suggest," X's voice continued, floating up from below, "the possibility of moving her to an assisted-living facility near us. You know that place Avalon Towers, by the park? It's supposed to be nice." Another pause. "But she didn't seem to like the idea. In fact, the message I got was Over My Dead Body."

A stared down the ladder at her, crumbling the rest of the bird's nest.

"Which, of course," X added lightly, "is another option."

So lame. Just stop. Stop trying so hard to be funny.

14

While Marika lay down for a nap and Adam continued to clean out the gutters, Lorna decided to go for a swim and fetched her bathing suit from the trunk of the car, where she'd tossed a few things into a bag that morning, including a change of clothes. The air had grown heavier as the afternoon advanced, until the shadows under the pine trees looked almost solid.

She was tired and hot, still upset over the incident in the car, and her headache was back. Why had she reacted so childishly to Marika's silly remark? Stamping on the accelerator the same way she used to hurl herself at Wade when he teased her by chanting her nickname, *LaLa, LaLa*, over and over, in a babyish voice. Shoving him for the sheer physical release of it, though she always got shoved back twice as hard. Ridiculous, to get so wounded. Yes, it was frustrating to have her offer rudely dismissed, but to be fair, she had sprung the idea on Marika suddenly, when she wasn't feeling well. An idea about which Marika would, of course, have conflicted feelings. An idea Lorna had sprung on *herself*. No wonder something unreasonable had taken place.

She changed quickly in the bathroom, and then paused to open the medicine chest to look for aspirin. Inside was the expected collection of creams and ointments, stool softeners, a mentholated salve, and some ancient Band-Aids, the wrappers gone nearly transparent. On the top shelf sat a squad of prescription bottles. Pain medications, in different strengths—though no aspirin—and something for acid reflux. But nothing that would indicate high blood pressure, or a heart condition.

Lorna closed the medicine chest and stared at herself in the mirror, at her flushed skin and windblown hair. By contrast her expression was composed. Eyebrows slightly raised, eyelids slightly lowered. She recognized her "listening look," one of neutral inquiry, worn to mask when she was not actually listening. Adopted from years of hearing clients retell anecdotes she'd heard many times before. A look she wore with Adam when he complained for too long about a school friend or a teacher he thought was unfair. Worn, also, in her early days with Roger whenever he started describing in detail one of the viruses being researched in his lab.

Stop, she would finally have to say. Please. I don't want to hear any more. And genuinely perplexed, he'd say, Why not?

Forgetting, of course, about Wade, who had died of one of the worst viruses of all time. Though Roger wasn't being insensitive when he talked for too long about antiretroviral therapy and the progressive depletion of T cells; he was just excited about his or a colleague's research. He had never met Wade.

Being careless without meaning to be careless was no more typical of Roger than it was of anybody else. He was a kind man. Whenever she was sick, he used to bring her tea and toast on a tray. *How are you feeling?* He'd meant it just as solicitously the other night when they were talking about Adam. *How are you feeling?* It was of interest to him, how she was handling what Adam was going through. Undoubtedly he was also interested in how she felt about Angelica, now that they were living together. Though generally speaking, what mostly interested Roger was whatever he was working on.

There had been a time, however, when Lorna was what interested him. For their honeymoon, he'd taken her to the Bow River, in Canada, for a few days of fishing. Their cabin was dark and full of spiders, but the sun came out every day and Lorna was happy to watch Roger fiddle with his gear, his rods and lures and collection of dry flies, and to applaud the trout he caught for dinner. They ate the trout with little boiled potatoes and butter, bought from a store a few miles away, and drank white wine they cooled in the river, and talked about whether they should try to have children.

Their courtship had been relatively quick. Both were at an age when one tried to be realistic about whether a relationship was "going anywhere," and then acted accordingly, and their amazement at finding themselves together, of having life leap one track into another, was still fresh. Roger had been married once before, briefly, unhappily, and figured that was it for him. After several failed romances, Lorna had worried if she was somehow unqualified for marriage. Young women felt differently now, thank god, but she'd grown up believing (while pretending otherwise) that not being married by your late thirties denoted a failure of character as well as of attractiveness, and worse, some sort of fundamental lack of warmth. So it had seemed, on principle at least, that if the opportunity presented itself by that point, one should seize it. And Roger was intelligent, maybe even brilliant, and kind, and nice-looking, with thick curly dark hair and large melancholy dark brown eyes that had reminded her of Omar Sharif's eyes in *Doctor Zhivago*, and also, just slightly, of her father's. Roger had wanted to marry her by their fourth date, saying that no one had ever understood him as well as she did. This had touched her, though she didn't feel that she did understand him. And now here they were, on their honeymoon in Canada.

Fly-fishing was something Roger had loved since boyhood, and eager to please him, Lorna agreed to let him teach her how to cast. Every morning Roger would hand her a rod and they'd stand in the river for a lesson. Roger would demonstrate how to lift the line, the leader, and the fly from the water's surface and fling the rod backward—not too far, or she'd snag the bushes onshore—and then snap the rod toward the water, carefully, to avoid making a splash and scaring away the fish, or tangling the line, or losing the leader. She would grow colder and colder, standing in the river in her rented pair of waders while Roger had her practice a simple cast, which was not simple at all, but required focus and coordination and instinct, and also a kind of relinquishment. She could not manage it, and the more he tried to help her the less she wanted to keep trying.

One evening she sat on a rock while he fished, glad for a little time to herself, watching him cast. On the opposite bank the fir trees were already black and jagged against the sky, but the sun still shone strongly on the water. Roger had waded five or ten yards into the river, far enough that she could no longer see his line. The lowering sun lit up one side of him and every time he lifted the rod, his arm was lit, too. Again and again he made those dramatic, arcing movements with his rod, like a wizard trying to summon something out of the river. Even now, as she closed her eyes, she could see the glowing shape of him, absorbed in his unanswerable gestures.

MARIKA'S BEDROOM DOOR was still closed when Lorna returned from her swim to change back into her clothes, refreshed by the cold water and hot sun. She'd swum back and forth past the dock, looking at neighboring cottages and their flagpoles. Small waves had sparkled around her, each catching a point of sunlight so that it had been like swimming through diamonds.

The kitchen was hushed and shadowy and smelled of rusting aluminum screens. On the counter sat the box of doughnuts she'd bought that morning, empty save for a few crumbs. So Adam hadn't minded her buying them, after all. She threw the box away and then stood looking through the screen door at sun-dappled branches and leaves and shining green needles.

It was still too early to start making dinner. She drank a glass of water and considered trying to fix the dripping kitchen faucet; then suddenly unable to bear that hushed house any longer, she carried her wet bathing suit outside to hang on the line strung from a corner of the deck to a pine tree, where a bird feeder lay at the base of the trunk amid a scatter of birdseed. A few yards away, Adam was raking up the leaves and twigs he'd pulled from the gutters into black mounds.

"Are you hungry?" she asked. "Did you have any lunch, besides doughnuts?" He ignored her and began raking with more energy.

"Okay," she said. "Well, then I think I'll go for a walk." Knowing that he expected her to add "Want to come?" and was already preparing a monosyllabic refusal, Lorna instead whistled for Freddy until he emerged from under the deck, garlanded in dirt and cobwebs. "See you later," she called to Adam, picking up Freddy's leash from the back of the Adirondack chair.

Ranks of spruce and pine, maples and oaks lined the road that ran along the Neck, broken every so often by a half-hidden dirt driveway and glimpses of the glittering lake. Patches of Queen Anne's lace stood out amid tangles of bull thorn and blueberry bushes, and swords of sunlight crossed the road whenever there was a break in the trees. It was very quiet. No cars passed by, though voices could be heard now and then from the direction of the lake, mixing with the breeze creaking through branches overhead and the occasional questioning cry of a mourning dove. As she walked along, Lorna occupied herself by reading last names painted crudely on boards nailed to pine trees at the ends of driveways, sometimes three or four, one above the other, indicating an invisible cluster of cabins. She was trying to make out a faded name painted on the remnant of a gray oar, when she realized that someone was standing in the deep shade beneath it.

A tall, heavyset man in a blue cap set low over his eyes, wearing a black T-shirt and dusty-looking jeans. Late sixties or early seventies, with a gray beard that reached down his neck and up the sides of his cheeks. He was leaning to one side, one arm resting on top of an aluminum mailbox. Beyond him, visible through the trees, were a cabin and a dock. Tied to the dock was a skiff with an outboard motor.

She raised her hand and called out hello. Without changing his posture, the man raised his hand in return, but as she stopped at the driveway he shifted his gaze to his boots as if he had dropped something.

"Met your boy earlier," he said. "And your dog."

Startled, she said, "You must be Dennis." As often as Dennis had been discussed today, she had not actually expected to meet him, or not in this way, by chance, while he was out checking his mail. She reached up to touch her damp hair. "I'm Lorna, as I guess you already know. It's nice to meet you in person."

She waited for him to say something in response. When he continued to stare fixedly at the ground, she gave him a puzzled look before continuing. "I've wanted to thank you for calling to let me know about Marika's ankle, and for doing so much to help her out. I don't know what she would have done without you since she stopped driving."

He said nothing, but seemed to lean more heavily against his mailbox. She began to wonder if he might be drunk. Worrisome, given that he'd been driving Marika back and forth to town. Though he didn't seem drunk, she decided, more like uncertain, noting the intent way he seemed to be studying the ground, like a man gauging the distance before trying to leap across a creek.

"It's good to know Marika has some friends up here." Lorna smiled. "Though I understand from Adam that you're moving soon to Florida?"

A curt nod. Again she waited for some further response. Maybe he had a cognitive impairment, or a speech impediment? He'd greeted her readily enough as she was walking down the road, had acknowledged meeting Adam and Freddy, but now would only stare at his feet and nod. Suddenly she felt exhausted. Not another one. Not another person who was going to make her do all the talking.

"So will you be selling the cottage she's renting?" Despite her sunglasses, the sun was in her face and she regretted not wearing her hat.

Still staring at the ground, he said, "She can stay as long as she likes."

"Well, that's very generous of you." Relieved that he'd at last said something, she added, "It does seem like it would be hard for her to leave such a beautiful place, where she's lived so long. Though I'm worried about her being so isolated. Actually, I've just offered to move her near us, to an assisted-living facility."

Once more, no response. His reticence had begun to seem judgmental. He must disapprove of her, the neglectful daughter, swooping in only now, pretending to take charge. Claiming to be worried about Marika's isolation after not visiting her for nearly twenty years. No longer smiling, she said, "You're probably aware that Marika and I don't see each other often."

A slight shift in his weight, his head tipping an inch or so to the side so that his nose, bulbous and pink above his gray beard, became more visible.

"Not to make excuses," she continued, watching him, "but she doesn't exactly encourage visitors. Except, apparently, you."

Definite change in posture now. He straightened up and leaned away from his mailbox, leaving a large hand planted on it. With the other hand, he pushed up the bill of his ball cap. A series of movements that seemed destabilizing, given his earlier stillness, so that Lorna had the impression of something coming untethered, like a boat drifting away from a dock.

"Anyway," she concluded, "this is my first visit up here in a long time."

"How's it going?" His voice was so quiet it was almost a whisper. A southern accent? She'd taken him for a native New Englander, maybe because of the Red Sox cap.

"Well, her ankle is giving her some pain." Encouraged, Lorna smiled again. "But she won't see a doctor. And she insisted on doing errands with me all morning. She's a pretty tough old thing."

Then, afraid she'd overstepped by making light of Marika's toughness, she added, "By the way, I hear you and she play chess."

Dennis ran a hand over his beard, for the first time meeting her eyes. "People have been saying she's beginning to wander. But for what it's worth, that's not my impression."

The anger in his tone was so undisguised and so unexpected, especially given the softness of his voice, that it took Lorna a moment to register what he'd just said: "People" had observed Marika wandering. Maybe losing her way in the supermarket or roaming the aisles of the CVS, unable to recall what she had come in to buy. Further evidence of what Lorna already suspected, and yet Dennis seemed to be warning her not to believe it.

"Why isn't that your impression?"

"She takes care of herself."

"Well, she *has* been able to," Lorna agreed cautiously. Dennis continued to gaze directly at her. She was suddenly aware of how hushed it was on the road, how empty.

"But from what I've seen," she went on more firmly, "that's no longer true. You called me because she has a sprained ankle and can't get around on her own. Whatever comes next could be worse."

Was he blaming her for the help he'd given Marika? Or blaming Marika for accepting it? Something rustled in the bushes nearby. Freddy gave a low growl.

"Stop that." Lorna reached down to touch his warm, reassuring fur. Freddy quit growling and began chewing a stick that had been lying in the road.

"Well, I guess it's time to get back to start dinner." Anxious to put some distance between herself and this large man and whatever it was that had made him so angry, she turned toward the road. "Thanks again for everything you've done for Marika. And good luck with your move to Florida."

She had already taken a few steps, when she heard him say, "Sorry," and clear his throat. "Sorry," he repeated softly. "I thought Marika might have said something, or you might have recognized me."

"Recognize you?" She turned around.

He pointed to the pine tree and the oar with its faded letters, of which Lorna could make out ACK, then OUS E. "Worked for a while at your grandma's place. Used to see you and your brother playing around the stables."

A memory flared at the back of her mind: a tall, towheaded teenager in dungarees and a flannel shirt standing by the wheelbarrow. Angular face and light-colored eyes, ropy forearms. The one Wade had called Igor. Special agent from the Kremlin. Identified by the excessively casual way he sauntered out of the stables to smoke, afterward flicking the butt onto the dirt to grind it out with a superb twist of a boot heel, which Wade said was a torture technique. Also called Dennis the Red Menace. And then her grandmother's drifting voice: *That Stackhouse boy? Went in the army? Heard he lost a leg over there. Nineteen years old. Such a shame.*

"Dennis?" Lorna said hesitantly. "Dennis Stackhouse?"

"I've changed some," faint suggestion of a smile, "since then."

She stared at him. Why hadn't Marika said anything? For the last twenty years she'd been renting a house belonging to someone from Lorna's own childhood. Someone who had worked on the farm, who had watched Lorna and Wade run through the stables, and known those same low stone walls fronting the road, the turf-green pastures and white board fences. And never said a word about it.

"Yes," Lorna said slowly. "I remember you."

"No reason why you should." Dennis was once more looking at the ground. "You were just a kid."

Another memory, this time of herself standing on the veranda amid wicker chairs, still and empty in the afternoon heat, watching a tall figure on crutches haltingly cross the far edge of crisping lawn, by the boxwoods. He continued downhill, past the kitchen garden with its huge wilting squash leaves and dried up tomato vines, past the rusty swing set, heading toward the shaggy stand of cedars that surrounded the old pool.

It was the fieldstone kind you never see anymore, spring-fed and smelling of muddy nickels. At one end, mossy stone steps led into tea-colored water. In summer the surface was covered in green duckweed, rendering the pool almost invisible within that deep cleft of shade. Nobody had used it in years except Lorna and Wade, daring each other to put a foot in, a whole arm. A swamp creature was hiding down there, Wade claimed, waiting to snatch you under and suck out your eyeballs. And yet twice that summer, they had gone down to the pool to find that someone had been clearing away the duckweed. Clumps of twigs and black leaves were piled up by the side.

Who could have done it? *The creature!* Wade cried the second time, before pushing Lorna in. That had been a couple weeks earlier.

By the time she arrived at the cedars, breathless from running down the hill, the figure she'd seen crossing the lawn was already in the pool. His clothing in a heap, crutches leaning against a tree. His long pale body thrashing back and forth in the dark water like a white eel trapped in a tank. Though what had shocked her, she remembered now, was not his nakedness. It was who was also there, sitting on the stone ledge, smoking a cigarette, skirt pulled to her knees, bare ankles in the pool.

"Yes, of course," Lorna said, shading her eyes to look up at Dennis. "I recognize you."

15

A was napping on the sofa when the screen door from the deck banged open, followed by X saying, "Why didn't you tell me?"

G was in her armchair, also napping. At least, it seemed to take her a while to say, "Tell you what?"

"I just ran into Dennis." X came into the middle of the room and faced G's chair. "Why didn't you share with me who he was?"

G said, "Didn't think of it."

"You didn't think of it?" For a long minute, X stood staring like someone at a busy intersection. Then she walked out of the room and stayed for a while in the kitchen, rattling things. But then she came back and stood again by G's chair. Serious Accomodation face. More discussion of D, who turned out to be somebody X had known as a girl, or anyway from her same town.

"I told you he was my landlord," G interrupted. "You didn't ask me anything else."

"I asked why he came over so often."

"What else did he say?" G was frowning at the window.

"Nothing. It was getting late, so I left."

Long pause, during which G stuck out her chin and X put her hands on her hips, the way she did when she was surveying the garden after planting something.

"But," she said, "I invited him to dinner tonight."

G jerked in her chair. "Who said you could do that?"

"I'm making dinner. And I invited him as my guest. It seems like a good evening," X added cryptically, "for a little gathering."

A decided it was time for a swim.

An hour later, the house was saturated with the heavy aura of People Not Speaking. Like walking into a damp sponge. A red sauce simmered on the stove, filling the kitchen with the smell of onions, tomatoes, and meat. So *hungry* after all that work on the gutters, plus had just swum for half an hour, and spaghetti Bolognese was an all-time favorite meal. But *vegan*, something X had obviously once more forgotten. Or hadn't forgotten, but would pretend she had, because spaghetti Bolognese had been planned and it was too much trouble to make something different, and because she thought being vegan was a phase, a fad, instead of being the only sustainable choice to make on a dying planet.

In the living room, X was gazing at the spotty red-checked plastic shroud covering the picnic table. "Let's take this off and wash it. Maybe we could use a sheet as a tablecloth."

"Not one of my sheets," said G, gripping her stick.

X had already begun rolling up the plastic shroud. With a little furniture polish, she declared, the wooden tabletop should be fine.

"I don't have furniture polish." G thumped her stick. It made a hollow, knocking sound against the floor.

In a strained voice, X said, "Adam, please don't eat peanut butter from the jar. And I could use a hand." She always made such a big deal about setting the table when she had people to dinner, especially for events like Thanksgiving, when she had candles going up and down the table and made a fancy centerpiece of flowers and tiny pumpkins. A table sets the stage, she liked to say. Another way for her to try to control everything.

With wet rags they scrubbed the top of the picnic table and then oiled it using vegetable oil and paper towels. The result was actually not bad if you ignored the rusty nail heads. On to table setting: knives here, forks there, X inspecting each one as if searching for germline mutations.

Holding a water glass up to the light, she said, "I thought it would be a nice gesture, inviting Dennis to dinner, since he's been so nice to you."

"A lot of fuss over nothing," growled G, "if you ask me."

"All right." X set the glass on the table. "If this is your version of fuss. Then I guess we're making one."

Some kind of subterranean conversation was flowing like dark magma between them. Recalled X's tense look after she and G came back from their errands. Maybe they'd had a fight in the car. Maybe they'd finally "talked." Fingered a sore bump on chin.

Though what could they have said? Nothing good, apparently. Some things best left unsaid. Like admitting what a total crap person you were. *You did what you did*, G had said last night over cognac. *We all had our facts*.

Exactly. So leave them alone. Because if you ever *did* admit what a total crap person you were, what you were really hoping was that someone else would try to argue that you *weren't* a total crap person, that the facts weren't as bad as they seemed, which would be a total lie. Hence: Shut the fuck up.

"Don't you want to change, Adam?" X looked up from the table. "Get out of that damp bathing suit?"

Shrug. "Whatever."

Five minutes later, X was still fretting over the table, now asking whether G had any candles. Negative. Followed her into the kitchen, where she began searching through drawers and then under the sink, eventually excavating three white plumber's candles, and knocking over a coffee can, sending a scatter of chicken bones across the floor.

"What are *those* for?" The chicken bones were dry and withered-looking, like something from an ancient Etruscan burial site.

"Compost," X said. "Fertilizer, I think."

She gathered the chicken bones and replaced them in the can. Next, she unearthed an old green china pitcher. "Look at this. Genuine Fiestaware. Probably worth something." She stood up cradling the pitcher and handed over a dented aluminum colander, also just exhumed, and asked for a collection of pebbles from the lake.

"What? Why?"

"I have an idea."

Returned with a couple handfuls of dirty pebbles. By then, the green pitcher held a bunch of wildflowers and three glass jelly jars stood on the counter. X rinsed the pebbles under the faucet, and then dropped them into the jelly jars and filled the jars partway with water. Into each one stuck a plumber's candle.

"Voilà," she said, stepping back to view her handiwork. "Instant atmosphere."

"For *what*?" Had not meant to sound quite so nasty.

She continued to gaze at the jelly jars, eyes unreadable. "For whatever," she said, at last, "I suppose."

CLOUDS HAD BEGUN GATHERING above the dark pines to the north. By seven o'clock the sun was starting to set, turning the sky a deep mauve that was reflected in the lake. Cooler air was on the way from Canada, according to the radio's weather station, creating the potential for a lake effect that could mean rain. All the windows were open, and like a ship at sail, the cottage was full of sound: water slapping against rocks, dock piles ringing, the plastic tablecloth flapping on the clothesline outside. Watery laughter and snatches of rock music drifted through the windows, and every few minutes a speedboat bumped across the lake, out for an evening cruise.

Oh, to be on one of those boats! On a warm summer night that smelled of sunscreen and other people's barbecues! Instead of being trapped in a half-empty cottage in northern Vermont with two women who basically hated each other. In truth, the scourge was too great.

Everyone seemed relieved when D arrived with a bottle of red wine. D took off his baseball cap, revealing a bald head that made him look smaller, and stared at the candles and the pitcher of flowers on the scrubbed picnic table. For a moment it looked like he might put his cap back on and make a run for it. But X was already saying, "So nice of you to come, Dennis, you didn't need to bring anything."

They sat down at the table while she brought in the food, sat down herself, and poured everyone water. Looking somber but determined to get the party going, she passed around bowls and plates, keeping up a steady patter of boring small talk. ("What a lovely evening, look at the sunset, shall we open your wine?")

And yet, as they all began eating, something was not right. D seemed half afraid to lift his fork, responding to any question X directed at him with a nearly inaudible yes or no. G stayed focused on her food, steadily chewing spaghetti noodles. When X asked, "How's the pasta? I was worried the sauce might be too heavy for tonight," G ignored her and kept chewing. Though X's expression remained calm, the dark undercurrent between them seemed more molten now.

"Who needs more wine?" asked X, pouring more wine for herself. "Anyone?" As she put the bottle down, she said, "So I went swimming today. The water wasn't as cold as I expected. Adam, you went swimming today, too. How did it feel to you?"

An innocuous-sounding question. On the other hand, red flags whenever X brought the word *feel* into anything. In fact, the timing of this dinner party suddenly seemed suspicious, given what had happened between X and G in the car when Avalon Towers came up, and then their argument this afternoon over why G had never "shared" anything about D. Maybe this gathering wasn't just a "nice gesture." Maybe it was some sort of psychological ambush, devised by X to show G what she'd be missing by refusing to go to Avalon Towers. A theory that explained the flowers, candles, etc., and why X was now yakking on and on. Setting the stage: *See how nice this is?* This *is sharing. This is what living with people is like.*

In which case, go Team G. Fuck social life.

Okay, unfair. X was not devious. She had not pretended to forget the vegan thing tonight, for instance, but had made a special no-meat dish of spaghetti, with peppers, which was actually decent, and she was talking so much because no one else was saying anything. Also it *was* pretty nice of her to offer to have G live nearby, considering that G had gone off and left her without so much as a *See ya, kid.*

Pushed away plate. No. Do not dwell on X's sad childhood, which she had so obviously tried to use yesterday as sympathy-bait, to get A to "open up."

Also it was her fault they were all here in the first place. Also: tomato sauce on T-shirt. Looked like a stab wound. Death by annoyance.

"Adam, would you like more spaghetti? Anyone need anything?"

No one needed anything. The conversation foundered. X tried going around the table and asking each person how they learned to swim, and then, getting mostly nowhere, resorted to describing her own first experience with swimming, which was when her brother had pushed her into an old pool full of green muck and then had to drag her out.

"We used to think a monster lived down there," she said. "Funny that there's one here, too, at the lake. Do you remember that pool?" she said, looking at G. "Under the trees?" she went on. "Just before the back pastures."

What was she talking about? Weird vibes.

The sunset was fading now to streaks of pinkish gold, and the room seemed to darken, drawing the four of them closer around the table, lit only by the three candles in jelly jars. Their hushed, candlelit faces suddenly gave the impression of a séance.

"So, Dennis." X raised her glass. "What about you?" Her tone had grown even calmer, and seemed strangely detached.

"What brought you up here, Dennis?"

D seemed to hear something strange in her voice, too, and shifted uncomfortably on the bench. But then, with a condemned look from under his bristly eyebrows, he cleared his throat and began talking about fishing. The lake was full of trout, perch, pike, largemouth bass. A began listening with more interest. Watching seven hours of *Slow TV: Salmon Fishing* equals learning something about fishing. At least about fishing in Norway. For instance, spring salmon running up river got tired and needed to rest in depressions in the riverbed. Never considered that fish got tired and looked for specific places to rest—river*beds*, haha.

D revealed that he did most of his fishing from his boat, but was a fly fisherman, too.

"My husband used to like fly-fishing," said X, still in that detached voice. "We spent our honeymoon on a river in Canada."

Despite the breeze, the room was getting hot. X drank off her glass of wine. She began talking again, but A was no longer listening, having left the table for a river in Canada. Tall dark firs, mountains, rocky cliffs, rushing water. Birds wheeling in a sapphire sky. Then, in a shaft of sunlight, there *she* was. She. Who Could Never Be Named. Face golden, wearing a plaid shirt and jeans. Watching A wade into the river, catching a trout and holding it up. Both of them drinking wine by a campfire, shoulders touching, leaning toward each other, smiling. A shuddered and held on to the edge of the table.

Outside, the sunset's last orange streaks were reflected in the opalescent lake. How cool it would be to glide across the lake in the evening, listening to your paddle dip into the water as the light sank farther into the trees. Paddling away from everyone forever. Never having to see any human being ever again.

"So how did you two come to be up here together?" asked X.

The lake faded away, replaced by the same candles in jelly jars, the same plates and silverware, the same tired old faces. X sat gazing at the candles. Across the table, G and D stared at her like they'd come across a sleepwalker in the living room, holding a box of matches.

A took a deep breath, only then registering that X had asked a question and no one had answered it. Most of her questions this evening had been met with some kind of resistance. But as the current silence became more prolonged, it no longer seemed like a pause while she figured out what to say next; it had a deliberate, waiting quality. And in that same instant, A understood what had created the séance-like feeling around the table.

It was her tone. The one she'd used in the car yesterday when talking about trauma theories, her tone a few days before when she'd said, *It must be painful to care about nothing*. That detached therapisty tone. That's what was going on here, the real purpose behind this "gathering."

X was trying to conduct some kind of group therapy session. She was trying to get them all to open up.

The breeze itself had stalled, as if the whole world was holding its breath, and then a sound did enter the room: a whisper, a hiss, a barometric shift, like the creaking of boats just ahead of a storm, as they swung the other way on their moorings.

16

A drop of wax slid down a plumber's candle with a tiny *zizz* as it hit the water in the jelly jar. In the middle of the candles sat the old green pitcher Marika kept under the kitchen sink, used occasionally as a chamber pot in the winter if the pipes froze. Something she'd decided not to mention tonight when Lorna filled it with daisies and whatnot and set it on the table. Candles and flowers. Food too spicy. Too much jibber-jabber. A lot of fuss over nothing. The boy had his mouth hanging open again. And Dennis was staring at Lorna across the table. Old fool.

Peering more closely at the wildflowers in the pitcher, Marika noticed that Lorna had also picked a few sprigs of lavender. Why couldn't she leave things alone? Interfering where she had no right.

"I asked you a question." Lorna's voice again.

"What?" Marika transferred her gaze to what was left of the bread on the breadboard, surrounded by crumbs. The light had drained from the windows, and except for the table and the faces glowing around it, the room had gone dark.

"I asked how you and Dennis came to be up here together."

Marika continued to consult the bread heel on the breadboard. It came to her that she didn't feel well. Not well at all. The dinner had not agreed with her.

"Is this question upsetting for you?"

"Is what?" said Marika.

"I'm wondering how you feel about me asking you this question."

The boy was shaking his head. Marika groped in her sleeve for a tissue. She discovered she was sweating and felt a spasm deep in her bowels.

"It seems like it's a difficult question for you to answer."

Where had she heard that voice before? Marika closed her eyes. And there in the window was a pair of mirrored sunglasses and a chapped-faced young policeman with a brown mustache, telling her he was taking her car keys.

"I'm wondering why it's so difficult? Why you feel you can't answer me?"

Marika shook her head. I'm fine. Give me my car keys back. I want to go home.

"The question is a simple one," came the policeman's voice. "Would you like me to repeat it?"

And then Dennis's voice said softly, "Stop."

Marika opened her eyes. Why was Dennis here? Why had she invited him?

"I'm sorry?" said the policeman.

Dennis said, "I think you should stop what you're doing."

"What *I'm* doing?"

No, it was Lorna, not the chapped-faced young policeman, who was sitting across from her. Lorna seemed surprised to see Dennis, too. Good, thought Marika. Maybe she'll quit talking and tell him to go home. I'm tired. I need to use the toilet.

But instead Lorna said, "Go ahead, Dennis. It sounds like you have something to say."

"She left with me."

Across the table, the boy tipped back in his seat. From outside came a splash as something slid into the lake.

"Left with you," repeated Lorna.

A dull anger had begun burning in Marika's cheeks, replacing her worry about those missing car keys. Lorna and her fussbudget questions. Where's your dishwasher, where's your toaster, why don't you fix that lamp? Aren't you lonely? It's not a crime to be comfortable, let's find a good complex for you.

"Could you say more, Dennis?" Lorna's face had gone blurry above the candles. A child's face was now there instead, pale and round in the candlelight. A livid face that seemed to float out of the dimness, disembodied, like a small offended moon.

"Say more about what you mean, by left with you?"

Dennis was stroking his beard. "We left together."

"I see. You left together. But just so I understand, that means—?"

"For godsake," Marika snapped as an ugly spasm seized her, deep in her bowels. "*You* know what it means. Don't be so stupid."

For a long moment no one spoke. Then there was a hard rusty scrape, like the sound the woodstove latch made when it opened. Lorna had pushed back the bench where she and the boy were sitting. She stood up and looked at everyone at the table, and then at Marika.

"What is wrong with you?" she said.

"Mom," said the boy.

I don't feel well, thought Marika broodingly, looking into her plate at the worm-like remains of spaghetti. That's what's wrong with me.

"Do you have any idea of the pain you caused?"

A pair of small gray birds flew into the room and landed on the table to begin pecking at her plate. Each had a gray cockade and a smooth buff front. Hello, little birds, Marika said to them, trying to remember what they were called.

"Do you have any idea," one of the birds said, "what it's like to find out that your mother left you for a teenager she hardly knew? Just drove off one day without even saying goodbye?"

Marika tried to stop listening, but twittering filled her ears. The bird tilted its gray head and fluffed its wings, at her with a bright black eye.

"And never called, or wrote? Do you have any idea what it was like to know we had a mother somewhere in the world, but not know anything else? Except that she didn't care about us?"

"*Mom*," said the boy.

"How could you just leave us like that?" The birds were now perched on the edge of her plate, both regarding her with their hard shiny eyes. "Did you ever think about how that *felt*?"

"No," Marika said angrily to the birds. "Never thought of it." And with a sweep of her arms she shooed them away.

The pitcher fell over, the candles, the empty wine bottle went clattering onto the floor. Water and flowers spilled everywhere. Dennis jumped up. A paper napkin caught on fire. The boy had to dump his plate over it. A singed smell drifted up from the table, and in the sudden darkness, as if from a great height, Marika saw herself lying on the ground by a campfire in the Hilversum forests, gazing up at the stars.

But when she opened her eyes she was still at the table. Someone switched on the hanging lamp. Marika sat blinking in the sudden glare, dazed by the feeling she sometimes had in her armchair, waking to find herself still halfway wherever she'd just been.

From behind her came voices. Someone said, "upsetting." Someone else said, "yes, I see." Then Dennis was saying, "Maybe it would be better." And Lorna, muffled and faraway, as if she were speaking from inside one of the kitchen cabinets, said: "Adam, go get your things." But across the table, piling plates on top of each other, the boy was shaking his head, saying no, he wasn't going. "I'll stay here," he said. "I'll clean all this up."

Once again Marika felt herself slipping away, now to a street in snow, where she leaned her bicycle against a shop window, and someone said in Dutch, Don't put it there. What is wrong with you? There was a bang and she woke up. But it was only the screen door banging shut. Then a sound like a plane flying over the driveway, a roar that grew fainter and fainter, until it disappeared.

"*Waar is dit*," she said.

"What?" said the boy, bending toward her.

"Where is this?" she asked impatiently.

He looked like he'd swallowed a chicken bone. He seemed even younger than he had before, with his stupid scared astonished eyes. Young in a way she'd forgotten, until that child's face floated toward her across the table.

17

Eleven ten, read the illuminated digital clock on the nightstand. A little while ago it had started to rain. Lorna got up for a glass of water and then lay down once more to stare at the motel ceiling, where raindrop shadows ran and merged across a watery rectangle, reflected by lights in the parking lot.

It had been such a simple plan. After meeting Dennis on the road, after realizing who he was, she'd thought, Let's do this now, while we're here together. It had made so much sense, the idea to get everything out in the open. As she walked back to Marika's cottage in the ordinary light of the afternoon, she had thought it all out: If she and Marika were to go forward, if Marika were persuaded to move to Avalon Towers, for instance, if Lorna was to take care of her, then it was finally time to confront why Marika had left. The central question of Lorna's childhood. Get it out on the table. It would be done calmly, frankly. The way she and Roger spoke about Adam when he had issues. The way they had discussed Roger's move to Seattle and what that would mean for them both. No recriminations, just a clear look at the events of the past. I need an explanation, Lorna would say. I need some closure. If we are to have any kind of real relationship, I need to understand why you did what you did. That's all I'm asking. And Marika would have Dennis there, for support, or corroboration, or as a friend, or whatever he was. And Adam—Adam would see two people talking about something difficult. He would see how freeing it was to face hard things.

A benign intervention, that's all it was supposed to be. In her own house, while having a good meal, Marika might finally be able to say a few words about what she had done and why. Then the healing, or something like it, might begin.

But it had not happened that way. And what happened instead was Lorna's fault.

There again was Dennis, saying quietly, *I think you should stop*, and Marika, lurching against the table, thrusting out her arms like a blind swimmer. Tumbling candles, the green pitcher spilling, a spurt of fire. Dennis and Adam both leaping up, rushing to help her. And Adam, his face a frightened knot.

Eleven sixteen, read the clock.

Lorna rolled over to look at the streaming motel window. In Seattle, Roger would probably be having dinner. At a restaurant, or maybe Angelica had made dinner for him. Or maybe they'd both bought sandwiches from a food cart or a vending machine and gone together back to the lab.

How are you feeling?

I feel terrible, she thought, rolling onto her back again and staring at the ceiling. I have never felt worse.

Eleven nineteen.

For some time now she had been aware of a noise, which at first seemed to be coming from inside the room. A low, glottal, backed-up sound, accompanying the rain coursing down the roof, a kind of obstructed channeling. Above her motel window a gutter must be clogged. She thought of Freddy, outside on Marika's deck. Though Adam would have brought him in by now, and put him in the kitchen.

Rolling over once more, she reached for her cell phone on the nightstand. He would hear it in the uncertain way she said, *Roger?* What's wrong? he would ask. Are you all right? It would be such a relief to hear his deep familiar voice, to have, even for a few minutes, someone concerned about her.

But then she'd have to explain everything: who Dennis was, and how he came to be at dinner, and then what she had done. How, as she'd looked across the candles at Marika, she'd intended to ask only: So why did you feel you had to leave your children so abruptly? She had meant to say: It must have been very painful, to leave us like that, without saying goodbye. I wonder if something similar happened to you? Being left, so suddenly? But then that calm, empathic self had stood up from the table and walked away, and someone else took her place. A cold, enraged person, intent not on asking questions so much as using them as knives to carve up the cowering old woman across from her. That was what she would have to explain to Roger. I drank too much wine. I let my anger get away with me. And even if she did manage all that explaining, she'd then have to hear him pause and consider his response.

Why, after all this time, could it matter so much to find out that Marika went off with someone? Haven't you always thought so?

Yes, and no, it doesn't matter, not anymore. But how could it *not* matter? A boy? Nineteen? *Adam's* age?

What Roger would say then was: So you left? You left Adam there?

I didn't leave *him*. I left. He wouldn't come with me.

And then Roger would not say: Can you blame him? But he would think it, and she would certainly hear it.

She put her cell phone back on the nightstand and closed her eyes.

18

It was Wade's fault. He had insisted on it.

He had found a letter in Marika's dresser drawer, written in code. Sent by someone in her spy network, probably orders for her next mission. And because he had found that letter, he'd "blown her cover." He explained all this to Lorna as they walked up and down the hot driveway, kicking at pebbles and stopping to pick at patches of softening tar. Once you blow a spy's cover, the spy had no choice but to vanish. Lives were in danger. But who was she spying for? You're not supposed to know with spies. Even *they* sometimes don't know. Wade followed *I Spy* on television, which Lorna was not allowed to watch, and spoke with authority. If I had that letter, I'd show you. Couldn't read a word.

Children always blame themselves when their parents abandon them. The reasons are painstakingly logical: they were too noisy, fought too much, cried too much, talked back, asked for toys they couldn't have, didn't clean up their rooms when they were told. Wade's claim that Marika was a spy justified why she was so remote and uninterested in him, just as his investigations of her dresser drawers explained why she had left. All Lorna knew back then was that a week earlier Wade had been caught before bedtime with something he'd taken from Marika's bedroom. Marika caught him as he was sneaking out the door. Snatching up her hairbrush, she chased him through the house, into the kitchen and down the cellar steps, grabbing his shirt collar in front of the furnace room door, and struck him in the face, making his lip bleed. Lorna watched, frozen at the top of the stairs as Marika came up the steps a few moments later, where she'd given Lorna a hard slap, as well.

That should have been the end of it. When Marika got angry, she struck out at whatever child was nearby, usually Wade, and then her anger was spent; almost immediately she seemed to forget whatever had just enraged her. But that night, Marika had beaten Wade in a kind of frenzy. Face blank, arm rising and falling faster and faster, as if someone who had no connection to him or to her, or to any of them, was in charge of turning up the speed on a machine.

Even more unaccountably, long after Lorna had finished crying and was almost asleep, Marika appeared in her doorway. It was rare for her to visit Lorna after she was in bed, so she must have been troubled about what had happened, although she didn't say so. Smelling strongly of cigarettes, she came into the room, closed the door partway behind her, and sat on the bed, light from the hallway illuminating a long stripe of her body as she crossed her legs. For a few minutes she sat staring at the half-closed door, her face still blank, and then she said, I have something to tell you.

What Marika had related that night, and over the handful of nights that followed, wasn't so much a story as a series of fragments. She offered no introduction for the incidents she described, came to no conclusions, and as if recounting someone else's memories, referred to herself throughout as "she." It was left to Lorna, later, to assemble what she'd heard into a narrative: the nurse sister, messages on medicine jar labels, bicycle deliveries, children in a cupboard, arrests, an escape, the convent school. In fact, over the years Lorna had sometimes wondered if she'd made up those nighttime visits, created a set of false memories, to give herself that brave girl bicycling through Amsterdam. A girl she would have liked to be herself. As Lorna recalled those nights now, it seemed to her that she had never since waited so anxiously for anyone's arrival or felt as much anticipation as when she heard her mother's steps on the carpeted stairs leading to the second floor, heard her breathing for a moment on the landing, and the soft creak of the door opening.

Then one morning she was gone. Three days later, Lorna's father called her and Wade into his den.

It was a small, low-ceilinged room at the far end of the house, steeped in pipe smoke and perpetual shade from two hemlocks standing sentinel outside the windows. In one of the bookcases, a row of rusty leather book spines swung outward when you tugged on them, revealing a cavity that a hundred years before had probably held a pair of flintlock revolvers, but now concealed bottles of Old Crow. A room their father rarely left except for meals, or to attend to farm business, never very demanding. The stables were rented out to DC people who kept horses to ride with the hunt, and the stable hands saw to the tack and the feed; the back pastures let to neighbors for their cattle. For most of each day he read in his armchair, though on summer evenings he would venture out to sit on the veranda with Granny, nodding every so often while she talked about engagement parties of people who'd been dead for twenty years, and second cousins she hadn't visited in five decades, and her great-aunt who had seen Abraham Lincoln ride a white horse down a street in Gettysburg and turned her back.

He was the only one with the patience for Granny's reminiscences, perhaps because he couldn't hear most of what she said. *When people are talking, it's common courtesy to show you're listening*. He had repeated this instruction to Wade and Lorna whenever he noticed them ignoring their grandmother during one of her stories. *Listen and you might learn something*. That was another. His thick gray mustache hung over the top of his mouth, hiding his missing teeth. He refused to go to the dentist. Perhaps there wasn't money? Perhaps he was afraid? People in those days thought dentists put truth serum in Novocain. If you needed to tell him something, you stood in front of him and spoke slowly.

Well, said their father, pulling on his pipe. Your mother has gone on vacation with a friend.

A few nights earlier Marika had been sitting on the end of Lorna's bed, describing bicycling across Amsterdam with a jar in her basket. The night before that, it had been soldiers in the doorway. Children led up the back stairs in their socks.

On the sofa beside her, Wade kept picking at his scabby lower lip. When he saw Lorna looking at him he contorted his face into a leer.

Their father puffed out another blue cloud. Don't think she'll be back.

Watching his pipe smoke spiral upward, Lorna felt herself float upward with it, and then curl toward the window and out into that pinkish twilight, wafting through the dark hemlock branches and away over the pastures. The window grew smaller as she drifted over the hills and watched herself become even smaller, sitting on the plaid sofa next to Wade, pulling at loose threads in the armrest, the soles of her saddle shoes sticking up like a pair of exclamation points.

A common effect of trauma, dissociation. Something Lorna had pointed out many times to her clients. Less recognized was traumatic reasoning, how convincing and convinced it can be. That evening in the den, observing herself on the plaid sofa from somewhere over the dusky pastures, Lorna understood exactly why her mother had left, and it had nothing to do with Wade's spy stories. Something had been expected of her on those nights when Marika came to sit on the end of Lorna's bed to talk about herself as a girl. Some encouragement, some sympathetic word or gesture, even a nod, to show that she was listening. It was common courtesy. But afraid of breaking whatever spell had brought her mother to her room, Lorna had lain there silent and unmoving, night after night, hardly allowing herself to breathe. And so Marika had gone somewhere else. "With a friend."

Lorna was staring once more at the watery rectangle on the motel ceiling. As she watched patterns of raindrops merge and slide, there it was again, that obstructed murmuring, audible even with the window shut.

A hosiery bag dropped into her mind. Pink satin, trimmed with black lace. There used to be such things as hosiery bags and Marika had owned one, hung on a hook near the bathtub. Unearthed by Wade from under a pile of rags in the laundry room later that summer, saved perhaps by their grandmother to turn into a pincushion. Printed across its pink satin front, in silken black script: *Little girls count on their fingers. Big girls count on their legs.*

There was nothing mystifying about why Marika left. People are always simpler than you think, though their situations might be complicated and usually were. In this case, it was the usual story. Boredom. Frustration. Loneliness. Married to a man she didn't love, whom she'd met as a volunteer nurse at a convalescent hospital outside of—Lorna couldn't remember—maybe Luxembourg, where he'd lain for months, his bandaged head "like a big old wasp's nest"; before he was unbandaged, they were engaged. The best way to get out of Europe was with an American officer. But what had Marika imagined while he was still wrapped up? Probably not a deaf man missing half his teeth, who would spend his days reading Civil War histories and drinking bourbon from a tarnished stirrup cup starting at noon. Who would bring her, at eighteen (nineteen?), to live in an old house in a Virginia backwater run by an addled old lady toddling around in a housecoat and flat sneakers, talking to herself all day and clutching things she meant to "fix," cracked gravy boats, torn pillowcases: *A stitch in time saves nine.* To become mother to a fat neurotic boy obsessed with her lingerie drawer and to a prim little girl who lay listening to her war stories, the one time she decided to tell them, as impassively as a doll.

So she'd legged it. Using a shell-shocked teenager as her getaway car.

She left with me, we left together.

Stupid.

Lorna winced in the darkness of the room.

How had it begun between them? A chance meeting in town outside the courthouse, or by the post office or the Ben Franklin. Dennis on crutches, watching people stare at his pinned pant leg. Or by accident, along the farm's long driveway, or at the stables, where Dennis had stopped for a visit. Or maybe the first time had been at the old stone pool. Knowing it was there, and rarely visited, Dennis had quietly cleared out the duckweed, grateful for a cool, private place where he could be alone with what was left of him, until one day he wasn't.

A few weeks, a month later, they were gone. It would have been Marika's idea, vanishing without a word. Figuring that by committing an act of such utter selfishness she was absolved of anything else. Because once you've done the worst thing you can think of to people you're supposed to care for—hurt them, betrayed them, left them for dead—you're free. Nothing you do will ever be as bad. You're on your own.

Though Marika hadn't been all on her own. There was Dennis who, for a time, she may have loved, or something like it. In some way he must have loved her, too, even after marrying someone else and moving across the country, having a son. At least here they were, still together.

And Marika hadn't completely freed herself, either. There had been that postcard of the lake, eighteen years ago. With an address and a phone number, above which had been printed neatly: *If you care to contact me.*

Lorna rolled onto her stomach and pulled the pillow over her head, but the gutter on the motel roof continued its obstructed murmuring long after the rain had stopped.

19

Rain began just before eleven, a light tapping on the roof, bringing the cool scent of pine needles and mud through the window screens. Yet the rain wasn't what woke A on the sofa. It was something else, a deep hoarse groaning, followed by a savage, tearing cough. A heart-walloping, bear-ripping-open-your-tent sound.

But outside the window, there was only Freddy's dark shape on the deck, curled between the lee of the Adirondack chair and an overhang of eaves. The next moment it became clear that someone was in the bathroom, that the door was not closed, and that this someone was the source of that savage noise.

"Uh, hello?"

The noise came again. Awake enough now to recognize retching, followed by a bodily explosion that must not be identified.

"Uh, hi? Are you okay?"

Outside, the world was quiet except for the rain, which in the past few minutes had gone from tapping to drumming. Trembling, stood up from the sofa and felt around on the floor for T-shirt and shorts. Dressed quickly and then sat down again on the sofa, eyes beginning to adjust to the dark. Don't just sit there. Get up. Go. Barefoot, marched past the shadowy picnic table and toward the hallway and the half-open bathroom door.

"Everything okay?"

Another explosion, followed by a rough drawn-out groan and a terrible smell. A word emerged from the bathroom. It was repeated, in a pant.

"Garlic."

More retching. Remained in the hall to one side of the bathroom door, spread-eagled against the rough pine wall, T-shirt collar pulled up to cover nose.

"Uh, let's call my mom?"

Nothing.

"Okay? We should like call my mom." Then stopped short, blinking in the darkness. My mom. *My mom.* Those two syllables, powdery in the mouth, felt like they belonged to someone else.

A moan from the bathroom. "No."

"She can help. She can get you to a doctor."

"No."

The rain on the roof now sounded like coins spilled from a jar. There was an old black telephone in the kitchen, noticed tonight when cleaning up all those dishes and washing pots. Call X. But if called, would she even come? Should she come? After what happened at dinner?

Though it had been expected, ever since that shocker in the car. Some kind of confrontation. It had to happen. Various allegations would be traded, followed by some kind of therapeutic truce. This, at least, was what happened in novels about dysfunctional families (preferred genre of X's book club). Had totally expected some kind of cringeworthy horror show. But not that the horror would be X. Not that she would be cruel. To an old sick woman.

Had not, ever, expected that.

Another explosion from the bathroom. More moaning. Crouching in the hallway, tried to remember X's cell phone number. Always went to "FAVORITES" on phone, but phone dead. She must be at the motel. But which motel? Was playing *Tetris* last night when she went to check in and hadn't even looked at the sign. Maybe call every motel in town and keep asking for her until got the right one? (*Hi, this is like an emergency? Is my mom there?*)

Was inching down the hall toward the kitchen, feeling for a light switch, when there was another deep groan, followed by what sounded like a sack of grapefruits hitting the floor. Then nothing. One moment, two, three, ten.

Only the rain, clamoring against the roof, and the sound of a heart pounding. Slid a couple feet, peered into the bathroom. On the floor a dark hump. Jerked away and stood again with back pressed against the wall.

What if she was dead? Shit. Shit. Oh *shit.* Call an ambulance?

Rain closed like a curtain around the house. A grumble of thunder. Out on the deck Freddy began to howl. Shit, shit. *Shit.*

And yet, at the same time felt curiously calm.

"We need to call an ambulance." Announced from the hallway, still with T-shirt masking nose. Palming the wall, finally found the light switch. In the sudden brightness, two electrical sockets stared back in astonishment.

A moan. "No ambulance."

"We need to get you some help."

"Leave me alone."

"You passed out." Voice sounding deeper than usual, but also somehow familiar. "You're probably dehydrated."

Thunder, louder this time, followed by a shock of lightning. Moved a few more inches to the right and peered again into the bathroom, and then yanked away, flattened once more against the wall. Had seen what now could never be un-seen: nightgown twisted above her waist, knobby spine, pale shrunken—

For an instant, teleported to tenth-grade Bio, watching a video of an anatomical model of the small and large intestines, molded in beige and lavender, listening to a voice intone: *And here is where fecal matter is formed and stored before its eventual expulsion. The large intestine is a truly amazing organ, over five feet long, beautifully compacted.* Then back in the bathroom doorway.

The body on the floor had begun to shiver. "Do not call."

"Well, you can't stay like this." Squinted over T-shirt mask. "If we're not calling an ambulance, at least we need to get you cleaned up and back into bed."

"Leave me alone," she repeated, but more weakly.

"It's okay." Again that weirdly deep voice. Stepped across the threshold and into the dark bathroom. "You're going to be all right. We're going to take care of you."

Reached down to pat her shoulder and then stepped over her to flush the toilet. "It's okay." Pushed aside the shower curtain to turn on the bathtub faucet.

She offered no resistance to being helped into a sitting position. Or to having nightgown dragged carefully over her head and sleeves disentangled from her arms. Damp cotton underwear had to be tugged from around her knees, down her thin calves, and off her bony ankles, and then she had to be lifted, hauled, and settled back onto the toilet, where she gave a little grunt, maybe of pain, maybe of relief to be once again upright. Tried to avert eyes, but in the yellow light from the hallway glimpsed sunken breasts, white and flaccid against the folds of her belly, and a crevice between her thighs, almost hairless.

Once she was securely on the toilet, the floor had to be faced: a biohazard. Must contain before further action could be taken. Folded the soiled bath mat to use as a mop, before throwing the whole mess into the hall. Opened window above the towel rack to disperse toxins. Next, test the water from the bathtub faucet with wrist, as X had done with baths, to make sure it wasn't too hot, before pulling the knob at the base of the faucet to redirect water through the showerhead.

She made a small, frightened noise.

"Don't worry," came that convincing voice through the T-shirt. "We've got you."

Moving cautiously, almost formally, reached under her armpits. Once on her feet, she seemed to have no muscles at all. Managed to wrap both arms around her waist and then did a two-step stagger to the bathtub. A long pause while she seemed to be catching her breath. Finally, grunting again, she raised one leg over the side of the tub and by degrees, while still supported, raised the other. There was an awful moment when it seemed both would lose balance under her full weight and fall together into the tub; but using every last spark of strength, still trying to avert gaze, was able to stand her up under the shower spray.

Billows of steam enveloped them. T-shirt now became smothering; plucked it from nose and reached for a washcloth from the towel rack. A bottle of green liquid sat on a corner of the tub. Squirted what was hopefully shampoo onto the washcloth and held it out, expecting her to say she could take care of herself. Instead she stood with her head bent, eyes closed. Water dripped from her nose, her chin.

With the washcloth, sponged her backside and then, very quickly, between her legs. Her skin had turned pink.

At last stepped back, own face flushed. "Ready to get out?"

She didn't answer, but when the taps were turned off and an arm placed once more around her waist, she stepped slowly, with great concentration, out of the tub. Keeping an arm around her, grabbed a towel from the rack. She clutched the towel to her chest and seemed not to understand what to do with it, so did best to swab her dry. An old gray terrycloth robe hung on the back of the bathroom door. Helped her into it and sat her down on the closed toilet lid.

"How about some water?"

She nodded, eyes still closed.

"Be right back."

Shakily, stepped over the wad of foulness thrown into the hall and went to the kitchen. Washed hands and filled a glass at the sink and drank it down before filling it again. Then opened the back door and stood for a few moments taking in gulps of fresh wet air, grateful for the sudden coolness, forehead pressed against the screen, gazing out at a dark world gemmed with rain.

20

After locating a clean nightgown and her slippers and, eventually, her eyeglasses—which required hunting around in her bedroom and on top of her dresser and finally under her pillow—it was after midnight. The rain had slowed, though it was still coming down. Closed all the windows except in the bathroom, and then helped her into her armchair, and switched on the little lamp beside it. Because she wanted a cup of tea.

Into the kitchen to put on the kettle. While she had her tea, cleaned up the rest of the bathroom, gathered up her dirty nightgown, the bath mat, and the wet towels, carried them into the kitchen, opened the screen door, and threw everything into the driveway. When finally returned to the living room, expecting to find her asleep in her chair, there she was, blinking behind those smudgy glasses, waiting. Instead of asking to go to bed like any normal old lady who'd just nearly died, she wanted to sit up for a while. Dropped onto the sofa across from her, too worn out to argue.

For a while sat staring at nothing as she finished her tea, only gradually aware that something seemed to be shifting, something had changed. Somehow a feeling of "different." Maybe just exhaustion, but a kind of visual disturbance took hold in that dim, half-empty room: one moment the picnic table, the stove, the rug were distinct, the next everything seemed doubled. It felt like peering at an eye chart as an ophthalmologist slipped one lens over the other, asking which was sharper, which was less.

Tomorrow, heard G say, you need to hang up that bird feeder. Not: *Thank you for saving my life, my grandson, my hero.* No, tomorrow you need to get up on the ladder and hang the bird feeder over the deck. Her birds would think she'd forgotten about them.

At the word "deck," realized that Freddy was the one who had been forgotten, outside all this time in the rain. Sat up straight, heart skidding. Idiot!

Two seconds later had flung open the back door, crying, "Here, boy! Freddy!"

Lying on the wet deck was Freddy's leash, attached to his collar. Nothing else but black, dripping woods. Freddy was terrified of all loud noises, but especially thunder. Once the thunder started, Freddy must have strained at the leash until he managed to slip his head through the collar and then run off to hide.

Into the wet night with a flashlight, wearing an old yellow hooded raincoat found hanging in the kitchen. Calling, "Freddy, Freddy!" hurrying around the cottage to look under the deck, shining flashlight into a crawl space full of spiderwebs and the remains of folding chairs, and then down to the dock, slipping on the rocks, twice nearly falling, playing the flashlight along the shoreline and onto the choppy rain-dimpled water.

Back in the driveway, spotted a dark lump close by the kitchen steps and cried out, "Freddy!" But it was only the pile of dirty towels and bath mat pitched out earlier.

Light from the kitchen window illuminated the driveway for several yards, ending in liquid darkness as abruptly as if it were the edge of an ocean cliff. Still calling, searched behind the woodpile and behind the trash cans, each arc of the flashlight revealing glistening black trunks and trembling ferns, beyond which shadows darted up and vanished. Pine branches groaned and swayed overhead, rain blowing hard, and everywhere was the smell of the lake, cold and coppery.

SHE WAS ASLEEP in her armchair. From the doorway, watched to make sure she was breathing before peeling off the wet raincoat and hanging it back on the hook by the door. Had been outside for over an hour, walking up and down the dark, streaming road with the flashlight, calling for Freddy until hoarse. Pulled off soggy sneakers, discovered toes as white and wrinkled as an old man's. The lamp flickered as she opened her eyes.

"Didn't find him."

"What time is it?" she asked.

"Late. Almost two. Time for you to go to bed."

She shook her head. "Not tired."

"You should be." Slumped onto the sofa and tugged the blanket across legs. She frowned. No sign of her twiggy stick, but on the floor by the sofa sat the half-finished bottle of cognac, and beside it a glass. Sometime over the past hour, she must have gotten up on her own to get them. She pointed to the bottle.

"No thanks." But reconsidered. Why not, you deserve it after a night like this. Ignoring the glass, picked up the bottle, unscrewed the cap, and took a swig.

Instant tears. Throat ache. Coughing, banged on chest with one fist. She watched this coughing fit without speaking until it subsided.

"You need to learn how to drink," she said grouchily.

You need to learn how to eat garlic. Old vampire.

Shared silence. Arms crossed on knees, stayed hunched on the sofa, while every so often she gave a sniff and shuffled her feet in her slippers. Was planning to get up and go back outside as soon as warmed up a little. But so incredibly tired. And that strange shifting vision was back, like overlapping lenses going clear, blurry, clear, blurry. *How is this?* inquired an imaginary ophthalmologist. *Better or worse?* Worse. So tired couldn't see straight.

Had almost fallen asleep, in fact, when that grouchy voice said, "Your mother says you had a bad year. Says you're trying to find yourself."

Sat up and stared at her incredulously, but she was looking at the black window. Why would X say something like that, especially to *her*, something so *undermining*? A bad year? You had a bad year when you didn't make the math team. You had a bad year when you got a C in organic chemistry. You tried to "find yourself" when the whole world wasn't lost. Not trying to *find* anything—hadn't anybody been paying attention? Trying to *delete* everything.

"So what happened?" she said.

What happened? Total annihilation, that's what happened.

Yet maybe it was the cognac, and that throat ache, but could not help wondering what it would be like, to tell someone. Had not, until now, even considered this possibility. Certainly could never tell any of it to X. Even the thought of confiding in her was like slowly extracting every single fingernail. Her sympathy would be unbearable. Worse would be her attempt to listen, because whatever she thought she understood would fall so far short of what had really happened as to be crucifying. *That must have been a very painful experience.*

The one person who should be able to help would offer no help at all.

But what about telling someone who wouldn't try to help? Who wouldn't even think of it? As if they had been consulted, the pine knots on the walls stared back impassively.

Suppose, for the sake of argument, you described just one or two things about that night. If she ever repeated anything, you could deny it, say that she'd been delirious following her attack of whatever.

Even if she did repeat anything, who would care.

With a surge of revulsion, thought of the past weeks of extravagant shame, of grandiose repentance. Self-erasure? What a DQ. What a fraud. Who cares if you stopped using the first person? Who cares that you watch mindless crap videos? Calling your parents X and Y, like that's some big statement. Who's even noticed? Delete yourself? You're already nothing, you conceited moron. And now you've lost your dog, the only creature in the world that actually cared enough about you to never ask you anything. So go ahead and talk. Go ahead.

IT HAD BEEN a mosh pit on the quad, and he'd been as drunk as everyone else, and really high, for the first time all year, finally ignoring his mother's warnings about "dope" being mixed with rat poison. He'd been passed a joint and smoked the whole thing, not even passing it on. The band was a bunch of totally wasted UConn Biebers playing Zeppelin, so it wasn't really music, any more than the jumping around was really dancing. It was riot noise. A single spotlight threw a white circle that spilled past the band and onto the grass, and in and out of that pool of light, kids were laughing and jumping on top of each other and being carried around and then dumped onto the ground.

Some kid handed him a pill while he was standing in line at a keg and he swallowed it, not caring what it was. Today had been such an epic fail that nothing could make it worse. His roommate, Dan Q-tip, that total mediocrity, had ditched him for next year's housing and hadn't even bothered to tell him, blocking with a bunch of guys on the hall who had been *his* friends first, whom he'd just *assumed* he'd be living with; but Dan had just shrugged and said, Dude, we only had room for four. When the music started, he'd been in the library basement, working on his final Bio lab report, which was late, so he'd probably get a D on it, so goodbye to being pre-med, and his face was all broken out again. Thank god he was alone in the library basement, because he'd actually started crying. He'd been left out of everything; he didn't belong here, he didn't belong anywhere. He had to stop himself from calling his mother, to tell her he was feeling like absolute crap. Because she would offer to come get him and bring him home, which is what he wanted, and it would be all over for him then.

Girls in tank tops and shorts brushed past him; he could smell their warm skin and their hair. He poured himself another beer from the keg and stood at the edge of the dancing, watching people slam into each other.

The beer and the weed were starting to make him feel a little better. Over the library's dark tower hung a big white moon against a navy blue sky. He thought of slides his Art History professor had shown a week ago: a medieval tapestry about the Apocalypse. A knight on a horse was trying to save a woman while a dragon tried to pull off her blue robe, exposing one of her breasts. Blue, the professor said, pointing to the woman's robe, symbolizes imagination. A requirement for true compassion. *Imagination & compassion*, the girl next to him wrote in her notebook. He'd wanted to lean over and scribble: *What's the boob symbolize?*

Without Art History, he thought solemnly now, the sky would be just blue. And maybe that would be better. Because life was not a symbol. Life had no imagination or compassion, and if you were alone it was mostly just a daily apocalypse.

He was still gazing at the moon with half a beer in his hand, when he felt himself grabbed roughly by the shoulders and by the waist. Beer splashed all over his shirt. Some kids had pulled him right out of the crowd and were lifting him over their heads. Hey, bro! somebody shouted. Let's go for a ride!

Soaked in beer, he was raised up, borne aloft by eight or nine people. Hands supporting his back, his legs, they began carrying him around like some kind of prom king. I've got him, people kept shouting. I've got him!

They jostled him back and forth in front of the band. And as he felt all those hands supporting him, heard the shouts, the drunken, good-natured laughter, something that had been hard and compacted within him started to unfold. He saw that if he could only let himself go, *this* was life. His real life. A life surrounded by other people, his brothers, his sisters, people holding on to him. They *had* him. He was not alone. He was not worthless. He was so grateful he almost wept again. Love was everywhere. The sky was warm. The moon was a full white breast emerging from a deep blue robe.

The kids who were carrying him didn't even drop him, but set him down gently, like a leaf, on a pile of half-full trash bags at the edge of the quad. Where some girl kissed him, right on the mouth. He sat on the trash bags for a little while, cooling off, listening to the guitars screeching, and to people yelling and laughing, his shirt sticking to his chest, and he felt so happy. He hadn't known it was possible to feel so happy.

That's when the pill, whatever it was, must have kicked in, because suddenly he couldn't sit still for another second. He had to *move*. The drummer was on a tear, elbows flapping, sticks flying, and the rest of the band had stopped playing to let him go at it. Smashing at the cymbals, blasting on the drums. *Boom, boom-boom, de-boom-boom, pow!* It was like a command, a huge overture. People were cheering, calling out. As he listened, he realized it was for him, that they were calling for *him*. Because somehow he was standing in front of the band, in a cleared lit space on the grass, and everyone was clapping.

A few people started chanting, *A-dam, A-dam*. He recognized Dan's voice, and a girl from Chem. More people were chanting. Louder. *A-dam, A-dam*. He bowed deeply, touched that so many people knew his name.

Now the drummer abandoned whatever noise-riff he'd been on and began playing something more intentional. The beat slowed, deepened, and when he listened more carefully he recognized what he was hearing, he'd heard it a hundred times. The drum solo in Zeppelin's "Moby Dick."

He looked down at himself. Naked! Except for his socks.

But already he was dancing. All alone in that wide circle of light, dancing, naked, in front of everyone. And they *loved* it. He was amazing. He did ballet leaps. He did jazz hands. The crowd was going crazy. He was doing moves no one had fucking ever *seen*. Then the drums got quieter and he stopped listening to the crowd to pay attention to the beat. The tempo was slowing, going low, brooding and strange, like a secret, told only to him. Now came congas, like footfalls, like someone running. Slow, and then fast. Fast, faster, like something was after him, something was going to get him. Back to the sticks: Ba-da-ba-da-ba-*daaah*. Ba-da-ba-da-ba-*daaah*. Urgency building again, hoofbeats galloping. Go man, cried the drums, *Go*. Use your superpowers! Save us! *Save the world!*

It was then that he understood the secret of the drums: *He* was the music, he *was* that beat, that dark primal beat, submerged but emerging, rising like something vast and ancient, like a great stone bridge rising from beneath black waters, the bridge that connected everything to everything. He could not let the beat stop; he had to keep the bridge rising, he had to keep dancing.

Yah! he heard himself screaming. Yah! Yah!

And right then, in the middle of it all, he got a big boner. People were holding up their phones. Some girls jumped out of the crowd and started dancing with him, pointing and applauding, because his boner was so huge and beautiful, it was so amazing, and the beat shifted again, started to throb, and the girls were laughing, reaching out their arms, and he felt such a painful joy because he knew they wanted to touch it, touch that beat, touch life itself, and he started chasing them around and around, until he caught one of them by a long thin braid and the whole world went, *Aaaahhh*.

Because it was Ashley. Ashley Cray-Foster, from last semester's Revolution and Revolt First-Year French Seminar.

Ashley, whom he'd sat beside for two and a half hours each Thursday, from four thirty to seven, staring at the slim brown hinge of her wrist whenever she raised her hand. Who doodled question marks and "haha" in balloon letters. Who was shorter than he was, and got more check pluses on her responses than he did, and smelled of strawberry milk, which she drank during class, and damp Lycra, because she'd just had dance team practice. Her many long tightly woven braids were each the same width, some gold, some brown (had she braided them all herself?), and when worn piled on top of her head looked like a marvelous brain, a gleaming set of neural pathways. Do not exoticize her, he scolded himself. Do *not* look at her hair. It was no use.

But one night they'd talked in the library about her summer program in Paris and about *Charlie Hebdo* and the consequences of suppression and why violence is inevitable, and she'd looked at him seriously and said, You really get it, Adam. Most people don't, but you really get it.

Ashley. Ashley. On this night in which everything was being granted to him, everything under the moon.

What happened next he didn't remember, but people started shouting and piling onto him and shining their phones into his face. Then someone was crying, and he was lying on the ground with a huge girl from crew kneeling on his back, her moist hot breath wreathing his ear. *About fifty people got that on video, bro, it's probably already gone viral, it was like legitimate sexual predation, like you pulled out her* hair extensions, *what* are *you, anyway, straight guys are such assholes, you don't care about anyone but yourselves, you should all like be in fucking jail, we've just called security, and listen, dude, no offense, but I've seen bigger wieners on kids in preschool.*

21

"Finis."

Said sarcastically, to suggest that everything just recounted might possibly be some big goof. In case it had to be retracted.

Had not, of course, told her everything. But had told some of it. Against the dark rain-streaked window her reflected profile was pale and stern. Her Abe Lincoln face. She was drawing the belt of her bathrobe between her long bluish fingers while the lamp beside her flickered. Okay, time to make some comment. Say something judgy. Say, What a loser. Say *something*. At least ask what it had been like, to see that night replayed again and again, all over Twitter. "NAKED COLLEGE BOY YANKS OUT GIRL'S BRAIDS." Out there, forever.

"So that's what happened. Since you asked."

Did she even know what Twitter was?

She continued to finger her bathrobe belt until finally, after what seemed like a long time, she said, "Eh." Eh?

"Like, after that, the only option was to disappear." Face hot, itching. "Like, for a privileged cisgender white male, it's probably the best option, anyways. Since, basically, we're all, like, Nazis."

Quiver of horror. Had just said *Nazi* to her. Of all people. But her expression didn't change, except that she shifted slightly to gaze at her reflection in the window. Then, as the minutes ticked by and it became clear she wasn't going to speak, there began to be a gradual feeling of something at last being over, of relaxing, one vertebra at a time. Somehow her complete lack of interest was reassuring. Instead of detailing the worst night of human existence, might have spent the last fifteen minutes describing a lab report, or the convoluted but supposedly democratic process of the college housing lottery.

For a while the two of them stayed as they were, both staring straight ahead, like the last people on a train car, rain sliding across the windowpanes. And curiously, as if a kind of traveling was indeed underway, a sense of movement now came into that quiet room, not of going forward, but of moving from one stage of the night to the next. At some point she said, "More?" Indicating the bottle. Poured cognac into glass and managed to drink it without coughing, while she worked her bathrobe belt through her fingers. Then from somewhere out on the water sounded the same weird shriek from the night before.

Or was that a howl? Freddy. Forgotten again for the past fifteen minutes. Freddy, lost in the dark, alone, scared. Time to go back outside with the flashlight and start looking, but felt too drained to move.

The lamp threw unstable shadows against the walls. She had taken off her glasses to rub the bridge of her nose.

Perhaps it was that feeling of travel, or the unshielded look of her pink-rimmed eyes, that made it seem conceivable to ask, "*Est-il possible de vous poser une question?*"

From her chair came a reluctant creak, like an old paint can lid levered off with a screwdriver. Possibly *Oui*.

"So tonight, at dinner—"

She gave an irritable flinch.

"No, not that," went on hastily. "Not about Dennis. That's cool. People, you know, fall for each other. It happens. Like, what are you going to do? *Not* fall for each other?" A mature thing to say. Also agreed with it: People falling for each other was not a choice. Felt sadly proud to know this.

She said, "That wasn't it."

What did she mean by "it"? Tucked the blanket more securely around legs—the room had grown colder—and then looked at her again, picturing X's face in the car when she'd said: Of course I've tried to talk to her about it.

"Okay. It's just, was wondering, like why you didn't ever go back? To see them?"

"Go back?" she echoed huskily.

Whatever was wrong with the lamp's wiring had worsened in the last few minutes; the flickering was now almost stroboscopic, making everything in the room go jerky and seem to be heading in reverse. A gust of wind rushed rain against the roof and from somewhere deep in the house a wooden joist moaned. She didn't move or speak, her eyes fixed on the dark window.

"It's okay," sighed at last, looking at the sticky brown residue at the bottom of the glass. "Never mind." Set the glass on the floor, yawning, pulling the blanket up higher, wondering about X and whether to call her to say that Freddy was outside, lost in the storm. She would be furious. She had no idea what a crazy night it had been, how wild and strange. Get up, yawning again, get going, and the next moment was asleep.

22

The rain had stopped. For a long time Marika sat watching the sleeping boy on the sofa by the lamp's fitful light. Such a baby. With his spotty face and skinny legs, and his silly story of getting drunk and taking off all his clothes. When his mother walked out tonight, he'd looked like a calf left on the other side of a fence.

No sense of direction. No idea where the world was going. Nazis, he'd said, as if he knew. And for all her talk of disasters, Lorna didn't know, either. Refugees. Detention centers. Europe dissolving. But Marika knew. She didn't need a compass to see where everything was headed.

We all had our facts, she'd told the boy last night. You did what you did. On the sofa, he gave a short snore. The lamp flickered again.

No one cares, she said sternly to the lamp, about that old stuff. It was a long time ago and no longer matters. Now there are floods, fires to worry about. That boy to worry about. But up here was safe. Fresh air was good for him. Lorna said so herself.

Look how he cleaned out the gutters. How he helped her tonight and went into the rain to look for that dog. No silliness then.

Though he still hadn't hung up her bird feeder. Well, would do it tomorrow. Not a bad boy, she thought vaguely, trying to recall which boy she meant. Not like the other one, who kept running into an alley at the back of her mind. And that boy hadn't been bad, either. He just made a mistake.

No, little birds, she said as they flew through the room, I haven't forgotten you.

She plucked the tissue from her sleeve and stared at it. The lamp continued to flicker.

Outside, the wind had whipped up the lake, waves gulping and swallowing against the rocks, stirring up fish and things resting below. After a while she was asleep, too. Or if not asleep, then no longer wherever she was when she was awake.

23

If you see any Sipo, Ellie said, pinch your cheeks. Rika, are you listening? It will make you look younger. Stay on your bicycle. Don't use your bell. Don't smile at anyone. Don't tell anybody anything except what I tell you to say.

She had an address to give, if stopped, another address to go to, if followed. At a different address, leave the jar, wrapped in brown paper that smelled of wintergreen. Each jar labeled with typed instructions: *Apply to affected area. Rub until absorbed*. She was thirteen when she began her bicycle deliveries.

At first she rode straight home, heart thumping at every corner. But no one stopped her and it felt good to be out on her bicycle in the cold bright air. After the first few times she kept going, past transport trucks, past the new embankments, out to Scheveningen to look at the waves. Sometimes all the way out to Haarlem, past the police station on Heemstedestraat, past the convent and the empty schoolroom windows behind which she had memorized French conjugations, past the nuns' parlor with its prie-dieu by the fireplace and wallpaper of ivy leaf, and into the countryside to ride on the towpaths past windmills and fields. Fields so flat, people said, they could not hide a blade of grass.

A friend of Ellie's gave them the addresses. The woman in the stationery shop at the far side of Rembrandtplein, who sat all day at her window, rearranging boxes of pencils and envelopes, and watching the square with her pale bulgy eyes. How does she know everything? Stop asking questions, said Ellie, who thought she was boss because she was almost twenty. Though Rika was so tall and they were both so blond that sometimes people took them for twins.

Not Ellie. Rika was a brat. Not to be trusted. Hey, you, little sneak. Do some chores, sweep the floor, peel potatoes.

But sometimes those days no potatoes, no onions. Father had no customers. He went to the Docklands every day to sit in his shop and pull nails out of old cabinet boards, waiting for fishermen to stop by to play cards and listen to him describe again how his wife had died in the spring. At dinner one evening she'd put down her fork, laid a hand on her chest, and said, *I feel like I've swallowed a horseradish.*

The fishermen felt sorry for him and shared whatever they had to drink. Sometimes he fell off his bicycle. Once, he cracked a lens of his spectacles. That night Ellie's voice was so loud that all the neighbors could hear her: Listen, old man. Do something useful. Build us a new kitchen hutch. The old one has wormholes.

He made the hutch in his shop and carted it home in pieces in the wooden carrier fixed to the front of his bicycle. Holding his black umbrella over his head when it rained, spectacles cracked, long gray hair sticking out from under his blue wool cap. Something to keep him busy, Ellie told the neighbors, loudly. Poor old fool. Thinks his wife died from eating a horseradish.

Spies, she said of the neighbors. Sneaks.

The hutch was painted white, the top half open shelving and the bottom a cupboard. Behind it, a section of the wall had been knocked out with a mallet wrapped in a sock, a foot or two each night, and then planks set down for flooring. The cupboard shelf held pots and pans, when in place. Once the hutch was finished, it was one of Rika's chores to go down the back stairs to the alley and stand in the doorway holding a paper sack.

When there was a moon, she could see across the alley to a heap of loose bricks that she watched for rats.

If a neighbor asked what she was doing, she said she was going to the dustbins. Some nights she waited for hours for someone to pass by whispering: *Rubbish?* And she was to say: *Yes, time to take it out.*

When one of them came it was only for a few days. Only room for one at a time in that hole behind the hutch, so black and close, a crack here and there for a sniff of fresh air, a needle of light. Months might pass between them, or one could come right after another. Maybe six in all, maybe seven?

Visitors, Ellie called them. Where do they come from? None of your business. Keep your mouth shut and everything will be all right.

In the evenings they were allowed out for a little while, to sit in the kitchen, have a bowl of soup. A few could not stand the dark. For them Ellie had her bottle of laudanum, drops stirred into a cup of water. Some got sick, and though they had a basin for relieving themselves, there were accidents. Another of Rika's chores was to clean up after them.

Before sunrise one morning the visitor would be taken down the back stairs to the alley. Ellie had got in the habit of riding their father's bicycle instead of her own. When the Germans began taking people's bicycles, he'd handed over the rubber tires and kept their bicycles and then made wooden tires in his shop on the lathe. It wasn't so bad, you got used to it, the *knockety-knock* on cobbles.

The child would lie down in the bicycle carrier, under a quilted blanket that had been used for wrapping cabinets. If Ellie was stopped and the blanket pulled aside, she could say: Diphtheria. Typhoid fever. She had her nurse's badge, and a day or two behind the hutch made anyone look sick.

No one said where they went, but Rika guessed they rode out to the hospital on the Vecht River, where Ellie had done her nurse training. An infectious diseases hospital outside the city, in what had been an old castle. On a dark stretch of the riverbank a boat would be waiting. Their father knew enough fishermen to know whose herring boat had what kind of hold, and who was allowed to sail into what harbors. Off the child went, to Friesland, or somewhere else north.

ONE AFTERNOON Ellie came home talking about twin boys and a baby girl. An NSB widow across the square from the stationer's shop had a job cooking for a bachelor, an assistant deputy to a Generalkommissar. This widowed cook needed someone to mind her children during the day. Her flat was small and dark, and she wanted her children to be somewhere bigger, nearer to the park. The stationer asked Ellie: Your flat is nice. What about your younger sister?

Their father pulled his wool cap over his ears. A woman working for the Reichskommissariat? The children will be met at the door, said Ellie. And think about this: Now if a child cries in the kitchen, none of the neighbors will wonder or complain. Who would want to offend the cook of an assistant deputy to a Generalkommissar by saying her children were noisy? Also, she's sleeping with him so we might hear something useful. Also, child-minding will keep *that one* busy instead of making eyes at soldiers in the street. And you tell me where else to get a few extra guilders?

Something else extra: The cook brought along food for her three children—bits of cheese, a tin of sardines, a tomato, an apple. Slipped into her carpetbag as she left the assistant deputy's kitchen. Always a little more than the children could eat.

Rika liked taking care of the cook's children, especially the baby, with her warm curdled-milk smell and damp round head. She tickled their feet, fed them, washed their hands, and tied their shoes. If she heard too much scratching or crying from the hutch, she would pretend to take down a bowl from the top shelf and say, *Be quiet*. Or she would take the cook's children to the park. If the noise continued, and it was raining or too cold to leave the flat, she would say, *Mice!* and read louder, sing, march around the kitchen table with the baby on her hip. *Come, little birds*, she would call when it was time to go out. Once, she pulled apart an old blue sweater to knit scarves for the boys and a pair of booties for the baby. After that, paper screws of coffee appeared in the cook's carpetbag, sometimes a little sugar. For the old man: vinegar bottles filled with schnapps.

THAT FALL, the harbors closed. The trains stopped and all she had to care for were the cook's children. Winter came and everyone said the war would be over soon. Keep your head down. Keep your mouth shut. No, there's nothing to eat. Drink some water. But just before curfew one evening, as Rika was wheeling her bicycle down the alley past the pile of bricks, she heard someone whisper, *Hallo*, and saw a smoke-colored face above a man's black overcoat.

The Fashion Plate, women in the neighborhood called her. Before he died, her husband had owned a shoe store near the Royal Zoo and she used to dress up in a fox stole and alligator pumps, even to take out her rubbish. A snob, neighbors said. Never says hallo in the street. But now here was the Fashion Plate, beckoning from a doorway. The next minute, whispering about a family in her attic for almost a year.

A father and two children. Her husband's former clerk. Had promised him. Had done her best. But she'd just had a tip. Someone was about to inform on her.

Tell your sister to take the children where she takes the others.

I don't know what you're talking about.

Listen, hissed the Fashion Plate. An ivory hand snaked out, pinching Rika's arm, hard, just above the elbow. I can keep it to myself or not, what your sister has been doing. With her other hand she reached behind her and opened the door.

Sitting on the back stairs was a tiny pale girl, about five, with a runny nose and thin whitish-blond hair standing straight up with static, wearing a purple smock coat buttoned to the neck. Holding her hand was a bull-headed boy of ten or twelve with dark hair like dog fur and small crossed-looking eyes. In a gray jacket and black bow tie, tight pants and heavy-soled boots that were too big for him, laces wound around the ankles.

The little girl's coat was ridiculous. Lavender, with rhinestone buttons. It must have belonged to the Fashion Plate and been cut down. Under some delusion of making him presentable, she had made the boy wear that bow tie. Both children seemed freakish, unchildlike, almost elderly, with their sinister clothes and empty expressions. As Rika watched, the boy leaned over and wiped his sister's nose with his fingers.

Like a little mother to her, whispered the Fashion Plate. Doesn't talk, but does whatever he's told. You, she said to the boy. Hold on to your sister.

Rika should have turned away then. Got on her bicycle, flown up the alley.

But she was fourteen years old and used to doing what she was told, so she walked her bicycle to the half shed by the dustbins where it was kept, and then led the children to the back door of her building, made them take off their shoes on the stoop, and ushered them up three flights of back stairs to the kitchen.

Right away there was trouble. The boy would not let go of his sister's hand. Would not crawl through the cupboard door, even after Rika told the story about being a stowaway on a ship, going to an island with coconut trees. Don't you want to see a coconut? The boy stood by the stove with his big head lowered, squeezing his sister's hand until she started to howl like a child stung by a bee. Father stayed in his room, pretending to be asleep, probably drunk.

Then Ellie came home. While the boy squeezed the girl's hand and she howled in her lavender smock coat, its glittery buttons making her howls seem even louder, Rika repeated what the Fashion Plate had said.

Ellie was furious. How could you be so stupid? They were her problem and now you've made them ours.

It was a mistake, I'm sorry.

No one cares about sorry. You did what you did. And you'll be a lot sorrier if we don't get her to shut up. Then, turning to the children, Ellie said smoothly, So. We like to welcome our company with some cake. You like cake, don't you?

Down came a box from the top shelf of the hutch. In her palm were two tablets of chocolate. The little girl stopped howling. That is your frosting, said Ellie. She cut two slices of brown bread and sprinkled them with a bit of sugar. Here is your cake. While the children were eating, she mixed a few drops in a cup with water from the jug. Look at the pretty blue stripe on this cup, she said to the girl. Drink this.

To the boy, she said: Keep your sister quiet. Understand? Otherwise soldiers are going to come and take her away.

The girl was already half asleep, nose running again. The boy wanted to put on his boots. It took him a while to do up the laces. At last they crawled through the cupboard door. Blankets passed in. Panel closed, cupboard shelves replaced, pots and pans put back.

Ellie was buttoning her jacket. I need to make some arrangements. There's not enough room in there for two of them.

You're going out now?

There was a guard Ellie knew, stationed by the bridge in the evenings. On her way home she often stopped her bicycle for a chat. *Haben Sie eine zigarette?* Like most of them, he was stupidly grateful for any *haben sie*, and if you gave him a kiss he'd hand over half a bar of chocolate.

I'll say I need to check on a patient. He'll give me a pass.

You never told me about any guard. Don't go. What if she starts howling again?

This is your fault, Ellie said. You take care of it. And cut those damn buttons off the girl's coat.

Everything was quiet for a few hours. Around midnight she heard coughing. Then a few high sharp cries. A little while later the knocking started. *Knockety-knock, knockety-knock.*

Let them be, Ellie would have said, as long as there's no howling.

Finally, the knocking stopped. In the morning, sleet snicked against the dark windowpanes. No sun on winter days until near nine o'clock. Wearing two sweaters, she lit a candle and put the kettle on the Primus stove. Father stumbled into the kitchen, wool cap pulled over his eyebrows. He drank his tea standing up.

Visitors came last night, she said.

I thought that was done?

Ellie went out late. She hasn't come back.

He was at the door to the back stairs, his hand on the knob. Ah. Well. Do whatever Ellie told you.

After he left she cut up two slices of bread into pieces, put them in a bowl, and blew out the candle. Then she unlatched the cupboard door, took out a few pots and, leaving the shelf in place, slid the panel back.

Hallo, did you use the basin? Give it to me and I'll give you some breakfast.

When she didn't hear anything, she sat down on the floor and took out the rest of the pots and pans and pulled out the shelf.

In an instant, the big-headed boy was shoving out of the cupboard. She took him by the shoulders to push him back inside, but he was stronger than she expected. He squirmed through the cupboard door and into her lap, smelling of piss. No jacket, but still in his bow tie, gone askew, and his big boots. Over his shoulder she glimpsed a dark huddle, a glint, and then the white nape of a neck, bent like an elbow.

She reached out to touch that white neck, thinking to startle the child awake, even as some place in her mind stilled. The boy made a noise, the first sound she'd heard from him. It was a soft damp noise, like *Oh*. Oh, he said, scooting onto the floor next to her.

Her fingertips brushed a cool ridge of bone. She drew back her hand. Over her mind fell the same blankness as the night her mother had laid a hand to her chest at the table, a blankness reflected in the boy's wide-apart eyes.

At that moment someone began pounding on the front door. The boy stumbled up into a chair, fell over, scrambled to his feet and ran down the hall to the parlor. The cook and her children had arrived early.

Shaking now, she slid the panel shut. Quick, put back the shelf and the pots and pans. Close the cupboard. Drag a stool against it.

In the parlor the boy was running in circles with his head down. She tried to grab his arm but he jerked away. Around and around the parlor he went, those boots like anvils against the floorboards.

Bang, bang, bang at the door.

Think, she commanded herself. *Think*. A neighbor's boy, say that to the cook. Left here for the morning. But when she opened the door, it wasn't the cook and her three children on the landing. Two helmets above long gray coats filled the doorway instead, shoulders dark with melting sleet. The shorter one was coughing and had a sty in one eye. The taller one held a pistol by its barrel. Both had pink earlobes and pale girlish necks.

Your father and sister have been arrested, the tall one shouted. He was missing an upper tooth. We are here to search the flat! Show your papers!

Just then the boy ran into the hall. He stopped by the coat stand, gawping at the soldiers under his mat of dark hair. Before anyone could say anything or make a move, he lowered his big head and charged, taking them by surprise. He was halfway down a flight of stairs before they turned to look after him. On the second landing he ran into the cook and her children. Two of the children fell over, wailing, as the soldiers stumbled down, too, and the cook began scolding that she was the cook for an assistant deputy to the Generalkommissar and that her children were being trampled!

Through the noise Rika's thoughts darted back and forth. Had a neighbor heard the howling last night, seen Ellie ride down the alley and reported her? Had the Fashion Plate told what she knew after all? Handed over the children to save the father? *No, it's another building you want, three doors down, third floor, search the kitchen.*

Your fault, Ellie said in her ear. You take care of it.

Boots clunked back up to the landing. She stared at the mirror hanging by the coats and scarves, and then reached up and pinched her cheeks.

The soldiers were in the doorway again, the one with the sty still coughing. The tall one opened his mouth and drew in his breath. But before he could speak, she whispered, *Suchen Sie Juden?* A woman next door is hiding one.

The tall one began shouting, his missing tooth appearing and disappearing like a tiny trapdoor. Last night a raid by Resistance Scum on the distribution center by the Magere Brug! Your sister was observed with the guard beforehand, trying to distract him! Your sister has been observed stopping her bicycle at the bridge, asking for cigarettes! She has been observed riding along the canal with her headlamp off! He ran out of breath and had to pause before he could resume shouting.

She wears alligator shoes, said Rika.

Neighbors have observed sardine tins in your rubbish! Cheese rinds! Black Market items! Your father arrested just now has admitted to drinking schnapps!

The cook was still scolding her way up the stairs with her crying children. The short soldier coughed harder, while the other one stopped shouting to hit him on the back, just as the cook reached the landing, puffing out her cheeks.

She told the coughing soldier to cover his mouth. You have no business coughing on innocent people. My children are right here, do you see? She pulled a bottle of schnapps from her carpetbag and handed it to him. Here. Take some of that.

Now you, she said to Rika. Go after that child. Otherwise he will be lost in the street. I will wait here until you get back.

The soldiers began passing the bottle back and forth, watching Rika as she took her coat and scarf from the rack by the door, grinning and getting in her way as she unhooked her father's black umbrella. The cook glared at them and the soldiers stepped back to let her pass by on the landing. Slowly, tugging on her coat and then tying her scarf, she walked down the stairs and out into the freezing rain, where she opened the umbrella and forced herself to walk along the canal to the end of the block.

At the corner she turned and ran to the alley, checking first to see if soldiers were posted there, before hurrying to her bicycle in the shed by the dustbins. She closed the umbrella and hung it on the handlebars.

Only as she was backing out with her bicycle did she see him, squatting against the wall by the sleety pile of bricks, shivering in his thin shirt and crooked bow tie, his heavy black boots. Behind the bins, his face looked like a book left out in the rain.

Hallo, she whispered. He stared back at her. Listen, she said, slowly wheeling her bicycle backward into the alley, the wooden tires making their knuckly sound against the wet cobbles.

She stopped. I have to go out. To make some arrangements. No, stay here, she hissed as he stood up. Keep quiet. Don't move. He looked at her uncertainly, his big head wobbling.

You have to stay here, she repeated, one foot on a bicycle pedal.

Still, he hesitated. But as he began crouching back down between the bins, a horseradish rose in her throat. *A good boy*, the Fashion Plate had said. *Does whatever he's told*. She remembered the sharp cries last night, and Ellie's voice, saying, *Keep your sister quiet. Understand? Or soldiers will come and take her away*. Then the soft knock-knocking that had gone on for hours. The cupboard door opened.

Once more she saw that small bent white neck, felt the cool ridge of bone, heard the hushed damp sound of the boy's voice, saying, Oh.

He must have been watching her face. As she pushed backward on her bicycle, turning from him to ride away, he grabbed on to her front wheel. She tipped to the side and kicked out at him, but he lunged back, hands raised like bear claws. She kicked him again, but he kept coming, reaching for her scarf, pulling on her hair, his swollen face right next to hers. As she pushed at his cheek, he snatched her hand and bit down on the palm. Her bicycle clanged onto the cobbles. Holding her throbbing palm to her chest, she clouted him in the ear with her other fist and then with both hands shoved him hard. He fell down and lay on his back by the wall near the tumble of bricks.

Yanking up her bicycle, she glanced down the alley. Still empty. The boy didn't move, save for two fingers twitching. On her palm shone a bloody half-moon of tooth marks.

Pull him into a doorway, Ellie whispered. Take off your scarf. Wrap it around him. Someone will find him soon, and by then you'll be halfway to Haarlem. She leaned her bicycle against the wall.

As she took hold of him under the arms, he twisted away from her, catching her by surprise. The next instant he was on his feet.

He rammed her with his head, knocking her to the ground. Then he kicked her in the ribs with his boot. Kicked her shoulder, kicked her in the jaw. She reached for his ankles, he kicked her in the stomach and stamped on her wrist.

Under her cheek, the wet cobbles smelled like a sour dishrag. She buried her face in her hands as he picked up the umbrella and began driving its pointed metal tip into her head and shoulder, great sobs gouting out of him. Blood seeped into her hair. Blood not sleet, because it was warm.

Suddenly, he dropped the umbrella and walked away. She opened her eyes, peering between her wet fingers. He was bending down to reach for a brick in the heap by the wall.

As he came toward her she grabbed his legs, tumbling them both against the cobbles. They wrestled for the brick, she prying it out of his hand, finger by finger, while he closed his other hand around a hank of her hair, pulling harder and harder, their foreheads pressed together, eyes wide.

Until at last she worked the brick free and held it aloft. When he let go of her hair to grab for it, she pushed his face into the cobbles. Blindly, with all her strength, she slammed the brick again and again against the side of his head.

By the time she dragged him behind the dustbins the sleet had turned to snow. She found a loose piece of tin to cover him, and a scrap of filthy blanket. Then she wiped her forehead with her coat sleeve, tied her scarf around her chin, and pulled her hood over her head. Leaving the umbrella where it lay, she wheeled her bicycle away from the wall, climbed on, and rode out of the alley.

SHE TOLD THE NUNS she'd hit a lamppost with her bicycle.

They took off her coat and scarf, washed the blood out of her hair, dabbed her face with iodine, and brought her a warm compress. One of them offered her a clean pair of underwear, but she shook her head. After making her drink something that tasted of licorice, they led her into the front hall where the grandfather clock stood by the stairs. One nun pushed aside the clock; another opened a little door cut under the staircase.

The next morning the cook arrived at the convent door, stamping her boots on the doormat. I know she's here, she told the nuns. Let me in or I will walk over to the police on Heemstedestraat. Here is a jar of goose fat.

A few minutes later she and the cook were facing each other in the cold parlor, sitting on wooden chairs. Once the nuns had left, rustling their habits to show they intended to listen on the other side of the door, the cook dragged her chair closer.

Who beat you, *schatje*? The cook squeezed her knee. I understand you are frightened. Who was that boy?

Rika stared at the ivy leaves on the wallpaper.

I see, said the cook, taking her hand away. Well. Guess what's in a pot in my kitchen? Two metworst, an onion, and a carrot. You come home now, the children need you to care for them so I can go to work. I will find out about your sister and father.

While the cook talked, Rika turned to look at the prie-dieu by the empty fireplace and then back at the parlor's wallpaper with its repeating ivy leaf.

Are you listening to me? How do you think it would it be for the nuns, if you are discovered here?

They rode back to the city, pedaling along in the tracks that trucks had made in the snow, the cook puffing white clouds over her bent elbows.

From the post office at Rembrandtplein, the cook telephoned the assistant deputy. He told her that anyone arrested in the raid on the distribution center was being processed and never to call him at his office again. Frowning, the cook hung up and said they would visit her friend the stationer, who often heard things. Not there, she said, motioning Rika and her bicycle away from the stationer's shop windows. What's wrong with you? Wait in the alley. I may be a while. This one likes a chat.

But a few minutes later the cook was back, red in the face. The raid on the distribution center was big news, so were the arrests of the old joiner and his nurse daughter. The stationer knew all about the arrests, though not where they had been taken. As for the nurse's younger sister, *she* hadn't been arrested. And why not? Neighbors had seen a tall blond girl stop her bicycle in the evenings to flirt with a guard posted by the canal. Mooching cigarettes in return for a kiss. Informed on her own family. For a chocolate bar.

When this war is over, the stationer had said, all these whores will get what's coming. Just you wait.

Toad Eyes, scowled the cook. What do you have to say for yourself? she demanded of Rika. Is it true what she said?

It was Ellie talking to the guard. She asked him for cigarettes. I don't smoke.

Well, that may be, said the cook. But take my advice and stay away from your street. Now we must pick up the children and I must get to the assistant deputy's flat or he will have nothing for his dinner. Tomorrow I'll stop at your flat to get your clothes and whatever's in the larder. If there's anything left. Had to leave the door unlocked, no key, the neighbors have all paid their visits by now, poking through your kitchen cupboards.

No, said Rika. She gripped her bicycle handles. Don't go.

Don't be silly. It's no trouble. You need some clothes.

There is nothing there.

What? Don't you want your clothes?

The cook looked at her for a long moment and then said she supposed she still had a dress or two from when she wasn't so fat. And why don't you smoke? she chided as they got on their bicycles. It's good for you. Calms the nerves.

IN FEBRUARY the cook stopped going out with her carpetbag. The door to the assistant deputy's flat was padlocked shut. All one day the cook went out looking for him. Take care of the children, she told Rika. Stay in the flat. But the flat was small and dark, and smelled of kerosene and boiled cabbage, also the talcum powder the cook rubbed on herself, and it was a sunny day, the first sunny day in weeks, so Rika took the children to the park. They ran back and forth looking under the bare hedges, pretending they were trying to find the assistant deputy. When the cook came home, one of the boys had a long red scratch on his cheek from a thorn and the baby girl had a cough.

I told you to take care of them, she shouted.

Rations were cut by half, and then halved again. The cook used a teaspoon to measure out dried peas from a jar. The little boys' bellies grew into melons. The little girl's cough got worse. She wheezed and cried, a thin high cry that lodged at the back of the eyes.

Your fault, the cook said.

One day a roar began, low at first, like faraway motorcycles without mufflers. The cook told the little boys to keep away from the windows. The Germans are going to blow up the dikes and drown the city! The roar got louder. Planes flew over the streets and dropped parcels with tinned ham and crackers. People fought over them, pushing, shoving. Some parcels exploded or landed on rooftops or sank into canals. One of the boys fell into a canal while Rika was on the banks trying to fish out a parcel. By the time she reached the boy, the parcel was gone and he'd lost one of his shoes.

Look what you've done, the cook muttered.

The cook sat in the kitchen rocking the little girl, wrapped in a blanket to her pale neck. Rocking and rocking, while the coughing went on and on, on and on, until finally one night it stopped. Two days later, Canadian tanks rolled into the square. The cook did not get out of her chair or even look out the window.

Everyone else ran into the streets, crying and clapping, climbing onto the tanks, kissing the soldiers, everyone wearing orange ribbons or armbands, singing, "Wilhelmus," playing accordions, blowing whistles, banging on pots.

Look! the little boys cried to Rika, laughing and pulling on her hands. Look! Soldiers are throwing chocolate!

The next morning she slipped down the back stairs to the alleyway, where her bicycle was covered with a blanket. She rolled up the blanket and crammed it into her basket. Out on the street she rode east and after a while she was out of the city.

Knockety-knock, went her wooden tires. She was fourteen and a half years old. She took her bearings by the sun, as she had once been taught to do, pedaling past columns of marching prisoners, past windmills without sails and houses without roofs and dark fields full of ditches. *Knockety-knock.* Every so often a canal flashed in the sunlight.

24

The sun was rising and pine trees were just beginning to separate from each other when from over the lake came the high rending cry of a red-tailed hawk. It circled the house twice and landed on a branch above the deck, just as a garter snake slimmed under the kitchen's screen door where it was dented at the bottom and fringed with rust.

Opening his eyes on the sofa, Adam's first thought was that he was cold. The blanket he'd pulled around himself last night had slipped to the floor, exposing his bare legs and arms. But he felt something besides cold and sat up. After further inquiry, he determined that once again he felt "different," and at last, in the thin light of morning, he knew why.

All that had happened over the past few weeks had become a nightmare from which he had finally awakened. A dream that vanished as soon as he did not think of it. Fantasy. Meanwhile, this cottage by the lake, the old woman asleep in her chair, the sofa where he was sitting, were facts. Provable, physical facts.

His hand, for instance, held up to the light, was a fact. His T-shirt, worn now for three days and smelling like old cheese, was a fact. His fingers could move back and forth; the shirt needed laundering; the sofa felt like it was stuffed with wads of damp dryer lint. All facts.

Everything else was not. College, Q-tip, exams, Ashley, That Night. Untouchable. Illusions.

"The past does not exist," he murmured aloud, recalling something someone had said, maybe in Lit Core. Pretentious. But still.

Outside the windows, the deck was empty except for the Adirondack chair and the bird feeder, toppled beside it, and Freddy's old towel, soaked from last night's storm. His grandmother was faintly snoring, chin on her chest, glasses askew. On his way back from the bathroom, he stopped to settle the blanket over her.

She opened her eyes. Her mouth had a bluish cast.

"You should get in bed," he said.

"Coffee," she croaked.

"I don't know how to make coffee." He tugged at the collar of his T-shirt. "I need to go out and look for Freddy."

It felt both momentous and utterly ordinary, hearing "I" come out of his mouth. An amazing commonplace. The way it might feel to say "my wife" for the first time after getting married. *I, I, I.* He turned the syllable over and over, noting its similarity to *ay, yi yi.* You again, he thought, marveling.

His grandmother looked at him dully.

"All right," he sighed. "Coffee. I guess I'll figure it out."

In the kitchen he located a large red can of coffee and the electric percolator. Feeling keenly alert, he removed the percolator's lid and peered into its blackened interior. The laws of physics dictate that boiling water creates bubbles, which gravity compels to rise—in this case most likely through the greasy tube connected to a greasy metal basket. If he put coffee into the basket, poured water into the pot, and turned on the percolator, boiling water should eventually be forced upward through the tube to saturate the coffee grounds. Coffee would be the result.

He would have liked to share these deductions with someone, but no one was there. He plugged in the pot. How much coffee should go into the basket? Though he'd watched his mother make coffee hundreds of times, he'd never actually paid attention, nor had he ever asked how it was done. At ten tablespoons of coffee, the basket was full. After filling the pot halfway with water and clamping on the lid, he pressed the switch on the percolator. No light. A bird flew past the kitchen window. Wet pine needles shimmered.

Then he did hear something: a low *huh, huh, huh?*

Hoping it might be Freddy, he opened the door and looked through the screen. In the driveway stood a bulky, bald-headed turkey. Oily black feathers, scaly pterodactyl feet. Telescoping its long skinny bare neck, the creature glanced at the driveway as if deciding whether to cross or wait for the light, and then pecked at a bit of gravel.

At the edge of the driveway appeared a female, smaller, brownish, hesitant, followed by a hurrying bumble of gray fluff. As Adam watched, the big turkey puffed itself up, fanning its wide black tail, a red scrotum-like sac ballooning below its beak. Then it strutted off into the woods with a bossy *huh? huh? huh?* the other two hastening after it.

Mansplainer, a voice whispered in his ear.

"I am not," he said.

Just then the coffee started to perk. At the same moment, he realized he was already bored by the first person and that something was slithering across his bare foot.

25

When Lorna woke she had a headache and it was nearly nine thirty. Sunlight seeped through a parting in the drapes across the window, which at some point during the night she'd drawn shut. From the parking lot came the sounds of children's excited voices and a lower voice asking them repeatedly to *get in the car*.

Last night's events had retreated to a safer distance, and as Lorna sat up, listening to the voices outside her window, seemed now less absolutely damning and more simply regrettable. She had acted out. She had gotten angry. She was human. No need to analyze it much further than that. The same way she resisted analyzing Adam, as much as possible, or at least resisted applying terms and definitions to him that she used with other people. He was her son, not her client. "Depression" was a catchall. A word that covered an emotional spectrum from "feeling blue" to—the furthest shade of blue.

Lorna closed her eyes and once more there was Marika, arms flung wide, knocking everything off the table.

In the parking lot, car doors slammed and an engine started. With Marika, too, she thought, climbing out of bed with effort, there were terms she could use, but again something stopped her. She was responsible for trying to figure out what was wrong with her clients, who were in her care, and she was responsible, of course, for Adam.

She was not responsible for whatever was wrong with Marika. In fact, the sooner she and Adam could leave Marika to herself—as Marika wanted—the better. *Get in the car*. Go home.

For a few minutes she occupied herself with the small brown plastic coffee maker she'd used yesterday on top of the wooden dresser, noting gratefully that the amenities tray had been replenished, with a package of coffee, two packets of sugar and one of nondairy creamer, a waxed paper cup, and a wooden stirrer that looked like a minute tongue depressor.

As the coffee maker began to burble, Lorna sat on the bed in her nightgown, head throbbing, and reached for her cell phone, thinking to call Adam, to apologize (somehow) for the way she'd behaved the night before and to ask how Freddy had managed in all that thunder.

Her phone, she discovered, was on mute. There were two voicemail messages from Roger. One was from yesterday evening, which had not shown up on her phone until now; the second call was from half an hour ago.

Roger's first message opened with apologies for not calling back sooner: Got your message, a lot going on at the lab, hope Marika's ankle is better, good that Adam went with you to Vermont, let's talk later tonight. The second message began abruptly. Something had come up. Something he needed to talk to her about. But instead of explaining what that something was, and why he'd called her at six a.m., West Coast time, what followed was a long pause.

"I'll be hard to reach today," he said finally. "But call when you can." Another pause. "Take care." Then an amplified fumble, as if the phone had been dropped in a pocket without being turned off.

Lorna remained on the edge of the bed, listening to what sounded like someone walking through a snowfield, looking at the phone's screen and at the thin gray line indicating the length of the voicemail. One minute and forty-two seconds.

There was something Roger needed to talk to her about, and from the tone of "Take care," it seemed he wanted her to prepare herself. Was he sick? He'd sounded fine in the previous message. But "something" had come up. "A lot going on at the lab" could mean a grant for new research or a problem. Botched experiment? Falsified data? Could he be getting fired? (How quickly her mind moved from problem to ruin.) Maybe the "something" was about himself and Angelica. Maybe they had decided to get married, a decision he would guess, correctly, that would strike Lorna as impulsive. Could Angelica be pregnant? She was only thirty-five; she might want children. Roger was sixty-three. Maybe they'd had a fight over this very issue, not uncommon between couples where one was much older. Maybe Roger wanted to talk because he didn't know what to do; maybe their relationship was over.

Take care. Lorna continued to scrutinize the voicemail line on her phone screen. It had been years since either had ended a call to the other with "Love you." Long before Roger left for Seattle they'd usually said, "See you later" when they said goodbye on the phone. After he left, they'd graduated to "Take care," the modern farewell, though in the past few months, ever since she'd realized Angelica was more than a passing interest, Lorna had taken to saying simply, "Okay, then."

She thought back again to the early years of their marriage, and her relief when it had turned mostly comradely. They were both involved in their work and then with Adam when he arrived. After listening all day to clients talk about despair and confusion, she'd been glad to come home in the evenings to someone who was rational and self-possessed, who seemed to need little from her, except dinner and to listen to him describe the experiments he was running. She and Roger were friends. Partners, Adam's co-parents. That had not changed.

Although now it seemed that something *had* changed, something had come up. *How are you feeling?* Lonely. Frightened about being alone in a world that, more and more, seemed overtaken by sadness and disasters. Frightened enough that if Adam insisted he didn't want to return to college in September, she would have trouble pushing him to go. Lonely enough that yesterday she'd even invited Marika to come live nearby.

Take care. Why this morning did those two words sound like a warning?

The coffee maker quit burbling. Lorna got up and stumbled over to it, filled the paper cup with coffee the color of gutter water, stirred in powdered creamer with the tiny tongue depressor, and carried her cup back to the bed.

In his message, Roger had said he'd be hard to reach, but to "call when you can." It was past seven o'clock in Seattle. Should she call now?

He was probably shaving, eating breakfast, rushing to get to the lab, where there was "a lot going on." She was all too familiar with his impatient tone when he was in a hurry or distracted. A tone that, just now, she felt she could not bear. *Can this wait?* he'd often said when Adam was little and she called him at the lab to share a small milestone or concern. *Not a good time*. Yes, of course. Fine. Always she would hang up a little angrier than the time before, yet secure in the knowledge that if it were something really important, he would answer differently. A conviction to hold in reserve. So she'd stopped calling Roger at the lab, stopped asking him to pick up milk on the way home or whether he could leave work early and get Adam from day care. Although she was the one who began saying see you later instead of goodbye. Had he noticed? It seemed to her now that she'd been posing a question. See you later? When Roger was debating whether to move to Seattle, she had seen it as a test of her generosity not to stand in his way. But the truth was, she'd seen it as a test for Roger.

Lorna stared into the pale depths of her unappetizing coffee. She had never said, I want you to stay. More to the point, she had never said, I want you to *want* to stay. She'd believed she was being honorable by remaining silent. Instead she'd been stupid. It was people who asked for things who got them.

Time to get up, she told herself firmly. Get dressed. No more wallowing. If you're not going to call Roger, then drink your bad coffee. Go buy some doughnuts. Make your apologies. But she stayed sitting on the bed.

The truth was that she had never wanted Roger to go, had wished until the last minute that he would decide to stay, and in some distant part of her mind continued to hope, even now when it was too late, that he would come back. And yet, she had also been relieved when he left. Relieved not to have to think about what he wanted and needed, to worry that it was her fault when he was in a bad mood. Aside from Adam, they had few interests in common. Roger could be—and frequently was—careless, self-involved. Drank all the coffee and didn't make another pot, was annoyed when she got home too late to fix dinner instead of offering to fix it himself. Snored, left socks on the floor and nose-hair clippings on the sink. Looked at his phone while she was talking. Forgot to ask about her day. Forgot plans they had made to go to a concert or a movie. Forgot that she was not always fascinated by microbes and viral loads. He was self-important, frustrating, unremarkable, and he had not particularly needed her to understand him, despite what he'd said when they first met.

All true and not true. She had not wanted Roger to leave, and yet she'd been relieved when he left because what she had always been afraid of had happened, and now it was done. She could get on with things. She could quit being afraid. That's what she had thought.

Roger once said: I think you like the idea of me more than me. She had denied it at the time, but he'd been right. She had liked the idea of being married to him, but he had not been quite real to her. The truth was, no one was quite real to her, not Roger, not friends, not even her clients, whose problems had long ago run together into one endless sad story.

No one except Adam. And perhaps, in a very different way, Marika. Neither of whom wanted anything to do with her.

The only way to live in this crap world is to care about nothing.

Lorna set her untouched cup of coffee on the nightstand. Gazing around at her motel room, she noticed for the first time that the brown carpet was flecked with viral orange squiggles, and that the synthetic bedspread was patterned with brown amoeba shapes outlined in orange. The curtains matched the bedspread. On the brown vinyl chair in the corner rested a pillow in the same amoeba-patterned fabric, as if some kind of contagion had taken place.

26

Across the kitchen floor rippled a greenish striped snake. Adam chased it into the living room and around the picnic table. "Hey!" he shouted as it slid under one of the electric baseboards. "Hey!" he shouted again. His grandmother had been dozing in her chair but now opened her eyes. "There's a *snake* in the house."

"Oh, really?" she said, sounding unsurprised.

After much dodging and flinching, mostly on his part, he cornered the snake by the woodstove and clamped a pot over it. The same pot his mother had used to boil pasta. His grandmother watched without a word. She might have been inside the pot herself, for all the opinion she had to offer. But now what? A snake in an overturned pasta pot required an immediate solution. If only his phone weren't dead, he could google: "What to do with a snake caught in a pot?" And something would come up, a suggestion from someone, somewhere, who'd been in this exact same situation. The snake bumped around inside the pot, making it shift from side to side as if controlled by some kind of poltergeist.

At last a plan arrived: Slide the pot across the floor to the door to the deck, prop open the door, scoot the pot onto the doorsill, and punt it.

His kick was hard and true. Both pot and snake flew high across the deck. At that precise instant, something swooped from out of nowhere and caught the snake in its talons. Holy shit! A hawk, a big, motherfucking hawk!

Away they went, off across the lake, the hawk flapping its great black wings, the snake twisting in midair. Even if this scene had been on *Planet Earth*, he wouldn't have believed it. In fact, he didn't believe it, and yet it had just happened.

"Did you see that?" he cried to his grandmother.

Asleep again in her chair. Missed the whole thing.

What a world. Every ten minutes, something new. He'd like to see his father goal-kick a snake across a lake.

IN THE KITCHEN, he poured out two mugs of black coffee and set them on a tray, alongside two slices of bread scorched on a stove burner, half a stick of hard butter, and a saucer with three slightly bruised strawberries foraged from the fruit drawer.

"Breakfast," he announced, setting the tray on the picnic table. His grandmother woke up. Her eyes looked crossed as she swabbed at her nose with a tissue.

She wanted to drink her coffee in her chair. No toast. No strawberries. Adam opened his mouth in protest but then closed it. He'd never considered how rarely people want exactly what you want to give them; then again, this was the first meal he'd ever prepared for someone other than himself.

The coffee tasted bitter and much too strong, and as he tried to drink it, he kept thinking about Freddy alone in the woods, frightened, confused. Or lying beside the road, hit by a car, injured, panting, soft brown eyes filming over. He put his mug down.

"If Freddy shows up while I'm out looking, will you let him in?"

His grandmother blew on her coffee and didn't answer, sunk in some deep brooding. "Remember my bird feeder," was all she said as he stood up.

When he reached the road, he turned west and kept walking, pausing every few yards to call for Freddy, aware that it sounded like he was calling a child's name, as if he'd lost his little brother or a kid he was babysitting. Puddles pocked the dirt road, each one a muddy little pond. Sunlight began breaking through the clouds. The rain had ushered in a tropical humidity and the road steamed. Adam pulled his T-shirt away from his chest, luffing a tiny breeze toward his chin. What had happened to all those doughnuts from yesterday? He hadn't said he wouldn't eat them. He was being a stretchy vegan. Why hadn't anyone saved one for him? He was hungry and thirsty, his throat ached worse than ever, and he was trying not to admit that he'd already given up on finding Freddy who, along with the doughnuts, had entered the mysterious vortex of lost things, far outside the laws of physics.

But when he rounded a bend, he saw a hound with droopy brown ears lying beside a rusty mailbox at the end of a driveway, as if the force of his yearning for Freddy had produced a dog, just not the right one. Behind the hound, half obscured by a pine tree, stood Dennis, in his blue ball cap. He was also wearing long khaki shorts. One of his legs was a regular leg, fleshy and hairy; the other was a shiny metal prosthesis ending in a boot.

"Freddy's run away," Adam called out.

"So I figured," said Dennis drily.

Adam halted at the edge of the driveway, trying not to stare at Dennis's metal leg. It looked amazingly sci-fi: smooth, shiny, ingeniously fitted together. The rest of Dennis looked bad. The gray bags under his eyes were baggier and his beard seemed to have crawled farther up his face. He held on to the mailbox while Adam described waking up to the storm and to his grandmother's bout of illness—omitting, out of modesty, the shower he'd given her—and then Freddy disappearing, and searching for him last night in the rain, and this morning's discovery of a snake in the kitchen.

"She seems okay now, though," Adam concluded. "I made her some coffee. But my mom," he said, "still doesn't know anything."

He shoved his hands into his pockets, concern for his mother crowding in with all the other responsibilities he'd acquired over the past twelve hours, mixed with resentment and pride at having been left to take care of everything himself.

"It's crazy," he said passionately. "I mean, everything *sucks*."

"Had breakfast?" asked Dennis, using his metal leg to scratch the hound's rump with the toe of his boot.

27

To one side of the screen door lay a heap of wet towels that must have blown down from the clothesline during last night's storm. Although as Lorna parked by the woodpile and got out of the car, she couldn't remember hanging towels on the line, only her bathing suit, still dangling from two clothespins.

She'd come bearing a fresh box of doughnuts, prepared to spend part of the morning cleaning up the kitchen and setting everything to rights, but to her surprise and faint disquiet the kitchen was mostly tidy, the dish rack full of clean dishes, pots washed and put away, counters wiped down, the smell of strong coffee emanating from the percolator. Adam must have cleaned up, as he'd promised to do. Contemplating the quiet, shadowy kitchen, she felt a small but definite displacement.

In the living room all the windows were closed, as they had been the day she arrived. It was very hot. Outside the picture window the lake was full of haze that matched the sky, both a sullen shade of freezer burn. Marika sat hunched in her chair, pine stick beside her, wearing the same outfit she'd worn for the past two days. Her flat cheeks were colorless, scanty gray hair sticking up in tufts, head sunk between her bony shoulders. She looked to be asleep. But at Lorna's entrance, she turned her head to the side and lifted her chin.

"You," she croaked. "You practically killed me last night."

Lorna had intended to begin by apologizing for the previous evening—she hadn't been sleeping well, had a lot on her mind, should never have had a second/third glass of wine—but was so taken aback that she froze, holding the box suspended above the picnic table.

"Sorry?"

Marika had turned back to the window. What was visible of her expression looked as if she had flung her face open for an instant and was now refastening the latches.

I have misjudged her, Lorna thought in amazement. I have misjudged her feelings about me. But I have never spent enough time with her to see it.

Yet now everything was suddenly clear. Marika had always been secretive, that was her nature. But last night, forced by Lorna's accusations to confront what she had done, Marika had finally allowed herself to admit the crushing guilt she'd been hiding all these years. *Never thought of it*, she'd said bitterly. Of course not. Because she couldn't bear to.

Lorna lowered the doughnut box to the table, placing it next to a tray she hadn't noticed at first, set with a plate of blackened toast, half a stick of butter, and a saucer of strawberries. To give herself time to compose herself, she said, "Where is Adam?" looking through the windows to the empty deck outside.

"Out," said Marika.

"Well, I brought more doughnuts." Dazed, Lorna took a seat on the lumpy sofa and leaned back, a hand placed to either side of her as if for balance. "So," she said, "can you say more about how I practically killed you?"

Marika made a face. "*Garlic*," she spat. "In your fancy sauce."

Lorna sat up straight. Her first thought was: Again? Could I really have been so stupid again? Her second thought was: Naturally Marika would now try to hide what she'd felt. How could it be otherwise? Hiding was her normal state. Her third thought was that she'd been so distracted by her plans for dinner that she had forgotten Marika was allergic to garlic. Every year at Thanksgiving Marika peered suspiciously at the buffet loaded with dishes and announced, *Can't have garlic.* How could she have forgotten? It was one of the few things she knew for certain about Marika, that she could not have garlic.

"I am so sorry," she said. "I forgot."

"*Garlic*," repeated Marika. "Kept me up half the night."

"I really am sorry," said Lorna.

At the same time she was realizing that, no matter what conclusion she reached, she would always be mistaken when it came to Marika. Probably because Marika would always be mistaken about Marika. Garlic? That's all that nearly killed you last night? How much was it possible not to know about yourself?

"The boy had to give me a shower." Marika squinted at her balefully. "That's how bad it was. He wanted to call an ambulance."

"An ambulance?" Lorna was now fully attentive. "A shower?"

"He handled himself *very* well. A *very* intelligent young man." Marika glared over the top of her glasses. "*He* was sorry for me."

"I'm sorry, too." Lorna tried to picture Adam helping his grandmother into the shower, but all she could see was the white plastic shower curtain, like a screen around a hospital patient.

"I completely forgot," she said.

"Hah," said Marika.

"I'm sorry you don't believe me. People do forget things." To calm herself, Lorna focused on a column of spiraling dust motes. "So will you tell me what happened?"

"The boy dried me off." Marika pulled out a tissue to wipe her nose. "Made me a cup of tea. Treated me better than any doctor, I can tell you *that*." She dropped the tissue onto the floor and gave a hard sniff. "Then we sat up for a while. He wanted to talk."

"To talk?"

"Yes. Wanted to tell me about his trouble at school."

The dust motes stopped moving. Lorna's armpits had dampened and the backs of her thighs prickled against the sofa's rough fabric.

"So what did he tell you?"

Marika leaned back in her chair, shifting her hips. "Not my place to say."

"But you'd let me know, wouldn't you," said Lorna, "if there's something I need to worry about."

"Chickadee." Marika craned her neck. "Two of them. At the bird feeder."

"But you would tell me," Lorna held herself very still on the sofa, "if anything was really wrong?"

"He'll get over it."

Silence followed. A silence that began to have its own smell, damp and dank, with an undercurrent of fish.

"Had a cardinal here this morning." Marika pointed to the window. "A nuthatch and two jays."

Outside, the bird feeder hung from a low pine branch. Beside it rested the ladder Adam had used for cleaning the gutters, propped against the tree trunk. The sun had begun to appear, thinning the vapor on the lake and tinting it pink. There was almost no sound at all, save for a few birds in the trees, the lap of water against the rocks, and a faint, insistent *tick, tick, tick* from somewhere near the woodstove.

"I'm glad that he wanted to talk to you," Lorna forced herself to say.

"What?"

"I said I'm *glad* he talked to you. I'm glad that you and Adam are starting to have a real relationship."

Marika grunted, and then gave a coy smile that was almost girlish. "Always have had a way," she said, "with the boys."

A kind of wavering unsteadied the air between them, like heat rising, a molecular breakdown dissolving the definitions between things. The ticking from the woodstove grew louder as Lorna's heart began to pound. She pictured herself standing over Marika's chair and striking her with her fists. Pushing her to the floor. I wish you *had* died last night. I wish I *had* killed you. Nothing has changed. You left me fifty years ago to run off with a stable hand. And this time you are trying to make off with my *son*?

But all she said was "Stop."

Because amid that furnace-blast of fury, she'd had a chilling thought: Was it possible that she had, subconsciously, tried to kill Marika last night, by feeding her garlic? Acting on a buried impulse? How much *was* it possible not to know about yourself?

In her armchair, Marika was kneading the armrests with her knotty fingers. "He ran away," she said finally.

No, thought Lorna. It was not possible to be that insensible. Not for her, at least. She was a therapist. There was a vast difference between desire and action, even when driven by the subconscious. She blinked and shook her head as if to clear it. "Who ran away?"

"That dog. Last night, when it was raining."

"You left Freddy *outside* in the rain?"

"We forgot about him. We had other things to think about."

Trembling, Lorna stood up. "Where is he now?"

"The boy's out looking for him." Marika had returned to glaring over her raised chin. "Went out after making my breakfast."

"Did he say where he was going?"

"I asked him to hang up my bird feeder." Marika pursed her mouth sourly. "Asked him three times yesterday. Finally had to do it myself."

Lorna had reached the door. She was perspiring heavily now, and all that mattered was to get out of that stuffy room and into the fresh air. But she forced herself to turn around.

"You did what?"

"My birds were starting to think I forgot about them."

"You climbed that ladder?"

"Well." Marika smirked. "Didn't fly up it."

Stumbling slightly, Lorna returned to the sofa. She looked at Marika's pine stick and then at Marika, who was no longer smirking. "I don't understand. Are you telling me that your ankle isn't sprained anymore?"

Marika pushed out her lower lip. "No."

"No? So what are you saying?"

"Never was."

Clasping her hands tightly together, Lorna said, "Your ankle was *never* sprained?"

"Look there," said Marika. "Another chickadee."

"Why did Dennis call me if your ankle wasn't sprained? Are you saying you only pretended you'd fallen off the ladder?"

She looked searchingly at the old woman in the chair. "You pretended to hurt yourself because Dennis is leaving? Is that it? Because he's going to Florida? You faked spraining your ankle because you want Dennis to stay up here with you?"

Marika was once again staring out at the lake with the same blank rigidity as when Lorna had first arrived and found her motionless in her chair.

"But instead," Lorna said slowly, recalling Dennis's odd behavior when she'd met him yesterday afternoon, his unwillingness to look at her. "Instead he called me."

What she had first taken for reticence must have been embarrassment. Dennis must have known what Marika was up to, that her sprained ankle was a ruse. Maybe Marika's illness last night had been an act, too. A scheme to win back Lorna's sympathy and cooperation after her burst of anger. Maybe even Adam was in on it. But this last thought was unendurable and she dismissed it.

"Okay." She set her clasped hands on her knees. "I see. But for once, let's try to be honest." She took a deep breath and leaned forward on the sofa. "Can you at least admit what you've been hiding?"

A sudden movement in the chair. Marika's blank expression disappeared, replaced by something fearful and cagey. "Hiding?"

"Yes, hiding. Can you at least admit that you were afraid I'd find out about Dennis?"

Marika looked affronted. "I didn't care about *that*."

"You didn't?" Lorna stared at her. "Then what *do* you care about?"

The caginess was back. "Well, I'd like to know what's for lunch."

A bag of knitting sat at Marika's feet, needles poking out of a skein of blue wool, a long strand of kinked yarn trailing onto the floor. It's always the same question, thought Lorna, wondering how she could find this surprising.

"You know," she said, determined to try one more time, "you could have told me you needed help. You could have told me that you'd stopped driving, and that it was getting too hard for you to be on your own."

Marika frowned and lifted her chin. "I don't need any help."

The sun had come out and the mist on the lake was vanishing. Two gray birds at the bird feeder were pecking at the same opening. Birdseed sprinkled onto the ground. The bird feeder swayed and winked, sunlight glinting off its pointed metal cap.

"Why have you never tried to talk to me?" Lorna said quietly. "And please don't say it was because you didn't think of it."

"Don't have to." Marika dragged another tissue from her sleeve. "You said it for me."

Lorna unclasped her hands and looked at her palms. She was used to difficult people. She was used to denial, irresponsibility, selfishness, obfuscations, even real cruelty. She was used to unhappiness. Day after day, people came to her office with their disappointments, their rage and regrets, their longing, their loneliness, which they tried, gropingly, with much effort, to explain to her, or at least pretended to try. And it wasn't just in her office. Everywhere you went, you encountered people who held such pain; you knew this, because when told about someone else's suffering, most people made a supportive remark or shared a difficult experience of their own, to show that they, too, had been there. In its way, it was common courtesy.

But with Marika there was nothing to share. She had nothing to say, or would say nothing. She acknowledged no pain she had felt or caused. She did not care about Lorna enough to try to explain herself, even in the most basic terms. She was a missing person. She would never turn up. No matter how many questions Lorna asked, or how long she waited.

Outside, the bird feeder continued to bob and sway as the birds flew away from it and then alighted again. Just beyond the bird feeder was the urn of lavender, which had an unpleasant sheen this morning, the color of spoiled meat.

"So what's for lunch?" said Marika, tucking away the tissue.

"Nothing is for lunch." Lorna exhaled deeply. She rose and flexed her fingers. "I am going out to find my son and my dog. And then in a little while we are going to drive home."

The old woman peered at her.

"This week," Lorna turned toward the window, where the lake now reflected a hard brilliance, "I will make arrangements for a home health aide to start visiting you. Someone who can drive you to town for your shopping and errands and do some cleaning. There are agencies that provide help for people in your situation."

"I take care of myself," said Marika.

"When the time comes that you need more help," Lorna continued as if Marika hadn't spoken, "when it becomes unsafe for you to remain up here on your own, we will make other arrangements."

Once again she was at the door, a hand on the latch. "But now," she said, "I'm leaving."

"So," came a thin, childlike voice. "Go."

28

They had been in Dennis's skiff for over an hour, motoring up and down both sides of the Neck. Dennis sat at the helm with the hound between his boots; Adam crouched in the bow, sitting on a red life jacket and holding a pair of binoculars, hoping to glimpse a flash of golden fur onshore.

"Freddy's never done this before." He tried not to sound panicky. "He never runs off. He's like eighty in dog years. He barely leaves the yard."

The skiff was aluminum, painted a camouflage design, with a large outboard motor. Several rusted shotgun shells rolled back and forth in an inch of bilgewater at the bottom. Dennis was a duck hunter as well as a fisherman, he'd said over a breakfast of fried eggs, sausage patties, buttered toast, and glasses of milk. Adam had never met a hunter, or seen a shotgun shell; he would have liked to pick one up and put it in his shorts pocket, not as a souvenir, exactly, but as something to remind him of the past couple days, if he ever forgot. Instead he peered through the binoculars and pretended to be on some sort of military reconnaissance. So far he'd spotted birds and squirrels, a gray-haired woman skinny-dipping who didn't seem to mind that anyone could see her, two men fishing in a canoe, and a girl in a red bikini sitting on a dock clipping her toenails. But no Freddy.

The haze had evaporated and the sun was now strong on the back of his neck. He wished that he'd resisted at least the sausage patties at breakfast. But he'd been so hungry. They ate at a table in Dennis's living room, which looked like a mini-mart: every wall held shelves of canned, bottled, and packaged food, water, medical supplies. When Dennis saw him staring at the walls, he'd said, "Always good to be prepared."

Recalling those crowded shelves, Adam realized he wasn't wearing sunscreen and wondered how to ask Dennis if he had any with him. He also wondered whether Dennis was planning to haul all that stuff to Florida.

Two people on Jet Skis passed them, and people in sailboats and kayaks. A few waved, but mostly no one seemed to notice them, even when Adam trained the binoculars in their direction. Periodically he lowered the binoculars to call for Freddy and then raised them to scan the shoreline. Maybe Freddy didn't want to come home. Maybe he liked being out in the woods. Nosing deer droppings, eating a dead squirrel. Returning to an instinctive identity denied to him in the suburbs, amid mown lawns and pruned hedges, where the only snarls came from weed whackers. Fend for yourself, that's what you did in the wild. A breeze lifted Adam's hair from his forehead.

More likely Freddy was lost and afraid. Or hurt. Even dead. Fingering the binoculars, Adam pictured Freddy lying beside the road in much the same position as yesterday he'd pictured his grandmother.

It's *all my fault*, he told himself savagely. I *knew* Freddy was outside and I didn't bring him in out of the rain. I didn't even look out the window. *Everything* is my fault. I am guilty of everything. I wish I were a woman, he thought, shutting his eyes to the lake's insistent brightness. I wish I were blind. And in a wheelchair, and poor. I wish I were old and about to die. But after several minutes of trying to disadvantage himself further, he concluded that wanting to escape feeling guilty about everything was another sign of white male privilege, and returned to worrying about Freddy.

"I'm really worried about Freddy," he shouted over the skiff's motor, turning around to look at Dennis. "I really hope he's okay. What if he got hit by a car?"

"Probably back at your grandma's by now," Dennis shouted back.

"Maybe you're right," said Adam doubtfully.

They rounded the Neck again and motored along in choppy silence, the skiff smacking up and down on short waves. But as they approached a small island of scrub and boulders, one of several they had passed, Dennis slowed the skiff and then cut the motor so that they sat drifting and rocking on the water, the sun full on their faces.

"Time for a little fishing," he said. "Want a beer?"

Without waiting for an answer, he dragged a grimy Styrofoam cooler out from under his seat, opened the lid with a squeak, and handed Adam a brown bottle and a church key. The bottle smelled loamy, mushroomy, as if it had been buried in dirt. Nested inside the cooler, next to the beer, was a white takeout carton. Dennis extracted a night crawler and held it up, pinched between two fingers. "Snack?"

"Haha," said Adam, grateful Dennis hadn't asked if he was old enough to have a beer.

As he took the first pull, he watched Dennis take a fishing rod from under a gunwale near the stern and then bait his hook. He tried to imagine what Ashley would say if she could see him drinking beer with an old prepper in a camo boat full of shotgun shells in the middle of a lake, at ten thirty in the morning. The worm curled in tiny agony.

A few moments later, Dennis cast with a sidearm motion and an expert snap of his wrist. The line made a light whir through the air and a circular ripple appeared in the water. Adam watched in silence as Dennis cast, reeled in, cast and reeled in, observing fine points of adjustment in swing and wrist snap. Dennis didn't seem to mind being watched so closely, but after ten minutes or so, he pointed to the little island.

"Used to bring my boy out here sometimes."

Adam raised his binoculars to examine the heap of boulders, a few blueberry bushes, and a pair of skinny fir trees. Dennis said that Greg was his son's name. Greg was in real estate management in Boca Raton. Mixed-use developments. Wife just had twins. Adam drank the rest of his beer as he pictured Greg: tall and tanned, broad-shouldered like Dennis, bearded, too, but with corporate stubble. White shirtsleeves rolled to his elbow, large silver wristwatch. Eating a sandwich at his desk and reading the box scores in the paper, then leaning back in his chair, hands laced behind his head, taking a break from a busy day of mixed-use developments, thinking of all he had to manage.

Dennis was casting again. The line landed nine or ten yards away, and slowly he reeled it in. He motioned to his rod. "Want to give it a shot?"

Adam shook his head. "No thanks." Then while they continued to sit rocking with the skiff, he asked shyly, "So what happened to your leg?"

"Blown off." Dennis reached for his beer. "On patrol, outside a village."

"Was it a land mine?"

"Some kids threw a grenade at us."

"Kids?" repeated Adam, horrified. "What happened to them?"

A dragonfly landed on Dennis's ball cap. It was an extraordinary color. Not indigo, or cobalt, but something deeper and incandescent, like the color inside a flame. In another moment the dragonfly was gone, leaving behind the impression of a small hole burned into the day. "You can probably guess," Dennis said in his soft voice.

To Adam's relief, a cloud drifted over the sun. It was very hot now in the open skiff; he was thirsty and sunburned and starting to feel dizzy. As he sat watching Dennis fish, he thought of those shelves in his cabin, row after row of cans and packages and supplies, and for the first time it occurred to him that most of the disasters people prepare for had already happened to them.

"My mom thinks I'm depressed," he said.

Dennis cast again. "Sorry to hear it."

Adam looked at his empty beer bottle. "That's her diagnosis. But I think *she's* the one who's depressed." His dizziness was getting more pronounced, but then he glanced up and caught sight of Dennis's fishing line, glinting in the sun like a filament of spiderweb.

"My dad is seeing someone," he went on, keeping his focus on the line. "Though they've been divorced for like years. But I guess it still bothers her. He lives in Seattle. I don't really pay that much attention to them," he added after a moment. "I think it should be your right as a child not to have to think about your parents."

He pressed the beer bottle to his temple, grateful for the brief coolness. Despite being divorced, his parents did display a reliable comradeship, at least where he was concerned, and also a mutual tolerance. Which was probably why he didn't have to think about them. They were both reasonable people. They did not shout or make mean comments like other divorced parents he'd heard about. Beyond that, they also seemed, at times, to harbor a kind of friendly pity for each other.

A speedboat passed by full of shouting people and trailing a rooster tail of foamy wake. The skiff rocked back and forth. "I don't actually know why they split up, except for my dad's job being in Seattle. They pretty much like each other. They're good parents," he said, beginning to feel sick. "They're good people. Whatever that means."

The day after he got home, he'd texted Ashley: *I sincerely apologize for having been such an asshole. As part of the white supremacist capitalist power structure I have been acculturated to subjugate. I will struggle to overcome this ingrained identity and become an ally. In solidarity.*

After three days, she texted back: *Just don't become another kind of asshole.*

"Your mother seems like she tries hard," offered Dennis.

Adam stared at the lake wrinkling in the sun. "Yeah."

What a nice person, people always said of his mother. Teachers, neighbors, his parents' friends, even his own friends. Every so often they would run into her former clients, at restaurants or at the grocery store, who wanted to thank her for helping them. What would those same people think if they'd seen her last night at dinner, grilling his grandmother, who was about to pass out, and then yelling, *What's wrong with you?*

What was wrong with his mother, he decided, was that she was always looking for explanations. The world needed more people like his grandmother, who never tried to reassure anybody about anything.

"I'm really worried about Freddy," he said.

Dennis cast again. This time the line went taut as he slowly began reeling it in. At the end of it was a silvery, blue-green-spotted fish, maybe a foot long. For several moments the fish thrashed in the air beside the boat, its mouth open in what looked like indignation. Dennis rested the rod between his knees and reached out barehanded to grip the fish around its gills. With a small pair of pliers, he worked the hook free of its lower lip. Adam's stomach lurched. Dennis leaned over the side of the skiff and eased the fish gently back into the lake.

"Why'd you let it go?" he asked.

"Too small."

Adam looked over the side of the skiff, where the fish floated sideways in the water. A thin trail of blood floated beside it like a caption: *I Am Dead.*

"The thing is," he said, feeling dizzy once more. "I never heard my mom *ask* my dad to come back home. Maybe he would've said no, but she didn't ask. At least she never said she did." He began rolling the empty beer bottle between his palms. "I mean, I think she's kind of decided the only way to deal with people is not to expect much from them. Probably because of, you know, what happened to her.

"It's almost funny." He gave a short unhappy laugh. "Like, she's the hopeless therapist or something." Raising the bottle to his eye, he peered unsteadily through it like a telescope. "I mean, like last night was an obvious example."

"I don't know about that," said Dennis.

"Hopeless," repeated Adam. He set his beer bottle between his sneakers and stared again over the side of the skiff at the limp fish. But as he watched, the fish suddenly seemed to realize that it was not dead. With a lash of its tail it was gone.

Dennis sighed, putting away his rod. "I think it's time to go see about your grandma."

THEY HAD ROUNDED the Neck again and were passing close by a small sandy public beach, at the end of it, where a silver VW station wagon was parked in an otherwise empty lot. A figure stood on the sand. A woman, in a skirt and blouse and black sunglasses. She raised her arm and began waving. Dennis spotted her, and before Adam could protest, had turned the boat toward the beach. A minute later he cut the motor and they glided the last few yards into the shallows several feet from shore.

Adam scowled as his mother pulled off her sandals and waded into the water to meet them, hitching her paisley skirt above her knees. The hound stood up and whined.

"I've been looking for you everywhere," she called out. As they drew alongside her, she reached out to touch Adam's shoulder. He jerked away from her hand, making the skiff rock.

"I heard about last night. Are you okay?" She pushed her sunglasses onto the top of her head and eyed the beer bottle between his sneakers. Then he saw her eye Dennis's metal leg and quickly look away, as if pretending she hadn't noticed it.

"We've been looking for Freddy," he said coldly.

"I know. I heard what happened."

"Grootie got *really* sick last night. She got totally dehydrated."

Her face flooded with apology. "Yes, I was just there and I heard you took really good care of her. She seems fine now. But it must have been scary, to see her get sick. You must have been very worried."

If he'd been holding a paddle or a fishing pole, he would have swung it at her. How dare she accept what had happened? As if it was all over, and now they could go back to business as usual, with him sulking and her being sympathetic. You must be tired. You're depressed. You've been under a lot of pressure.

No, he wanted to shout, I am an asshole. But *you* need to get a life.

"I'm so sorry," she was saying to Dennis, "about everything last night. I was completely out of line. What happened is all my fault."

"It was the garlic," Adam said, hardly moving his jaws.

She returned her gaze to him. "I forgot she was allergic."

"How could you *forget* something like that?"

"I don't know." She gave him a humble, enraging smile. "The same way I suppose I forgot you were vegan."

"It's not the same thing at all. This is *life-threatening*." But as he glowered back at her, a dreadful suspicion crawled into his mind. He pictured her tense expression yesterday afternoon as she reported Grootie saying that she'd rather die than go to Avalon Towers. Her so-called funny remark: *Of course, that's another option*. Then last night's interrogation, the relentless way she'd attacked Grootie until the old woman basically collapsed.

"I'm sorry," she said. "I really am."

Dennis's hound chose that moment to try to leap out of the skiff. Though built low, he was a stocky animal and weighed at least sixty pounds. The impact of his first, unsuccessful leap caught Adam unawares and almost pitched him off his seat.

"Whoa," cried Dennis.

The hound's second leap cleared the gunwales, landing him in the lake with a splash. Adam had barely righted himself when he was knocked backward again, this time onto the floor of the skiff, awash with an inch of scummy bilgewater. When he was able to struggle onto his knees, he saw that his mother had also lost her balance and was sitting in the lake up to her waist, the hound floundering and splashing beside her.

Shaking, Adam climbed back onto his seat to find that Dennis's beard was moving up and down, emitting a rusty seesaw of noise, possibly laughter. Nauseated by the bilgewater soaking his shorts and T-shirt, reeking of gasoline, and by the thought that Dennis was laughing at him, after all he had gone through last night, Adam put his face in his hands.

His crazy suspicions about his mother had made a pit in his stomach, along with the fear that they would never find Freddy. He'd banged his elbow when he fell into the skiff, sending achy twinges up his arm as if rubber bands were snapping inside it, and with each twinge he understood more clearly that his life would be a series of injuries and humiliations. No one but his parents would ever love him. The Earth would become uninhabitable by the time he was fifty and he would probably die alone. Also, he never should have eaten those sausage patties before getting into the boat and drinking a beer.

It was too much. He could not bear it. Especially he could not bear the spectacle of his mother, sitting in the lake, laughing now, too, as the hound nosed her ear. Any compassion he'd felt for her earlier had vanished; he could barely contain his repulsion as she staggered up out of the water, skirt dripping, her bra showing through the wet fabric of her blouse, as exposed as an X-ray.

A few minutes later, the skiff had been pulled onto the sand. Dennis produced a green towel while recounting their search for Freddy, repeating his conviction that Freddy would soon return, and announced that they were on their way to check on "your maw."

"She seems fine," repeated his mother, returning the towel. Then asked if she could join them in the skiff, as if the morning's search had been some sort of joyride. "Adam? Would you mind grabbing my purse from the car?"

In the parking lot, he threw up behind a tree and immediately felt better. He peered through the car's open window, where her purse and the car keys lay on the front seat. Without glancing back at Dennis and his mother on the beach, Adam climbed into the car and started the engine. Dangling from the rear view mirror, the jade good-luck charm began to sway.

Smoothly, with a competence he forgot to distrust, he let out the clutch, put the car into reverse, and began backing up. He felt a rush of gratification, followed by a jolt of panic. He had not driven a car in over six months, and this was his mother's stick shift. But there is a moment in any gesture when you have committed yourself and so with a grinding screech, he changed gears into forward. Then he gunned the engine to keep it from stalling and bucked out of the parking lot.

29

"Adam!" Lorna shouted. "Adam!"

She turned anxiously to Dennis as the car vanished into the trees. "He's been drinking," she said. "And he only has a learner's permit."

"One beer." Dennis held up a finger. "Ate a big breakfast. And just got sick behind that tree over there. It's half a mile to the cottage. He'll be fine."

"I hope you're right." Lorna frowned, somewhat reassured, at the same time feeling it was irresponsible not to worry about Adam, given the situation. Beside her the lake was sparkling, a few small yellow birch leaves floating on the water. Under the surface, dark leaves and twigs wavered against the ridged sand. Automatically, she reached for her sunglasses, only to realize they were gone, knocked off the top of her head when she'd fallen into the water.

"He'll be fine," Dennis repeated. "We can keep looking for your dog," he offered. "And give the boy a chance to simmer down. Then I'll run you back."

"I guess that's a good idea." Lorna looked down and plucked her wet blouse away from her bra. Then she looked at Dennis's metal prosthesis, which she had noticed immediately, but in the confusion of the last few minutes was only really seeing now. It looked like many she had encountered during her two years working at the VA, her first counseling job. Her supervisor at the time was a rangy, middle-aged woman named Faye who called everyone "kiddo"; by her desk was a sign that read: COMPASSION AND COMPANY SHARE THE FIRST FIVE LETTERS. SO DOES COMPAZINE. On Lorna's first day, Faye had advised her not to comment immediately on a man's prosthesis, which would suggest it was the most noticeable aspect of him. Instead mention it later in the conversation. Bring it up, but be prepared to let it drop. A missing limb is as much a part of the dear body as any other limb, she had said, and the dear body deserves deference. If a client doesn't want to talk about it, that's to be respected.

Dennis had dragged the skiff back into the water while they were speaking. Now he offered his hand to her. Holding her sandals, Lorna climbed aboard. When she was seated in the bow, he lifted the hound, wet paws rowing the air, and set him down by her knees. Then he climbed into the skiff himself.

"I remember hearing about your leg from my grandmother," Lorna said. "I'm sorry."

He nodded briefly. "As for your dog"—he began pumping a bulb on the red gas tank at his feet—"there's no place to go once you're all the way out here."

"He's an old dog."

"All the more reason for him to come back."

"I wish I understood what's going on with him," Lorna said, meaning Adam.

A line of small birds flew low over the water like a string of dark beads. She watched them disappear and then lifted a hand to shade her eyes and studied Dennis for a few moments.

"So, while I was with Marika this morning I found out that she's worried about you leaving for Florida. And that she pretended to sprain her ankle to get you to stay."

"Ah." Dennis lowered the bill of his cap.

"You told me yesterday afternoon that she could take care of herself. Did you guess what she was trying to do?"

Instead of answering, Dennis adjusted the throttle on the skiff's outboard motor and yanked the rip cord. A waft of petroleum rose up. Nothing else happened. He readjusted the throttle and pumped the gas bulb again. He gave two more yanks on the rip cord.

"Is that why you called me?" Lorna waited. "What if I'd said no?" she asked finally, with genuine curiosity.

"Well," said Dennis, "but you didn't."

On the third yank, the flywheel caught and the motor roared. Dennis turned the bow of the skiff out into the lake as the hound settled onto a life vest at Lorna's feet and laid his head on his paws. The skiff smacked up and down on the short bright waves, the bow lowering as they gained speed until they were skimming flat along the water.

After ten minutes or so, Dennis slowed the skiff, letting it wash forward on its own wake. They were near one of the little islands that dotted the lake, two fir trees sticking up from a tumble of boulders like a pair of raised arms. He cut the motor and they sat drifting and rocking on the water.

"So," he said at last. "Where are we?"

"Where are we?" Lorna shifted in her seat to face him. "You mean in terms of Marika?" When he nodded, she said slowly, "I suppose where we are is that she's my mother, but I hardly know her. She's a stranger to me in almost every way." Then, afraid of sounding petulant, but wanting to be frank, she added, "And I don't feel that I owe her anything."

While Dennis bent down again to check the gauge on the gas tank, Lorna surveyed the island with its two spindly fir trees, picturing Marika in her armchair by the window, staring out at the lake.

"I'm arranging for a home health aide to visit a few days a week," she said. "It's not a great solution, but it will have to do for now."

A pair of mallards had splashed onto the water, wings lifted, a green-headed male and his brown mate. They floated away toward the island, and then out of sight behind a clump of low-hanging blueberry bushes.

"She may not appreciate all you've done for her, but I do." Lorna glanced back at Dennis. "But you shouldn't stay here any longer. You've done more than enough."

"I've done what I wanted to do." Dennis's voice held some of the same anger as yesterday afternoon when they'd stood by his mailbox discussing whether Marika could take care of herself.

"Well, I appreciate that, too," said Lorna. "But you have your own family."

She wondered if it was true that she didn't owe Marika anything. There was the fact of her existence. And those Thanksgiving visits, made so that Adam would know he had a grandmother. Also the hopeful sight of Adam on the ladder yesterday, bare-chested, sunburned, looking healthy and engaged, cleaning out the gutters—something Lorna herself could not have persuaded him to do. She thought of the men in her divorced men's group, most of whom she would never associate with in private life; but within the boundaries of her office, she did care about them and what happened to them. What were the boundaries in Marika's case?

They had rocked closer to the island. It was too small to be habitable, hardly more than a pile of rocks and a saddle of dirt. As if sharing this impression, the ducks sailed once more into view, quacking quietly as though conferring over where to go next.

"Not that I'm owed an explanation," Lorna said to Dennis, "but if it's all right with you, I'd like to know what happened after she left."

DENNIS HAD NOT CARED where they went, only that he was going with her. During the hottest part of July, they drove across the country, sleeping in his car and eating at truck stops. It took five days. For their first few weeks in California they stayed at a motel near Venice. Then Marika rented an apartment in Studio City for herself and found a room for him in a YMCA. She said she needed her privacy. She bought a small convertible.

"That must have been hard for you," said Lorna. "Alone in a city you didn't know."

Dennis had paused to examine the fuel tank gauge again. "I adjusted," he said, straightening up.

"Where did she get the money for a car and an apartment?"

"Your father, I think."

At some point during Lorna's childhood, land on the other side of the creek had been sold to a neighbor; perhaps it was then. As she waited for Dennis to go on, she pictured her father and grandmother sitting together on the veranda of the house where they both had been born, her grandmother talking about long-dead people as if they'd just stopped by for a glass of iced tea, her father nodding in his cane chair. In the spreading summer dusk stretched the stables and pastures, the creek, the spring-fed pool, and to the west the little graveyard circled by low fieldstone walls to keep out the cattle. A rusted gate squeaked thoughtfully when you opened it. Among the thin slate headstones, green with moss, lay a few flat stones half hidden under cedar duff and tight dry pine cones, marked only with a date. For babies, Wade used to say. All of it would have claimed their protection, that vanishing world, from a scandal that to those two shy, hindered people must have seemed a kind of contamination. Sending Marika money had been a desperate measure, a warding off of further disaster.

But there was never any question of Marika coming back. In the fall she began teaching French at a private high school in Santa Monica, while Dennis worked as a dishwasher and then as a line cook, and took classes at a community college. For a few months they continued to see each other once or twice a week, and then less and less often. That spring she helped Dennis enroll at UCLA, covering fees his GI Bill didn't cover, and over the next three years she continued to help with his tuition, and helped him again when he enrolled in law school. By then they had long stopped meeting altogether.

Though she would call him every now and again. Even after he moved back east with the woman he was going to marry, Marika got in touch every few years. She continued to teach at the private school, a job that suited her. Most of her students weren't interested in learning French, but they usually did what she asked of them, enough so that the school left her alone to teach as she liked.

There was always a man. Until twenty years ago, when during one of those infrequent calls she told Dennis that she'd retired, and was alone, and had been so for some time, and that she was tired of living in Southern California, which now seemed too sunny and too hot. She didn't have much money. The last man had gone off with most of it. That was when Dennis offered her the cottage; he owned several by then. Around the same time, his marriage ended. Marika was not the cause, but she had not improved matters, either, after his wife understood who was living in that cottage on the Neck.

LORNA LISTENED SILENTLY, rocking with the boat. When Dennis was finished, she said, "It was generous of you to offer her a place to live."

"She'd helped me. I helped her."

From the lake's far shore, deep in the blue-gray mountains, came the sound of a train whistle and then the long low faint rumble of cars passing.

"Did she ever talk about us?" Lorna asked when the train sounds had faded, replaced by the steady slap of water against the skiff's hull. "About me and Wade?"

"She never talked about anything. Not anything that wasn't going on right that minute." Dennis gazed at the stony little island off to their left. "In the beginning not talking was exactly what I wanted. But after a while even I couldn't take it."

Lorna nodded, waiting for him to say something more. When he continued to stare at the island, she said, "But she must have given some reason for leaving. Some explanation. Aside from wanting to be with you."

"I was never the reason. I just happened to be there."

With her sandal, Lorna nudged the wet life jacket at her feet, where the hound had gone to sleep. "She sent me a postcard not long after Adam was born. I have no idea if she knew about Adam, or how she knew where I lived. But she gave me her address and number, in case I wanted to be in touch. I've always wondered what made her do that, after so much time."

Dennis cleared his throat. "She didn't send it."

Lorna looked up. "What?"

"After she moved up here I decided to try to find you and your brother. That's how I heard he'd passed." Dennis's eyes were hidden by his cap. "I thought it might change things, if she saw you again."

A postcard view of the lake had slid one day through the letter slot. It lay on the floor along with bills, donation requests, supermarket circulars. When she picked it up, Lorna had stood for a long time reading and rereading that single line on the back, written above an address and a phone number. Printed, she remembered now. Careful, architectural print. Not the looping cursive letters she'd seen on Marika's yellow pad.

"I also thought," came Dennis's voice, "when I found out you were a social worker, that you might know how to talk to her."

He took out one of his fishing rods from where it was stored under the gunwale and examined it. Lorna looked away to watch a dark cloud of midges floating just above the water, remembering her fruitless conversation with Marika that morning. *Didn't think of it* described Marika's attitude toward any subject save her list of chores and the weather, and the birds that visited her bird feeder.

She had left Europe with a man who could not hear much of

anything she said and could therefore be counted on to ask her nothing. Later she'd run away to Los Angeles, where no one would notice her. She'd had a series of lovers, apparently choosing ones she knew were untrustworthy, bargaining that they'd be as incurious about her as she was about them. Even Dennis, who'd stuck with her, had done so on transactional terms, eventually because he felt sorry for her. Now here she was in that bare cottage, living as meagerly as possible, like a fugitive whom no one was pursuing, who had convicted and banished herself.

Consistent, except for one thing: Why had Marika agreed to those Thanksgiving visits? Despite not sending that postcard, despite showing no interest when Lorna had arrived with baby Adam, year after year she'd been willing to drive hundreds of miles for a single day, to sit at a table with strangers. An experience she could not have enjoyed, but felt bound to undertake. As further self-punishment? Or had she seen those visits as a last chance at connection?

Was it possible that for someone like Marika there was no difference?

"I don't know," Dennis said from the other end of the skiff, "if I should have told you."

Lorna reached down to pat the hound stretched out on the life jacket at her feet. "I'm glad you did." Without rancor, she said, "It makes sense that you thought I might be able to get Marika to talk, since therapists are supposed to be good at that." She stroked the hound's long muzzle. "It's true that we know how to help people come up with explanations for what's happened to them, and that talking usually makes them feel less alone with themselves."

She gave the hound a last stroke and sat back. "But in Marika's case, she seems determined to be alone with herself."

Dennis was doing something to the rod in his hands, untangling a section of the line where it had become snarled near the reel.

"I'm not her therapist, I'm her daughter. And as her daughter, I can't relate to her." Lorna watched him work at the knot. "I can't even figure out how to behave decently around her. As was unfortunately clear last night."

Dennis shook his head. As he freed the line, he said, "You're a sympathetic person." Perhaps meaning to encourage her.

"Not always," she said seriously. On the seat beside her lay a waterproof camouflage case. She took out a pair of military-style binoculars.

"I'll bet there's never been a person who wanted to talk that you didn't listen to."

But Lorna was no longer paying attention. She had lifted the binoculars and adjusted the focus wheel to scan the wooded shoreline with its doll-like houses and matchstick docks, and what she saw was Wade, lying on the floor in the front hall, dressed in his gray cadet uniform, crying about cannibals.

30

Something was wrong with the car. Adam had managed to get it back from the end of the Neck to his grandmother's driveway, only stalling a couple times on the way, and fortunately not when he was passing anyone walking on the road. But he was probably going too fast when he turned into the driveway, to keep from stalling again, and halfway down he'd hit something hard, a rock or a tree root. The car juddered once, twice, and then the engine cut out.

He released the clutch, pumped the gas pedal, shoved the gearshift into neutral, forward, and reverse. Nothing. After trying the ignition a few more times, he climbed out of the car and kicked one of the tires. An oily taint of skunk drifted toward him, strong enough that when he heard a raspy scuffle he started around to make sure a white stripe wasn't waddling toward him out of the woods. Only a chipmunk diving behind a tree stump. Overhead, a flock of starlings flew into one of the pine trees and began jeering.

Already a light scatter of brown needles lay across the hood. In the brief time it had been sitting in the driveway, the car had taken on the fixed look of something that had been there for decades. He opened the trunk, not so much expecting to find something useful there, but because, like kicking the tires, it seemed to be what you did when your car broke down. As he was lifting the hatch, he noticed something yellow at the back of the trunk.

It was a small spiral notepad. He opened it, startled by the round, childlike handwriting, then saw his mother's name penciled on the inside of the cover. Where had it come from?

Mostly it seemed like a notepad of lists. What a surprise. She'd been keeping lists since she was born. Names of girls. Boys' names. Names like *Champ*, *Scout*, *Taffy*, *Rex* that appeared to be dog names. A page of knock-knock jokes. Lists of ice cream flavors, apparently in order of preference. Then he reached the last page.

How to Be a Better Girl

---

close mouth while chewing
say please and thank you
keep hair out of face
change underwear every day
do not slurp soup
do not ask for seconds while others are eating firsts

The mention of underwear was so cringifying that it took him a moment to understand that this was a list of reminders. Judging by the reasonably steady handwriting, and the confident spelling, she must have been about nine or ten. Which meant this list was composed after her mother had left. A list of reminders, in other words, that a mother should have given a daughter about good manners (*close mouth while chewing*, *say please and thank you*), reminders that he himself had been given, plenty of times. But since her mother wasn't there, she'd had to supply these reminders for herself.

At the thought of a lonely child reviewing her own bad behavior, a choking sadness all but overwhelmed him. He leaned against the car, gazing up at the trees. Then he stiffened and glared at the notepad. What was it doing in the trunk, tossed in as casually as an extra pair of sneakers? He looked at the list again, and then closed the notepad and set it back where he'd found it. Or where it had been meant to be found.

Radioactive, this pathetic list. Should not be touched by human hands.

BY THE TIME he opened the screen door, it was past noon. The sun had shifted and inside the kitchen it seemed nearly dark. He washed his hands and dried them on a dish towel before opening the refrigerator and drinking directly from the milk carton.

In the living room, the tray still sat on the picnic table, the strawberries shriveled and the butter now melted in its saucer. His useless phone lay on the sofa where he'd left it. But there was a fresh box of doughnuts, and his grandmother was awake and clutching the armrests of her chair. Looking, if possible, even worse than she had earlier. Her thin hair stuck up in different directions, and the lenses of her pinkish glasses were more smudged.

"I think I need to call a tow truck," he said, halting by the picnic table.

She stared over the tops of her glasses. "Your mother was here."

"I know. I have her car. I ran over something and now the car won't start. I think I did something to it."

He lifted the lid on the box of doughnuts and selected a chocolate glazed. As he bit into it, he realized his grandmother was still staring at him.

"So what happened?" he asked through a mouthful of doughnut. "Did she say she was sorry for last night?"

His grandmother pulled a tissue from her sleeve. "Yelled at me."

"She *yelled* at you?" Adam was stupefied.

"Said you're leaving as soon as she finds that dog. Said she doesn't care what happens to me." She paused to wipe her nose. "Said she'd make *arrangements* for me."

"She said what?"

"Wants to stick me in an old folks home. Leave me there to die. And it won't take long," his grandmother said with a choleric sniff, "I'll tell you *that*."

"I don't believe it."

She turned partway in her chair, her mouth an angry horseshoe, long chin hairs catching the light from the window beside her.

"I mean," he said, "I don't believe my mom would say something like that."

But he did believe it. He pictured her sitting in the lake, laughing, her bra showing through her wet blouse. Preparing a sauce full of garlic to feed to an octogenarian who was deathly allergic. Bullying that same octogenarian until she practically fell into her plate. She had lost her mind. She was having some kind of nervous breakdown, triggered by having to deal with the woman who'd deserted her. Who had left her to scold herself for chewing with her mouth open and slurping soup. Away from her clients and her office, her garden, her small talk with neighbors, her book club, her shrink friends having wine on the patio, all her usual ways of controlling everything, his mother was having some sort of psychotic episode. From an overdose of self-pity, she had become someone who could—unintentionally, for sure—try to kill a sick old woman because of unresolved childhood issues. (Hadn't he heard stories like this all his life?) Or at least park her in a place that would kill her.

She would, of course, be incapable of recognizing any of this about herself. Even think it.

Half ashamed of these thoughts, but also half convinced by them, he dropped the doughnut back in the box and shoved the box off the table. "She's crazy," he said.

He was sorry for his mother. He was sad she was so screwed up. But she couldn't be trusted. Not right now.

His grandmother gave a harsh hiccup. "Just get a gun and shoot me." She was eyeing the box of doughnuts on the floor.

"Don't say that."

"Get a gun and shoot me," she repeated. "I'm not leaving this house."

Adam shook his head. "No one's going to make you leave."

"*She* will." Horrifyingly, her glasses fogged up as she started to weep.

"No, she won't," he said, keeping the picnic table between them.

His grandmother hiccuped again. "What can *you* do about it?"

"I'm going to stay here."

As soon as the words were out of his mouth, he realized that this was what he'd intended to say all along. He'd probably known since the first evening, when he and his grandmother sat up drinking cognac and speaking French; he'd known more definitely since last night, when he helped her off the bathroom floor, bathed and dressed her, and brought her tea, and then told her what had happened to him, and she, without meaning to, but even so, had made him feel better.

It was the first clear emotion he'd had in a long time: that he wanted to stay here by the lake, with his grandmother.

"I'll stay," he repeated, his throat swelling as if he had gulped too much water at once.

His grandmother blew her nose. A sly smile seemed to cross her face, which he hoped he'd imagined. It didn't matter. It was done. He'd said what he said and there was no going back. But before he could say anything else, there was a thump on the deck, just outside the screen door, followed by barking.

Freddy had returned.

It must be a sign, Adam thought, blood leaping in confusion. A reward for the pledge he'd just made.

Crying, "Freddy!" he threw the door open.

In a great golden heave, Freddy bounded into the room. Fur stiff with mud and pine resin, radiating skunk, trailing twigs and a long pair of bulrushes from his tail, he hurtled past Adam like an angelic beast from a medieval tapestry and launched himself straight as a thunderbolt at the old woman in her chair.

31

Lorna watched until Dennis and his skiff had disappeared around a point before climbing up the boulders to the flat part of the island. It was the island they'd been floating near as they talked, and she'd asked to be set down there to have a little time to herself. Dennis had promised to come back for her in an hour.

She settled onto a mat of moss under one of the fir trees and leaned against the trunk. It would be wise to calm her mind before facing Marika once more, to think logically about what to do next. Though she'd told Marika that she intended to drive home as soon as she found Freddy, Lorna had already decided to stick to her original plan to leave tomorrow. She had overreacted, again. No need to rush home. For instance, it would be a good idea to visit the assisted-living facility in town while she was here. She should buy groceries to stock Marika's kitchen while she looked for a home health aide, which might take a few days to arrange. And Adam might object to leaving early, might see it as running away from her obligations. Though he'd also probably be relieved to go back to his laptop and his phone, his shut bedroom door.

To either side were miles of lake, extending north all the way into Canada. The water had been flat while she and Dennis sat in his skiff, but now a slight breeze ruffled the surface, freshening the air around her face. As Lorna stared out at the lake, its small endless waves began to resemble a vast, radiant network, reflecting uncountable flashes, like millions of signal flares.

She fell asleep, shaded by the fir tree. When she awoke some time later, feeling heavy and sticky, the sun had vanished behind a thickening haze and the air had cooled. As she stood up, brushing off her skirt and the bits of twigs and needles clinging to the backs of her thighs, the lake seemed emptier than before.

The island was perhaps half an acre in total, most of it rocky. At the far end were clumps of blueberry bushes, the blueberries still green, small and hard. A tangle of wild grape swarmed over a crosshatch of dead branches. Blackened rocks were arranged in a crude firepit. Other signs of previous inhabitants: a rusted cola can, a few soggy cigarette butts, a fishhook. Her wristwatch had stopped after getting wet. Surely more than an hour had passed?

The sun was headed west and the breeze had subsided once more, though the temperature seemed to have dropped at least ten degrees. Rubbing her hands up and down her bare arms, Lorna picked her way to the edge of the island facing the widest part of the lake, where pale scarves of mist had started to gather over the water. That was the direction Dennis would be coming from.

Less than a hundred yards away, a couple of men were fishing in a red-hulled boat. Hesitantly, she waved to them. One of the men waved back. A few moments later, the other man started the engine. She listened to its stertorous putt-putt across the water as the boat slowly motored away.

When she could no longer see the pines on the opposite shore and even the island was engulfed in chilly gray mist, she climbed back to the highest point and sat down again on the moss under the fir tree. It seemed important to return to where she had been before, and the tree gave her something to lean against.

The day had been completely clear when Dennis roared off in his skiff, one hand raised. The sun had been warm, the water bright. Now everything was gray.

Something must have happened to Dennis. He said he was going to check on Marika and see if Adam had found Freddy, and then he would be back. He must be caught out in the fog in his boat. Once, she thought she heard an outboard motor and shouted Dennis's name, but when she stopped shouting to listen for an answer, there was only the water lapping against the rocks.

32

"Leave me alone," Marika was shouting.

It had happened at last, what she had known was coming. First a heavy shock, and then a hot tumbling weight. Followed by that sluggish blundering within her chest, like a fat sleeper turning over in bed. She lay back in her chair, gasping.

Men arrived to take her away. Arrest her? Show us your papers. She felt hands on her shoulders.

"Where does it hurt," a voice said.

Two doors down, she told them.

Hands were pulling on her, lifting her under her armpits.

"We need to get you to the hospital."

Just go ahead and shoot me, she cried.

"Can you stand up?"

And then it came again, that slow heavy blundering.

As she fell back into her chair, talons pierced her chest. A claw reached in to snatch up her heart and carry it away, twisting and writhing, over the lake.

33

Wade was running across the pastures and Lorna was chasing him. Grasshoppers flicked against her bare calves as he got farther and farther ahead, a butterfly of sweat between his shoulder blades, passing the red tractor and two barn cats dozing in a lozenge of sunlight, before disappearing into the dark mouth of the stables.

He's asking for you, his friend Paul told her when he telephoned to say Wade was in the hospital. Can you come out to see him?

Wade had never before asked her to visit him in San Francisco, though he'd been living there for years. Lorna hadn't seen him since he was seventeen, when he ran away from school to hitchhike across the country. He sent postcards once or twice a year, the touristy kind. They spoke on the phone at Christmas and on their birthdays, brief conversations, friendly enough. He hadn't returned for their grandmother's and father's funerals.

Yes, she told Paul. I can come.

She'd just gotten her job at the VA; she had a large caseload and no vacation time, and no extra money. There was also the fear of Wade's disease. Not much was known about it back then except that it was deadly and contagious, and she was afraid, as so many people had been afraid, that you could catch it just by shaking someone's hand or sitting next to him on the bus. But she asked Faye, her supervisor, for the rest of the week off, and on a frigid March morning two days after Paul called her she flew to San Francisco.

It had been very bright in Wade's corner room when she arrived at the hospital, late afternoon light blazing through the three windows. Then there was Wade, propped up by pillows in bed, one arm raised like a conductor holding a baton. As he caught sight of her in the doorway, he cried out, LaLa!

Come in! he cried, a tube dangling from one wrist.

Several people were standing around the bed, scrubbed youthful-looking men, clean-shaven or with neatly trimmed beards, dressed in pressed T-shirts and khaki pants or pressed blue jeans with penny loafers. They greeted her cordially and made her sit in the only chair in the room, introducing themselves and asking about her flight. But as soon as she was settled, they turned their attention back to Wade who, after his first enthusiasm at her arrival, had been watching this process impatiently. He raised his arm again. She had interrupted him mid-performance; he'd been describing last night's dinner. A routine she knew well: the magnificent complaint.

The chicken Kiev had required a panzer division to attack, the green beans were puce; the rice pudding defied analysis without going into highly scientific detail, most of it classified and involving whale sputum and gorilla semen. . . .

The air in his room was very warm and carried the sting of rubbing alcohol, and beneath it a spoiled sweetish smell, like overripe apricots. Whenever Wade paused for breath, one of the men by the bed offered him a cup of ice chips, but Wade would wave him away and keep talking. On his face were the purplish marks she'd known to expect. His chin was covered with dark stubble, his thin neck too exposed, rising nakedly from the collar of his hospital gown.

Soon another friend arrived, Paul, who had telephoned her. Paul was short and stocky, with an auburn handlebar mustache that was waxed at the tips, and he wore a leather vest. Almost immediately, he began asking brisk questions about which doctor had been in and whether Wade had been given a sponge bath and if the nurse had brought him a specific medication. Wade fell silent and put a trembly hand to his eyes.

Paul went back out into the corridor and returned a few minutes later with a nurse wearing a mask, a plastic face shield, and gloves. The nurse checked Wade's pulse and gave him a pill to swallow, along with a paper cup of water and a straw. Wade had just started an experimental treatment, Paul explained to Lorna after the nurse left and Wade was sipping his water through the straw. The treatment seemed to be working; he'd had more energy in the last couple days.

I'm General Electric, said Wade. He put the cup down on the metal table by his bed. Give me a salute. Everyone saluted. Then he was off again, this time describing his "fellow inmates" who shuffled past his door in their loose hospital johnnies, which were designed to be as ugly as possible so that you wouldn't mind if you died. Why not just issue everyone a black robe? There was something so elegant about Grim Reaper outfits, they had a nice drape, and the hood did wonders for anyone with a bad complexion. Everyone laughed.

It was becoming clear to Lorna that Wade's visitors were used to his performances and depended on him to keep them up, and also that Wade understood this. They all wore the same expression as they listened to him, like tired people sitting by a fan.

Your brother is a remarkable guy, said Paul in a low voice. He had come to stand beside Lorna's chair, gazing down at her over his mustache. Wade gave her a sharp look from across the room, as if only just then noticing she was there.

Sister here, he said a moment later, has just reminded me of the strangest old things. Did you know we grew up on a *plantation*?

He began describing the farmhouse, referring to it as "a decayed antebellum manse." In the den had been a row of false-backed books, concealing a hidey-hole where their father—"the Old Gent"—stashed jars of moonshine, but it had once contained the petrified arm of a Yankee soldier, presented to their grandmother by an admirer on the eve of her first cotillion. Above the fireplace hung a cavalry saber used to behead a Confederate traitor. Slaves were buried in the family graveyard. The cellar was crawling with rattlesnakes. *Sister*, he kept calling Lorna, in a drawling voice, as if they were characters in a Tennessee Williams play. *Sister* knows what I'm talking about. He gave lengthy descriptions of the stable hands, as dumb as roosters, but just as cocky, haha! We lived on a *stud* farm, Wade kept insisting.

The really strange thing was that much of what he said was true, or true in a sense (there had once been a rattlesnake in the cellar, stud fees helped support the stable), or could have been true (though not the petrified arm), but presented in such a way as to be cartoonish or ghoulish or outlandish, and nothing like anything Lorna remembered.

Occasionally the phone by his bed rang, answered by Paul in a hushed voice while Wade kept talking. The window beside her chair overlooked a small brick courtyard several stories below, which held a pair of squat palm trees and a stone fountain. Lorna watched the fountain as, one by one, Wade's friends left and were replaced by other friends, except for Paul, who stayed perched on the end of Wade's bed whenever he wasn't answering the phone. Around five thirty, almost mid-sentence, Wade fell asleep for a few minutes while everyone in the room kept quiet.

But just as Paul put a finger to his lips, Wade opened his eyes and said, Well, that's all for this evening, ladies.

The two friends who were there leaned over his bed, clasped his shoulder, and wished Wade a good night, sounding regretful about leaving, yet looking relieved; his stories had been draining in their determined outrageousness, and the room was close and depressing, as hospital rooms invariably are, even ones with three windows. Paul ushered them into the corridor, but stayed behind himself. Lorna took the elevator with the two men who'd left with her. In the lobby she declined their kindly, half-hearted dinner invitations and instead walked across the street to a Mexican restaurant, where she went into the little blue-tiled bathroom near the entrance and carefully washed her hands.

After dinner she walked to her bed-and-breakfast on Divisadero Street and sat in a parlor with grayish lace curtains and quaking glass lampshades while the proprietor, a handsome old man with long dyed-blond hair, explained what could not be flushed down the toilet and when breakfast was served, and then she went up to her room on the third floor and sat looking out at the glittering hills of the city.

Paul had asked her not to visit Wade in the mornings, but to wait until midafternoon. Wade was sleeping until then, Paul explained, or groggy from the medications he was taking. At first Lorna thought that Paul wanted time with Wade to himself. But then she understood that Wade was conserving his energy for that rotating group of friends who began appearing every day around three or four.

She spent each morning walking. It was foggy until nine or ten, and then the fog would lift and from the tops of the hills she would get a view of the city, laid out like a map, and the agate-colored bay. She recognized sights from postcards Wade had sent over the years. Golden Gate Bridge. Fisherman's Wharf. Out in the bay was Alcatraz, the military prison, swimming distance from shore, yet reportedly surrounded by sharks. As she walked she kept trying to glimpse Wade at seventeen, arriving alone in San Francisco after hitchhiking across the country—surely not in his cadet uniform, though that's how she pictured him, in gold braid and epaulets, climbing these same streets to get his bearings, saluting Alcatraz in honor of his own escape, still with that fold of baby fat under his chin, but also with something shrewd, even a little calculating about his youth. Not unaware of the sharks.

At the steepest crests, the houses on street corners seemed to hang in the air, while the wind blew brightly and sunlight skated along the cable car tracks. One thing she noticed everywhere was the smell of tar and of something burning, like the smell of burnt toast.

Brimstone, said Wade cheerfully, when on her second day in San Francisco she asked about that smell. The Hills Brothers coffee factory, corrected Paul, with a pitying smile, as if to say, *How much you don't know. Sister.*

ON HER FOURTH EVENING in San Francisco, her last, Lorna did not leave with Wade's friends, but stayed in the chair by the window. She had a red-eye back to Boston and had brought her suitcase with her so that she could go straight from the hospital to the airport. After a few minutes even Paul left, reluctantly, to pick up some dry cleaning, he said, and to feed his neighbor's dog, perhaps realizing he should give them some time alone. Lorna hadn't liked Paul, with his officious mustache and his leather vest that looked like it should have a sheriff's badge pinned to it. Yet she was grateful to him for taking care of Wade and as he left that evening she found herself wishing he would stay.

Wade seemed unusually subdued and didn't look like he was listening when she tried to tell him about her job at the VA. Someone had shaved him, probably Paul, and except for those purple marks his face was white and gaunt, and too bare. Nurses, shielded like beekeepers, came and went, adjusting monitors, changing the bag on his IV pole, looking away from him as much as possible. The overripe apricot smell, which had come and gone over the past few days, was stronger now.

At some point, a nurse came in with his dinner tray. When she began to draw the window shades, he told her to leave them open, but asked her to turn off the overhead light. After the nurse left, Lorna said she should go soon, to get some dinner before she caught her plane.

Eat mine, he said. She ate the package of crackers that had come with his soup. The window by his bed filled with twilight. In the cool San Francisco evening outside, the streets must have been full of people heading home or out to restaurants for dinner or a glass of wine. Spotlights came on in the courtyard around the palm trees and the fountain, enough light to filter in from the window and illuminate Wade's face and hospital gown.

Still he didn't speak. Lorna was afraid he had noticed how she'd stayed in that chair for the past three days, looking out the window, and hadn't touched his shoulder or held his hand, as his friends did when they said goodbye.

She had to be at the airport by eight and it was nearly six thirty. This was their last chance to talk about why Wade had wanted to see her, but she couldn't figure out how to begin. So she asked about Paul, if it was "serious" between them, and Wade shrugged and said something about feeding the dog. Then he went silent again. In that dusky light, the blotches on his face weren't so visible, and he seemed very young, lying against his pillows, like a boy tucked into bed. He reached for a paper cup on the metal table beside him. When he put the paper cup back down, it made an empty sound.

Know what I did? he said.

No, Lorna said, grateful that he was speaking at last. What did you do?

Sat on the landing and listened.

She pressed the empty oyster cracker package between her fingers so that the plastic crackled. Listened to what?

You remember. His voice had gone reedy. I sat outside your room and listened to those stories she told you.

I'm sorry, she said, heart beating faster, but I don't remember any of that.

He gazed at a point over her head with an abstracted expression, gave a hard cough, and touched his mouth with the edge of the blanket. Then he asked what she did remember. Tell me, he said. Tell me about us, when we were kids.

She thought for a few moments, and then said she remembered how sometimes he would hide under her bed at night and make ghost noises after the lights were out to scare her. And how they used to slip their father's medals out of the glass case on the mantel and pin them on their shirts. *Sir, you are the only one who can lead this mission. All right, Corporal, follow me.*

Then they'd run down to the stables, sleepy in the late afternoon, thick with the musty sweet smell of hay, horses moving their hooves deliberately in their stalls, and how they would stop at the wheelbarrow to slide oats through their fingers, chaff rising like gold dust, pretending to be Midas with his treasure while they sneezed.

Something jangled in the corridor. In ten minutes Lorna needed to be downstairs in the hospital lobby. Her plane was leaving in a little over an hour. She was worrying about how long it might take to find a cab, and whether she could ask someone at the front desk to call one for her.

What else, Wade asked, fingers fluttering on top of his chest.

Grasping the handle of her suitcase, she stood up and came to stand at the end of his bed. Remember picking watercress by the springhouse door? Remember sitting under the boxwoods in the snow? How Granny cut their hair with poultry scissors and Lorna told everyone at school that she used a butcher's knife. How they'd called the furnace Old Scary, sprawling with pipe tentacles down in the cellar.

Wade had turned his face toward the window beside him, picking at the blanket with his thin fingers. He whispered something. When Lorna leaned closer, he said it again:

Remember that time when I ran down to the cellar, and she came after me with a hairbrush?

No, Lorna said, drawing back.

He turned from the window to look at her. I took something from her room. Remember? Thought she was going to break my head open.

Lorna squeezed the handle of her suitcase. I don't remember.

Busted my lip. Gave me a black eye.

I don't remember that.

She hated me, he said.

Wade, Lorna said. Don't.

It had been the humane thing to do, she told herself later, cutting him off like that. What she'd meant was, Focus on your health. Focus on your friends. Stop chasing after her.

But she knew. She understood that it had shaped Wade's whole life, his belief that he'd driven his mother away with his ardent pursuit of her, sneaking and prying, hunting in her dresser drawers. A pursuit that, for whatever reason, Marika had viewed as an attack, requiring her to attack him back. Lorna could have said: She was probably projecting when she beat you with that hairbrush. She could have diagnosed Marika with behaviors she wrote on charts at the VA. Post-traumatic stress disorder. Narcissistic personality disorder. Schizoaffective disorder. But would that have made any difference? Wouldn't it just have made Marika the center of attention, once again, when Wade deserved all that attention himself?

Paul was right, Wade was remarkable. Battling on gallantly, despite his horrifying disease, with his marvelous complaints, his outlandish stories, his jaunty embrace of brimstone. Every afternoon in his hospital room taking the lead, showing how it could be done: It's an outrage what is happening, so be outrageous. I'll lead this mission. Follow me, corporals. Because he knew, and his friends standing around his bed knew, that what was happening to him could soon happen to them.

This is how to lose your treasure, by sneezing at it.

On that cool March evening in San Francisco, their last time together, in his darkened hospital room overlooking a fountain, what she should have done was let Wade talk. But she could not bear to listen. And so out of pity and cowardice and delicacy and dread, she'd changed the subject.

She said she was glad the new treatment he was on seemed to be working, that he sounded a lot better, that his voice was a lot stronger.

She said that Paul seemed like a nice guy, and how lucky Wade was to have such good friends who cared about him. She said she would come back to visit soon. Wade had turned his face back to the window. When it was clear he was not going to look at her again, Lorna said goodbye stepped into the bright corridor, squinting at the lights, suitcase bumping against her legs.

There was a memorial service in San Francisco, held at the library where Wade had worked, and almost three hundred people came, from all over the city. He'd become something of a local celebrity because of the programs he'd created for children, especially for ones in foster homes and shelters. Paul wrote to her later and sent her the obituary that ran in the paper. She'd saved the obituary for years, and then lost track of it. But one phrase came back to her now: "An irreplaceable presence."

The mist had thickened, become grayer, more clammy and obliterating. Lorna pressed her back against the tree trunk to feel its rough bark through the thin fabric of her blouse, and wrapped her arms around herself.

34

At first Marika thought she was in her chair, looking out at the lake. It took her some moments to realize she was staring at a blue curtain. Around her were white walls, above her bright lights. She was in a room full of machines. Or that was what she supposed they were, those blocky metallic shapes, which was all she could discern without her eyeglasses. Sounds reached her: dull clatters, things being wheeled, low jumbled conversations; the impression of people moving back and forth on the other side of the blue curtain.

She was lying propped up in a bed. An enormous hand was squeezing her arm, hard, and then releasing. "Let go," she muttered, pushing at the hand.

"It's a blood pressure cuff," said a quiet voice. Dennis.

"To track your vital signs," said the boy.

It was a relief to hear familiar voices in a place she could not recognize. But she seemed to be missing something. Something important. After thinking for a long time she decided it must be her purse.

From behind her a man's voice asked: "Can you tell me what day it is?"

"No," she told the blue curtain.

"Who is the president of the United States?"

She shook her head.

"You can't tell me?"

"I don't have time for that foolishness," she said. "I want a cup of coffee."

"Well, you can't have a cup of coffee just yet," said the voice. A head appeared against the blue curtain: bald, jowly, clean-shaven, a stethoscope around his neck. "We can't let you have anything until we've run some tests. It looks like you may have had a mild myocardial infarction."

"A heart attack," explained the boy, somewhere to her left.

"Thank you, Doctor," she said to the stethoscope.

"I'm the nurse. The doctor will be in soon." The blue curtain opened and closed again.

"You gave us a scare." Dennis's face appeared now where the male nurse's had been. Under the bill of his cap, the whites of his eyes were yellowish, webbed with broken red capillaries. The boy's face also came into view. His eyes were an excited clear light brown.

"Do you understand what happened to you?" he asked.

"I swallowed a horseradish."

"What?" said the boy.

"I want a cup of coffee," she said fearfully.

"Let's get you another blanket," he said. "You're shivering. It's cold in here."

35

They had been in the examining room for half an hour when the curtain was once again rung back. "Having *chest pains*, are we?" demanded a heavily accented voice. A prow-like bosom in a lab coat came into view, followed by a helmet of shining bronze hair, a pair of black horn-rimmed glasses, and a mouth coated in red lipstick. Dr. E. Krzhizhanovsky, according to the name tag pinned to her bosom. Flashing even white teeth, she introduced herself as the ER attending physician and then turned to Adam's grandmother.

"So, who said you could have *heart* attack, young lady?"

"Eh?" croaked his grandmother.

"I see here, Marika," Dr. Krzhizhanovsky consulted the clipboard she was carrying, "that you are eighty-eight years old. Until you are ninety, you must have *permission* to have heart attack. In Russia, no one gets permission until ninety-five. Things are too easy in this country." She pointed to Adam. "Who is this gentleman? Boyfriend?"

"I'm her grandson," said Adam, blinking.

"So they all say." Dr. Krzhizhanovsky plugged her stethoscope into her ears. "You, sir," she pointed the stethoscope bell at Dennis. "You are father?"

"Friend," muttered Dennis.

"*Two* boyfriends? No wonder you have chest pains. Can you describe how you are feeling?"

"No," said his grandmother.

"A common ailment." Dr. Krzhizhanovsky patted her arm. "Not to worry." She motioned to Adam. "Come help girlfriend to sit up."

Adam was too astonished to be affronted. He had never encountered a physician who treated patients and their relatives so clownishly, as if they were part of some Marx Brothers routine. His own pediatrician, a slender, thin-lipped older man who played the cello, had always behaved with elaborate courtesy, even when Adam was very small, asking him what he was reading these days, and whether he minded stepping on the scales to be weighed. Even Dr. Knapp, his dermatologist, a cheerful South Afrikaner whose office was decorated with ceramic turtles, became somber as soon as the examination began.

As he raised his grandmother from her pillows, he expected her to object, especially when Dr. Krzhizhanovsky loosened the cloth ties on her hospital gown, but she submitted quietly. Her eyeglasses had been left behind in the rush to get her into the ambulance and her watery blue eyes looked unfocused and defenseless. She did not respond to Dr. Krzhizhanovsky's repeated questions about how she was feeling, so Adam described her illness the night before and then her collapse after Freddy jumped on her in her chair.

"I figured it was her heart," he said. "Because of her being dehydrated."

Dr. Krzhizhanovsky listened without expression and then turned again to his grandmother. "Okay, Marika. So now I subject you to brief internal interrogation." She lifted a corner of the hospital gown and placed the stethoscope bell against his grandmother's chest. "We will find out what you are hiding in there."

"I want to go home," his grandmother whimpered. "I want a cup of coffee."

"So do all our prisoners." Dr. Krzhizhanovsky moved the stethoscope to a different spot. "Please take deep breath and hold for me."

After listening to his grandmother's chest for several minutes, and then to her back, Dr. Krzhizhanovsky looped the stethoscope once more around her neck. "You play hopscotch, Marika?"

"No," said his grandmother.

"Well, heart is doing little skips."

"Skips?" asked Dennis from the other side of the bed.

"Probably not serious," said Dr. Krzhizhanovsky. "I will order tests."

His grandmother was going to have an EKG, an angiogram, a chest X-ray, and a test where her blood would be checked for enzymes. Adam listened to this information carefully. He pictured himself in a white coat, delivering the same news to patients, but more soberly, answering their anxious questions with brisk accuracy while checking his pager for texts summoning him to other parts of the hospital.

A few minutes later he followed Dr. Krzhizhanovsky out of the examining room and into the hallway.

"So what's the prognosis?" he asked when Dr. Krzhizhanovsky had rung the curtain closed. Men and women in blue scrubs walked past them. An empty gurney sat under a glowing red EXIT sign, and from another examining room came a burst of loud laughter.

Dr. Krzhizhanovsky frowned. Her air of relentless amusement had left her and now she looked burdened and harried, even her bronze hair seemed dulled.

"We will see," she said, "what tests show."

His grandmother was being moved from the ER to the hospital's third floor, where she would spend the night under observation. Adam asked if she could have her own room, explaining that she lived alone.

"She is not people person," he said, unintentionally leaving out the article, and then worrying that Dr. Krzhizhanovsky would think he was making fun of her Russian accent, just as two nights earlier he'd worried his grandmother would be insulted when he'd echoed the way she said "ting."

But Dr. Krzhizhanovsky seemed not to notice. "No one is people person anymore." Moodily, she tapped her clipboard with a red-painted fingernail. "Is epidemic. As for single room, no promises."

"Thanks," Adam said, wishing his mother was there to take over this conversation. She *was* a people person, and her air of pleasant apology often persuaded people to do things for her they might not do otherwise.

For the past hour, he had been wondering why she was not at the hospital. After his grandmother had gone white and fallen back in her chair, he'd forgotten about his mother. But as they'd followed the ambulance to the hospital in Dennis's truck, Dennis explained that when they were in his boat she had asked for some time to herself. The idea of his mother relaxing by the lake was so inexcusable, given the circumstances, and so completely validated all the punishing things he'd been thinking about her, that he hadn't asked Dennis anything else. Her phone was in her shoulder bag, where he'd left it in the car in the driveway. When she got back to the house, she'd find Freddy there, and the note Adam had scrawled on a scrap of paper and left on the picnic table: *Gone to North Country Hospital.*

Yet now where was she?

Dr. Krzhizhanovsky had pulled her phone from the pocket of her lab coat and was frowning at the screen. "So," she said, looking up and catching him staring at her breasts, "I see by interested expression you are drawn to medicine?"

"Well, maybe," Adam said, blushing. "My dad's always telling me I should go to med school. He's kind of a big deal in Seattle," he added. "At least in epidemiology."

"Ah. Big-deal science guy."

"Yeah. I guess. So how about you," he said respectfully, "did you, like, go to med school here or in Russia?"

"UMass." She smiled. "I'm from Framingham."

"Sorry?" he faltered.

"The Dr. Strangelove accent?" Now she sounded like a New Jersey gangster. "Mostly a distraction for patients, but it works for me, too." She sighed. "Pain and suffering get to you after a while, buddy. We docs have to protect ourselves." Shaking her head, she leaned toward him and lowered her voice. "But you know what's the real killer?"

"Fear?" he breathed.

She touched her forehead. "Big deals."

Adam stared at her.

"I need to call my mom," he said. "Could I maybe use your phone?"

36

The house was silent when Lorna opened the door from the deck. Beside Marika's armchair, the plastic bag of knitting was tipped on its side, blue yarn escaping from the mouth of the bag, one knitting needle flung toward the window. The tray from that morning was still on the picnic table. Coffee had spilled on what looked like an old grocery list tucked under a saucer, turning the letters into a blue smear. On the floor under the picnic table was the doughnut box, now empty.

In the kitchen she searched for a note from Adam. The clock on the stove read six thirty. Could Dennis still be out in his boat looking for her? Had he reached the island only to find her gone? Were they all out looking for her, even Marika?

An old-fashioned paddle wheel boat had come to her rescue, chartered to cruise up and down the lake. None of the girls on board for a bachelorette party asked Lorna what she had been doing on a tiny island, alone, in a thin blouse, paisley skirt, and sandals. No one seemed interested. A Solo cup of sangria was offered to her, which she declined, though she gratefully ate a bag of potato chips and drank a bottle of water.

The boat's operator did ask where she would like to be dropped off. She didn't know. But by tracing the shoreline from the public beach at the end of the Neck, and counting flagpoles, Lorna was able to guess the location of Marika's dock.

In the kitchen she ate a piece of bread and two slices of cheese. Perhaps Adam hadn't thought anything was wrong when hour after hour passed and she failed to show up. Or nothing that required calling the police. Last night she had walked out of the house with no explanation, gotten into her car and driven away, leaving him to fend for himself with a scorched table, a sink full of dishes, and two old people staring at him.

Maybe he thought she'd done it again. Gone off and left him.

When she opened the kitchen's screen door and stepped outside, there was the shadowy hump of her car parked near the end of the driveway. Inside the car her shoulder bag was still sprawled on the front passenger seat, the keys still in the ignition. Her phone was there, too, though the battery was dead, she discovered, when she tried to turn it on.

She carried the phone into the house to plug the charger into the outlet by the kitchen sink. Adam and Marika must have left in someone else's car. Dennis had returned in his boat, perhaps after hours of searching for her, and driven them somewhere.

Lorna walked through each room, snapping on all the lights. At the threshold of Marika's bedroom, she paused. It was a small, narrow room with knotty pine walls, like the rest of the house, a worn braided rug on the floor. Marika's black purse was on a chair. The single bed was neatly made, a worn white chenille spread drawn up over a hard-looking pillow. The shades were pulled and the room had a stale, biscuity smell that seemed to come from a wicker laundry hamper in one corner.

She was shivering in her damp clothes, so she opened the closet and took a brown cardigan from a hanger. As she pulled the cardigan around her shoulders, something under the bed shifted and groaned, and a moment later Freddy's big head appeared beneath the hanging fringe of the chenille bedspread.

Lorna knelt down to embrace him as he crawled out onto the

rug. “Hello there, boy.” Freddy pressed his nose into her neck. “So *glad* to see you.”

She was relieved that he looked unharmed after all those hours on his own, and for a few minutes gave herself over to patting him and pulling twigs and mud out of his fur, and untangling long reeds caught in his tail. He seemed all right, though he smelled slightly of skunk, and his muzzle was sticky and gritty, with what on closer inspection turned out to be sugar.

In the kitchen she filled a bowl with water and set it on the floor. He began lapping thirstily. Only then did it occur to her that the empty house, and the rush with which it had been abandoned—Marika’s purse left behind, the doughnut box knocked onto the floor, not even water set out for Freddy—must have had nothing to do with her absence.

Her phone now had enough battery charge to reveal that she had a voicemail from an unfamiliar number, left several hours earlier.

“Grootie’s in the hospital,” came Adam’s voice. “Where are you?”

37

Adam sat in the green vinyl-covered recliner chair by his grandmother's hospital bed, waiting for Dennis to come back from the vending machines by the lobby. He wished he had a book or a magazine, even the newspaper. Already his grandmother had been through two hours of tests, X-rays, examinations. More were scheduled for the morning. Coronary heart disease was the preliminary diagnosis, also arrhythmia. A scan had revealed something about a cardiac shadow, which the X-ray technician did not explain. The cardiologist would be in tomorrow.

A short, very pale, portly nurse arrived carrying what she said was a nitroglycerin tablet in a tiny paper cup.

"I want a cup of coffee," said his grandmother, keeping her eyes closed.

"How long will she be here?" Adam asked the nurse, noting that her skin was not just pale but the blanched color of white asparagus. "She's been kind of babbling."

"As long as she needs to be here," said the nurse. Even her cropped hair was blanched-looking, as if she had just emerged from years of sunlessness. Behind her steel-rimmed spectacles her eyes were pinkish and sensitive looking, and seemed irritated by the fluorescent lights overhead. But she gave his grandmother a worn smile. "Here, hon," she said. "Take this. The doctor wrote you up."

His grandmother shook her head.

The nurse set the cup on a table by the bed. "You don't want to feel better?"

"No," said his grandmother listlessly.

"Well, sorry to hear it, but we're short two nurses tonight. Sit up and stick that under your tongue."

Monitoring this exchange, Adam saw that empathy was not always called for when it came to the sick. Also of interest was the nitroglycerin tablet. He'd always thought of nitroglycerin as something used to make dynamite. Who knew that what could kill you could also save you.

"What's a cardiac shadow?" he asked the nurse. "Also I think she's hallucinating."

"*Ik wil naar huis*," whimpered his grandmother, lying back against the pillows.

"What, hon?" said the nurse. "What say?"

"I want to go home," said his grandmother.

38

Lorna tried the number Adam had called from, but got the voicemail of someone called Ellen with a long last name full of consonants. According to Lorna's phone, the closest hospital was North Country. At first her car wouldn't start, but after pumping the gas and shifting to neutral, she got the ignition to turn over and in a few minutes, guided by Google Maps, she was driving away from the Neck.

The hospital's front desk attendant confirmed that Marika had been admitted earlier in the day, gave Lorna the room number, and directed her to elevators leading to the third floor.

Now, standing in the doorway of the hospital room, a hand on the door, Lorna paused to catch her breath and to take in the tableau inside: Marika in bed, eyes shut, a white blanket pulled to her chin; Adam in a chair, Dennis standing at the window, rubbing his beard. No one spoke and yet there was an air of interruption, as if an intimate conversation had been halted mid-sentence when she appeared.

"What happened," Lorna whispered as Adam and Dennis turned their faces toward the door. "Is she all right?"

"She's had a myocardial infarction," Adam said, not whispering.

"I went over to the cottage after I left you," Dennis explained, "and found her."

"Having a heart attack. Caused by dehydration," interjected Adam meaningfully. "And also Freddy jumped on her."

They all looked at Marika, who had acquired the sarcophagal stillness that comes to people pretending to be asleep. Lorna asked what else the doctors had said and Adam listed a series of tests and their results and the tests to be run tomorrow.

"It looks like a *mild* heart attack." He sounded slightly disappointed. "The doctors think she's okay. But she'll need to stay here for a couple days, until she stabilizes."

He yawned and then shut his mouth. "Anyway, where have you *been*?"

Dennis gave Lorna an apologetic look. "Sorry I couldn't get back. I figured someone would stop and pick you up."

"Someone did, eventually. But you didn't tell Adam where I was?"

"He told me," said Adam sharply, "that you wanted some time to yourself."

"Well, I got plenty of that." She came all the way into the room.

It was a story for later, what had happened to her and her improbable rescue; she'd tell Adam in the car when they drove back to Marika's cottage tonight. Tomorrow she would begin calling clients to cancel appointments for the rest of the week. There were other calls to make, arrangements and decisions. But for now she said only, "It seems like Grootie is being well cared for and that the doctors think she's probably all right.

"I brought her purse, by the way," she added, setting it on the floor by the bed, where limp balls of Kleenex were scattered like clumps of melting snow. "Have you had any dinner?"

Adam held up a Snickers bar wrapper. Dennis had also bought them both sodas and some pretzels from the vending machines.

At the mention of dinner, Marika opened her eyes. Against the white pillows her skin had a sallow, varnished tinge, like a portrait by a Dutch master. She looked at Lorna and frowned deeply for several moments.

Finally, with an effort, she said, "You're wearing my sweater."

Lorna looked down at herself. "Yes, I guess I am."

"It needs a wash," said Marika, and closed her eyes again.

39

When Dennis had gone, promising to come back in the morning, Lorna straightened the blanket on the hospital bed, and cleared away plastic cups and pretzel crumbs on the tray table. She switched off the overhead light and then adjusted the window blinds, opening them farther instead of pulling them closed.

"Look at that moon," she said, before sitting down on the end of the bed.

Adam was glaring at her, though even he would have to admit the room was more restful now, lit only by a fluorescent emanation from the half-open door, and by the glowing monitor on the wall, recording Marika's heart rate. A phone began ringing at the nurses' station. Out in the corridor were unhurried footsteps and the squeak of rubber soles. From her many visits to hospitals over the years, Lorna recognized the feeling of being in a world where night and day functioned more or less the same. Hospitals are like casinos, she remembered Roger once saying. No one ever gets enough sleep and it's always too cold.

The monitor's greenish screen continued to record the electrical signals pulsing from Marika's heart. Adam had closed his eyes and now looked to be dozing.

Marika reached for a tissue from the box by the bed; she was raising it to her nose when Lorna leaned toward her.

"I want you to know," Lorna said quietly, "that I don't have to understand what you did. But if you do ever want to talk about it, I'm ready to listen."

The old woman stopped wiping her nose and gazed back at her blankly.

"Mom." Adam made a restive movement in his chair.

"That's it." Lorna held up both hands, sitting back. "That's all I have to say."

Marika shut her eyes, clutching the tissue in her hand. Once more they all lapsed into silence, broken only by footsteps and mechanical summonses, bells, beeps, from the recesses of the hospital. Outside the window the moon was as white and round as a gaming chip.

ADAM INSISTED that he was going to spend the night at the hospital. When Lorna tried to argue that they should return to the cottage, that Marika would be fine tonight in the hospital with the nurses to look after her, that it would be best for her to be alone, to get some sleep, he said only "No."

They were standing in the long corridor between the elevator and the nurses' station, currently unmanned. The corridor was painted half beige, half green; the linoleum floor was also beige and green, in alternating squares; outside one of the patients' rooms was an oxygen tank on wheels. Otherwise the corridor was empty. Earlier Lorna had gone out to speak with one of the nurses, who assured her that Marika's condition was stable, her blood pressure had returned to normal, and that her heart rate looked fine. But when she repeated this information to Adam, he crossed his arms and gave her a stony stare.

"What is it you think you can do by staying here?" she asked finally.

"Keep her company."

"Keep her company?" Lorna echoed. "There are nurses right here." But seeing that he was determined, she changed course. "Okay, fine. Then I'll stay, too."

Adam snorted. "Not after you like basically told her to die."

"What?" Lorna was so surprised that she dropped her shoulder bag. She bent down to pick it up. "When did I do that?"

"Just now. You said you forgave her."

"I did not." Lorna returned the bag's strap to her shoulder. "I told her I was ready to listen if she wanted to talk."

"Same thing," he said stubbornly.

"It is *not* the same thing," she retorted and immediately regretted it. His stony look turned belligerent.

"Anyway, even if I *had* said I forgave her," she went on more carefully, focusing for a moment on the oxygen tank, "what would be wrong with that?"

"You tell people in the hospital you forgive them," Adam said icily, "when you think they're about to die."

"Well, I don't think she's about to die, first of all." Lorna wished she could smile at him, but knew that would be another a misstep. "Second, people forgive each other in all sorts of ways. And third," she added, "if I want to forgive her, when and how I do it is my business."

Adam shrugged and then pointed out that there was only one chair in the room, and cited a hospital rule, probably fictitious, that permitted only a single overnight visitor per patient. Lorna was not sure why he was so opposed to having her stay the night at the hospital, or why he was so resolved to stay there himself. Marika's vital signs were good and he'd be much more comfortable on the sofa at the cottage. But clearly he felt it was necessary. He believed that his grandmother needed his protection, including, apparently, from Lorna. He probably wouldn't feel the same way tomorrow, but tonight he felt he should stand guard.

For years she'd been telling him to think about other people. And now what she had hoped for was actually happening. Adam was thinking about someone else, and what's more, someone who was not easy to find sympathetic. She understood he was probably using his grandmother as a way to accuse Lorna of not seeming sympathetic enough herself. To punish her for coaxing him away from his bedroom and his videos to come to Vermont. To rebuke her for not solving his problems, even while refusing to tell her what they were. He needed to separate. He needed to grow up. Shutting her out, making her a villain, was one way to do it.

Lorna understood all this. But in that long empty corridor, made ghastly by fluorescence, her mouth had gone dry.

"Can I at least get you something from the cafeteria?" she asked.

After a hostile pause, he said he would eat a ham sandwich.

"What about being vegan?"

"Egg salad," he said, in an injured tone, "is the only other kind they have right now. Dennis asked the nurse."

"Well, that's sort of vegetarian."

"Do you even *know* me?" he said. "I hate egg salad."

"All right." Now she did allow herself to smile, relieved to hear him sound so much like his old self. She turned toward the elevators. "Anything else?"

"I'm not going home."

"Not going home?" she repeated, turning around again.

"I'm staying with Grootie." He had his eyes on the green and beige linoleum floor tiles, where he was standing as still as a chessboard piece. "I'm not going home," he said. "I'm not going back to school. I told her I would stay up here and take care of her."

From the direction of the elevators, a bell chimed.

"Adam," Lorna struggled to say, feeling as if she had taken a hit of pure oxygen. "That makes no sense."

"Maybe not to *you*."

Fighting a swell of panic, Lorna tried to think clearly. On Friday Adam had been a boy at home in bed with his laptop, watching people bake cupcakes and eating Cheerios from a bowl balanced between his knees. A kid who couldn't be counted on to take the dog for a walk. Three days later, he was standing in a hospital corridor volunteering to take care of a frail, bad-tempered old woman he hardly knew, in the northern woods, with no Wi-Fi, in a house that was little more than a shack. It really didn't make sense. Things change, but they don't change that quickly.

"Adam," she said, her heart pounding. "What are you doing?"

"What someone has to do." He lifted one shoulder in an imitation of recklessness, looking instead as if he were ducking something being thrown at him. "And *obviously*," he added with desperate malice, "it's not going to be you."

"Listen to me," she said, "listen."

"She *told* me what you said," his voice was rising. "She told me about your arrangements. How you said you're leaving. So you should just, like, *leave*."

"Adam," Lorna tried to keep her own voice low. "Please, calm down."

"Don't tell me to calm down," he snapped, starting to shake.

"Sorry. I'm just trying to understand. I just want you to explain a little more clearly what's going on here."

"Explanations," he hissed violently, "don't matter."

She stared at him. "Who told you that? Of course they matter."

"No, what you *do* matters. You said it yourself. And I said I would stay." He looked like he was about to cry. "And I'm going to."

"All right. I hear you. I understand what you're saying. But do you honestly think," Lorna continued, gripping the strap of her shoulder bag, "that you could ever do enough for someone like that?"

A short, pale nurse had emerged from a room and was walking down the corridor, her rubber clogs squeaking. Now she stopped just behind Adam.

"Everything all right here?" Her steel-rimmed spectacles made her gaze seem penetrating as she turned her attention to Lorna. "Can I help with anything, hon?"

"No, thank you." Lorna smiled faintly. "We're okay. But thanks."

For a moment, the nurse continued to examine them both. Then, apparently deciding that whatever was wrong with them was beyond her abilities to remedy, she nodded and walked on, her footsteps squeaking more and more faintly as she disappeared down the corridor. A monitor began bleating from a nearby room.

Lorna was aware that Adam had been watching her intently during this exchange, to see how deeply he had wounded her, to see how she would respond. Now he clamped his arms tighter across his chest, his face clenched into a sneer. Under the harsh light of the corridor, the sores on his forehead and chin seemed to grow more inflamed. She knew he wanted to be rescued from what he'd just said. She knew he was terrified. At the same time, she knew that he would not back down. He couldn't back down. Not now, not if his very life depended on it. To argue with him further would be a grave mistake. He would only cling more obstinately to the notion that he was behaving like a hero. He *was* behaving like a hero. On that chessboard of linoleum squares, he looked like a young knight, declaring his intention to slay a dragon or die trying.

You're in charge of your own behavior, Lorna had told him in the car on their way to Vermont, when it seemed impossible he would believe her. But now it appeared he had. After weeks of miserable indolence, he was taking charge. He was going to sacrifice himself for someone old and weak, thereby rectifying some dishonor he'd brought on himself, or thought he had. He had made his promise.

And yet, at this very moment, in that too-bright corridor, he must also be realizing that his pledge to his grandmother had little to do with nobility. He had been seduced.

Lorna recalled Marika's coy look when she said she'd always had a way "with the boys." Details from the last few days floated before her: Marika and Adam speaking French; Marika asking Adam to do chores. Then last night Marika had fainted, had needed to be bathed, dressed, revived with tea. (*Took care of me better than any doctor, I'll tell you that.*) Afterward she had gotten Adam to confess whatever it was he'd been hiding all this time. He had made her breakfast. This afternoon she had complained to him about Lorna, had needed to be consoled. And then Marika's final attack, the coup de grâce: rescued from the brink of death. It was the law of empathy, when you take care of someone they come to matter to you.

But this was the same woman who had never taken care of anyone herself. Who by her own admission had not thought about what became of the children she abandoned. Never wrote or called or tried to come see them. Her son had died without ever hearing a word from her. And now she was willing to eat *this* boy alive, her own grandson, to keep him caged in that primitive cottage, taking care of her until she died, which could be ten years from now, given the steady pattern of peaks and valleys displayed on that heart monitor. It was grotesque. It was absurd. It was a fairy tale come to life with the moral upended, as always happens with fairy tales when someone tries to live by them.

Aloud Lorna said, "You have no idea what's going on."

"Neither do you," Adam said, the blood leaving his lips.

Everything faded: the humming lights in the corridor, the beeping monitor, the phone ringing again at the nurses' station, and from within that gray hush, which seemed like a cessation of all the noise in the world, Lorna heard herself say, "Maybe not exactly, but I have a pretty good idea."

She moved closer to Adam, though she did not try to touch him. "You can stay with your grandmother tonight," she said firmly, "but I am not leaving you up here. This is not your problem to solve. You have done enough. I'll figure out how to get her what she needs. I promise."

Adam looked appalled at his own relief. He pretended to scowl, but she could see a wave of gratitude sweep over him mixed with exhaustion, and probably a distinct but inadmissible feeling of absolution.

"Whatever," he muttered, and shivered, shoving his hands into his shorts pockets.

"Here," she said, shrugging off the brown cardigan she was wearing. "Take this. It's freezing in this place."

She stepped back and stood regarding the shivering boy before her as he clutched the cardigan around his bony shoulders. So many mistakes stretched before him. He would fail tests. He would be careless and brutal by accident. He would stupidly hurt himself. But Dennis was right: he would also be fine. He wanted to be brave. He wanted to behave well, to help other people. Sometimes he would fail, or be short-sighted, but he would try to correct his mistakes when he could. And when he really needed help, if it was offered he would accept it. Would it be enough? It would have to be enough. There was no other way.

"I know it doesn't matter what I think," she said, her heart full of aching. "But I love you and I think you will do great things with your life. As embarrassing as it might be to hear that from me."

She saw him try not to smile. "It's no big deal," he said.

40

The cafeteria was closed. By the time Lorna returned with two more bags of pretzels from the vending machines on the first floor, Adam was asleep in the chair by his grandmother's bed, mouth ajar, the brown cardigan draped across his chest. Marika was also asleep, nose pointed toward the ceiling, mouth sternly set.

Lorna laid the pretzels on the tray table by the bed and then stood in the doorway, watching the two sleepers. Here they were, her mother and her son, her nearest relatives in the world, together in this small room where they would stay all night, wrapped in their separate mysteriousness. She would have liked to whisper something, some kind of benediction. But nothing came to her except *Take care*, and finally she closed the door.

Outside in the parking lot, she took her cell phone from her purse as she walked to the car. No messages, nothing from Roger, and the battery was nearly dead. She'd charged her phone at the cottage only long enough to get her voicemail, call all the area hospitals until she located the right one, and use Google Maps. Then, unthinkingly, she'd given her charger to Adam so that he could use his phone. There might be just enough battery to get her onto the highway.

Knowing that she'd mostly have to find her way back on her own put her in an oddly positive mood. Unlike all the other challenges of the last few days, this one was purely practical, and she felt somehow ready for it, like a Girl Guide who had learned to navigate by the stars and would now have to prove herself. She was in the North Country, she knew that much. All she had to do was head west toward the lake. Even in the dark she could stay oriented if she read the signs, and paid close attention to landmarks and geography. Just as she'd found Marika's dock that evening by studying the shoreline and counting flagpoles.

Above were the moon and the open night sky. Somewhere in the distance lay the vastness of the rest of the continent, Canada, the Yukon and the Northwest Territories, all the way to the Arctic Circle.

In the car she turned on the ignition, her thoughts once more with Adam, preparing to spend the night in a chair in that chilly hospital room, keeping watch over his grandmother. Then she wondered where Roger was right now, and what he would tell her when they spoke again.

How are you feeling? he'd asked, this man who didn't like to talk about feelings, who considered unhappiness a phase. Who had once said that childhood was not worth talking about because it was pre-rational. *How are you feeling?* There had been that note of self-conscious apology, which usually indicates some sort of revelation.

Lorna had figured it would be about Angelica: that they might be getting married, or they might be breaking up. But now as she replayed Roger's question, she detected something more tentative, something that may well have to do with Angelica but also went beyond her. Was it possible Roger was asking for advice? As in: How do you go about it, this feeling business. How is it managed?

Proceed slowly. That was the only advice she had for him. Or for herself. So much had happened recently that she'd barely sorted through any of it, and the days ahead would be just as unpredictable and difficult. Yet, sitting in her car in a mostly empty parking lot on a clear starry night, it also seemed to her that she was living in a period of great innocence, as before wartime, and that not long from now she would look back in amazement at how easy her life had been.

Driving along dark roads back toward the lake, Lorna fell to thinking once more of where she had been born. Of the old house surrounded by pastures and old stone walls, its small, low-ceilinged rooms, the cane chairs on the veranda, the warm gloom of the stables, the spring-fed pool under the cedars with its tea-colored water. Down in the creek, where they often went wading, Wade once found a brass button embedded in the mud banks. He'd pried it out and washed off the mud, and told her about Gatling guns firing and horses screaming as they fell to their knees, seen in a filmed reenactment on a school trip to the Manassas Battlefield. For months one winter, soldiers from both sides had camped on those pastures, divided by the creek. Sleeping, eating, cleaning their guns. Fitting brass buttons through stiff buttonholes, never guessing that a hundred years later one of those buttons would find its way into a boy's pocket.

All of that had shaped her, whether she knew about it or not. She should have asked more questions of her father and grandmother. She should have asked about her grandmother's great-aunt, who had turned her back on Lincoln as he rode by on his white horse, and about who was buried under those unmarked slates in the family graveyard. She should have asked about her father's weeks in the Ardennes, where he had lost more than his hearing, and what he had seen as he marched across Europe. But by the time she'd thought to ask them questions, her father and grandmother were gone, and even if she had asked, they might not have answered.

Water under the bridge, her grandmother might have said.

LORNA HAD FORGOTTEN to leave a light on for herself. As she pulled into the driveway, she could just make out the roofline of Marika's cottage, and behind it the lake, where the moon cast a lit path across the water. Inside the kitchen Freddy was waiting, his tail a plumy metronome. She let him out into the driveway for a few minutes before calling him back inside. It was too late to go back to the motel, and she didn't want to leave him alone again. The sofa had done for Adam and would do for her.

On the counter by the stove sat the bottle of cognac she'd brought, almost empty. She took a glass from one of the cabinets, poured what was left of the cognac into it, and carried the glass into the living room, where she switched on the lamp by the armchair.

Immediately the lamp began flickering. Nothing else moved in the room, and yet in the unreliable light, she thought she saw a small shadow crouched in the corner by the woodstove. She did not feel frightened. Whatever this presence was, it seemed somehow familiar, as if it had been waiting a long time for her to admit that it was there. When she turned fully toward it, the shadow was gone. She switched off the lamp and waited a moment in the darkness, as if to invite it back, and then turned on the light above the picnic table.

"There you are," she said to Freddy, who had come to stand beside her.

Carrying her glass, she walked slowly around the living room, looking closely at first one thing then another, objects that over the years had become Marika's nearest companions. The lamp, the woodstove, the yellowed map of the lake thumbtacked to the wall. She stopped by the armchair and then, hesitantly, turned over the cushion.

From the doorway of Marika's bedroom, she confronted the threadbare coverlet and the laundry hamper with its biscuity smell. Freddy had followed her and now stood in the hallway.

"You want to know what am I doing?" she asked.

He wagged his tail uncertainly.

"Snooping," she told him. "That's what I'm doing."

The top dresser drawer was full of underwear and white socks. The next held a few folded knit shirts and turtlenecks; in the third were several faded cotton nightgowns. But toward the back of that drawer, Lorna discovered an old metal Band-Aid box containing a gold wedding ring and two snapshots of Adam, one as a toddler, speaking into a toy telephone, and one from his high school graduation, wearing a jacket and tie. At the very back of that drawer, wrapped in a dish towel, were stashed three or four doughnuts, already quite stale. Saved, apparently, for after Lorna and Adam had left.

As she was pulling out the doughnuts, she felt something underneath them. At first she thought it was just a sheet of liner paper. It wasn't until she had pulled it out that she saw she was holding a stiff manila envelope. Inside was a letter, folded in thirds.

It was handwritten, in a large confident feminine hand on a sheet of onionskin. Lorna sat down on the bed to examine it. The paper was not particularly yellowed—not as yellow as the map on the wall, for instance—and the ink had not faded, so it must have been kept in that manila envelope, out of the light; the creases at the folds were sharp, suggesting the letter had been unfolded only once or twice, before now. She got up again to search the rest of the drawer and then carefully searched the other three drawers, and the fourth she had not opened, but found no other sheet of paper.

In memoirs, people were always discovering boxes left in an attic or at the back of a closet that revealed family secrets: boxes full of old journals and letters, passports with surprising stamps, photographs, newspaper clippings. Even after staring at the letter for several minutes she couldn't escape feeling that it was not real, but a trick, something that had been planted for her to find, knowing that this was just the sort of discovery she would have hoped for.

She recognized that the letter was in Dutch, and she could tell that there must have been at least another page, since the last line at the bottom seemed to break off mid-sentence. Why had Marika kept only the first page?

15 juni, 1968

Beste Rika,

Ik heb de afgelopen twintig jaar zo vaak geprobeerd contact met je op te nemen en deze brief te verzenden met weinig hoop op een antwoord. Jouw adres is aan mij verstrekt door een particulier onderzoeksbureau dat ik heb ingeschakeld. Ik wil je geen pijn doen, gewoon om erachter te komen wat er van je geworden is. Ik begrijp wat je

Who had called her Rika? A nickname. Something you would call a child. Of all the things Marika might have saved along with her wedding ring and those snapshots of Adam, why this one sheet of a letter in Dutch?

Wade ran across her mind, holding an envelope.

Lorna looked up at the pine walls. A letter in code, that's what he said he had found. A letter in code had been the reason why Marika had beaten him in the cellar. Was it possible this sheet of paper was from that envelope? She could not recall what became of the envelope that night, or its contents. The timing of that terrible scene and Marika's departure, a week or so afterward, could not have been a coincidence. But there was no one now but Marika to ask, and she would not remember, or would not say.

Lorna sat down once more on the bed, looking more closely at the letter. *Beste,* probably meant "dear." She recognized a few other words: *contact*, *adres*, *bureau*. *Je*, as in French, might mean "I." If she could use her phone it would take no more than a few minutes to scan the letter and translate it. But her phone was useless until tomorrow when she drove back to the hospital and recharged it.

She continued to examine the sentences in front of her, trying to puzzle some meaning from them. It seemed that someone had wanted to contact Marika, had found an address for her, through a *bureau*, perhaps an investigative office. Someone who knew her as

Rika. Relative? Old friend? Had Marika held on to part of the letter as a memento, or as a warning? Either way, it would have been a reminder that someone was looking for her.

Who would have wanted to find Marika as late as June 1968?

Lorna stood up and replaced the letter in the dresser's third drawer, telling herself she would translate it tomorrow, once she could charge up her phone. Tomorrow, I'll figure this out. But now it's late. I'm tired. My head hurts. I need to make up the sofa and get some sleep.

She carried the doughnuts to the kitchen and, after hesitating at the garbage can, put them in the refrigerator. But instead of getting ready for bed, she drank some of her cognac and began opening drawers and cabinets, pushing back cans and looking again into the dark jumbled recess under the sink. She slid her hand into the pockets of a yellow rain slicker hanging on a hook by the door and moved the umbrella also hanging there. Figures seemed to gather outside the room as she searched, pressing against the window, as real and insubstantial as the mist that had enveloped her on the lake.

The letter, the armchair facing a picture window. Clues, Wade would have said. Somehow they revealed the workings of Marika's mind, and why she had left her children without saying goodbye. Why she had fled across the country, had not wanted to see them, had tried to distract herself with a series of men, and why eventually she exiled herself to this little house, as if she'd no other choice. It couldn't be guilt alone that did such a thing to a person. Guilt carried at least the hope of making amends.

Lorna leaned against the refrigerator, feeling its quiet electric current.

Marika had done something. Something shameful, added to the shame of surviving when the rest of her family had not. She would have been hardly more than a child when it happened. She was only eighteen or nineteen when she left Europe; her crime, if that's what it was, would have been committed earlier. A teenage girl who had done something shameful. Or had something done to her, but was convinced it was all her fault, and now her life was over. Not so different from girls Lorna sometimes saw in her office, brought in by anxious, bewildered parents. *She won't talk to us. She won't say what's wrong.*

Like any teenager in the grip of self-loathing, Marika would have made vows: I will never speak of it. I will never tell. I will never want anything, care about anything, if only *this* can remain a secret. Usually with time shame grows less vivid. Someone is told, the offense fades, becomes something unfortunate, deplorable; yet not ruinous.

But if no one was ever told—

It was not uncommon, with traumatic episodes, for the brain to flicker out, like an overloaded electrical circuit. Lorna had seen it with men at the VA. Sometimes they'd done things they could not remember. Even when questioned in detail later, nothing came back. They did not deny they had done those things, once confronted with evidence, they simply could not remember doing them. But with Marika it seemed different. Whatever she believed she'd done was not gone; it had stayed with her, locked into a shut place her mind. How else to explain why she had never wanted anyone to understand her? How can you talk about something you're keeping concealed from yourself?

She might, with time and patient encouragement, eventually have confided in her husband or his mother. They were well-meaning people, and proximity sometimes breaks down resistance; but one could not hear and the other couldn't listen. And so, in her aloneness, she stopped talking.

Lorna took her hand from the refrigerator and looked at the kitchen's closed cabinets, their black latches.

Marika had indeed been a spy, Wade was right. A spy by virtue of whatever secrets she carried. Sitting at her window, day after day, scanning the horizon, watching and listening in on a world she could not join. A spy with no passport, at home nowhere, with no past she could lay claim to, or future to count on.

In the living room Freddy settled heavily onto the rug with a sigh. Lorna walked around the room again, pausing to look at the box of safety matches on a shelf above the woodstove, the picnic table, the brown sofa where Adam had slept for the last two nights. She thought of the incomplete letter she had just tried to read, and the writer's desire for whatever *contact*, *adres* might bring.

At last she stopped to stare at the old map tacked by the kitchen door. There were many dots that could have been the island where she'd spent so much of the day; on closer inspection some were not even islands, but flyspecks. She thought of a photograph of a map of Amsterdam in a booklet Adam brought home after his class visited the Holocaust Museum in Washington, showing where Jews had been concentrated. Each dot on the map stood for ten.

Over a hundred and twenty thousand people were deported from Amsterdam during the Occupation. This fact had also been in the booklet. Eighty percent of the Jewish population, the highest percentage of anywhere in Western Europe. People had stood in lines at the railroad station, holding suitcases and the hands of their children, wearing in many cases their best shoes. Waiting to board crowded trains under a watery sky that has been captured so luminously in landscapes by the Dutch School, where often the sky is greater than anything else in the painting, to give an impression of infinite space.

Most never came back. Some vanished without being deported, according to the booklet, along with Dutch people who had tried to help them, buried in the dunes of The Hague, where German bunkers had lined the beaches. As far as Lorna knew, Marika had never tried to find her father and sister. Perhaps she had tried and failed, another of the many things she never said. But during those Thanksgiving visits over the years, Lorna had noticed in her a childlike fatalism toward things she mislaid. As soon as Marika couldn't find something—her purse, her sunglasses, the car keys—she was convinced it was lost, and gone for good.

Was it possible that Marika's sister had written that letter? That she had not died after being arrested, as Lorna had always assumed, but survived the war and then began hunting for Marika? And eventually found her—her *Beste Rika*—after more than twenty years of searching. Could being discovered in June of 1968 be the reason Marika had fled for Los Angeles a few weeks later? If so, whatever her sister knew about her (if her sister wrote that letter) must have been something Marika could not face.

Freddy lay on the floor, twitching his eyebrows from side to side as Lorna resumed walking around the room, holding the glass of cognac. Knowing something is not the same as understanding it—she often said this to clients. But perhaps the opposite could also be true. Perhaps you could understand something without knowing what had happened. Though why try? Why not leave it alone, as Marika would prefer, fold the page back in its envelope, slip the envelope back in the drawer. Because whatever was in that letter had shaped Lorna, too, whether any of it was ever explained, as it probably would not be. Lorna thought of Adam in the hospital corridor that evening, shaking as he said that explanations didn't matter. Of course they do, she had said. Meaning, how could anyone learn anything without them? But now she found herself unsure.

Did she need an explanation for that heroic girl, for instance, cycling across Amsterdam, whom Marika had once conjured for her and whom Lorna in turn had conjured for Adam, a girl she'd spent years conjuring for herself. A girl in an alley doorway. A girl on a narrow back staircase, leading a child by the hand. A girl facing down soldiers and a pistol.

A better girl than any she could really have been.

Given in compensation, for company, after Marika herself was gone. Something to stash at the back of a drawer, for lonely afternoons. Because company, all these years, was what that girl had been. A slight figure in a gray convent skirt, cycling through a darkened city. Lorna had had that girl for comfort, for guidance, and in the end it probably didn't matter whether she had been real or not.

However, the question remained why that girl had been necessary.

It was late. Lorna had hardly slept in three days. Her head ached. Still she kept walking. Past the map of the lake, past the picnic table. Past the dark picture window, which held her own pale reflection. At last she stopped in front of the woodstove.

A Vermont Castings iron stove, squat and black, with a stovepipe that ran up through the ceiling and a square black door with a handle like a latch. The door opened with a rusty complaint. Inside, mixed with ashes, was a small heap of bones.

41

A grayness had come into the sky above the hospital parking lot, the beginning of brightening. Morning. Or almost morning.

Adam lay on the reclining chair by his grandmother's bed, covered by the itchy brown sweater his mother had given him. He'd hardly slept all night, and when he had nodded off, he woke almost instantly, feeling there was something he should be doing. His grandmother, however, had stayed deeply asleep; she was still sleeping, breathing regularly. The monitor behind the bed showed regular, steady cardiac activity. Greenish lines jigged up and down, like a secret musical score.

It was almost embarrassing, he thought, being able to watch her heart working this way. Seeing what no one should ever see, eavesdropping right into the heart of another person, where those four beating chambers produced their own private rhythm. A rhythm that one day, maybe with no warning, would simply stop. And then, what? Really nothing? Unbidden, an image rose before him, glimpsed once before, the ancient bridge surfacing beneath black waters, connecting everything to everything.

He shifted in the chair. His arms and legs ached and he felt a kink in his neck, as if someone had hugged him too hard. Who had kissed him on the mouth That Night? He wondered if it would be possible to find her.

The monitor continued its recordings. For now, the old girl was holding on. Soon his mother would arrive, probably with something to eat. Dennis would come back. The cardiologist would stop by this morning and explain the shadow. It would all be okay.

Adam looked at his phone, which he'd finally been able to charge. At first he was pleased to be reunited with it, with YouTube and Instagram, especially. Yet when he woke in the night and turned on his phone, his thoughts had often drifted from the images sliding across the screen, mostly to unimportant things. His application to Wegmans was still sitting on his desk at home. He'd forgotten to return a library book. Email must be accumulating in his school account, left unchecked for weeks: end-of-semester announcements, his grades, reminders about course registration, advertisements, campus club invitations, requests for money from candidates and Green groups.

He'd spent some time looking at the news on BuzzFeed, amazed that all this time the world had been producing it. Most of it bad, and getting worse, but a few inspiring stories were in there, as well: stolen artwork recovered; a baby fallen down a well saved by a human chain; new ways to purify water; breakthrough medications.

It's not all dark clouds out there, his father often said when he spoke to foundations to solicit grants for his lab. *We're making some remarkable progress.*

Sometime today or tomorrow he would call his father. Just to tell him what had been going on, up here in Vermont. Hey, his father would say. Good to hear from you, buddy. So what's happening?

Oh not much. Just, you know, helping out.

Then he'd tell him about Grootie's heart attack, probably brought on by dehydration, and the tests she'd been given at the hospital, for which they did not yet have all the results. How he'd stayed the night because there weren't enough nurses. He would describe the way two nights before he, Adam, had cared for her alone, in a storm, when she'd collapsed in the bathroom. That sound she'd made as she hit the floor, and how he felt he'd known what to do. How he'd even had to give her a shower. No way, his father would say. Yeah, I had to. A tricky operation, but we both survived. Good job, son. Not sure I could have managed that one.

And maybe he would even mention, as a joke, that weirdly confident-sounding voice he'd assumed as he tended to his grandmother, which had sounded deeper than his own voice. But that was, actually, his own voice.

42

The grayness outside was lightening. Lorna stood up from the sofa to see better what was happening. Outside the window the light was changing so quickly. Magenta, then lavender, and then the lake was dark gray streaked with pearl. Now the trees on the island opposite had begun to turn blue.

She'd been awake for hours. Already she'd washed her face, brushed her teeth, and then let Freddy out into the driveway, fed him, and refilled his water bowl. She had made coffee and eaten an apple. But before she'd done any of those things, she'd gathered the chicken bones from the woodstove into a pan, carried them down the dark stone steps to the end of the dock, and thrown them into the lake. She knew they were for bonemeal, ash. Fertilizer for that stone tub of lavender. But they were also bones.

She brought a second cup of coffee into the living room and sat down in Marika's chair at the window to watch the brightening sky reflected in the lake. Soon she would telephone the hospital from the phone in the kitchen, to talk to Adam and hear how Marika had fared last night. She would tell him about the letter she'd found, perhaps bring it to the hospital, and they'd scan it and translate it together. Or maybe not.

Maybe better to wait till things had settled down. She hadn't decided. In any case, as soon as she had recharged her phone, she would make calls to various agencies. A consultation with Dennis about practical matters: for instance, installing a dishwasher in the cottage, a dryer, to make things easier for now. Possibly a call to Avalon Towers at home, to see about their waiting list. Calls to clients, to cancel appointments. A call also to Roger, a message left on his voicemail, if he didn't answer.

Sometime, this afternoon or tomorrow, they would talk. Lorna wanted to get his opinion on what kind of follow-up care Marika might need. And he would tell her whatever he needed to tell her. Maybe she'd guessed correctly: he and Angelica had decided to get married. Or Angelica was pregnant. Angelica was a young woman, but not that young. Not unlikely that she'd want a child. Lorna closed her eyes and listened to the water slip against the rocks below. The sound of things going on.

It had not broken her heart when Roger left. But she had loved him. She loved their son. During the years they had all lived together, she'd thought and wondered about them every day, driving home from her office, guessing what they might like for dinner, trying to remember what they needed from the grocery, ready to listen to their worries and hopes and complaints, kissing them good night and again in the morning before they all went off for the day. Even after Roger had left for Seattle, she continued to think about him, and wonder how he was doing, just as she thought about Adam while he was away at school. For years now she had been wondering about them. They were always on her mind whether they were with her or not, and those years of thinking and wondering about them had worn within her the deep habit of care.

People love how they can.

It was almost time to call the hospital, but for a little while longer, she wanted to sit with her second cup of coffee, watching the sky turn pink and purple over the lake, the lightening trees. Facing the window and Marika's view, she felt that Marika herself was very close. Though it was not an old woman's presence she felt, but that of a younger one, just barely recalled from childhood. Fingers strong and deft as they brushed and braided her hair, a large warm hand resting on her shoulder. The sensation of leaning against a wide soft chest.

When Lorna's father was dying in a Richmond hospital, and slipping in and out of consciousness, he would sometimes shout out panicky, incoherent phrases. One of the nurses had asked if he was religious. When Lorna said no, the nurse had said, that's a pity. Easier on the ones who know where they're going.

It must have been for this reason, she guessed now, that Wade had wanted her to visit him, so that she could describe the farm that night in San Francisco. If you don't know where you're going, you go back to where you began. But Wade had been away for a long time, and for a return like that he'd needed help. She wished she had described more to him. There was the old house, which you couldn't see from the road until you turned in at the gates and drove down the long driveway, pastures and white fences to either side, as far as the stables, where the driveway forked and the boxwoods began. And then the four chimneys above the cedars surrounding the house, the cedars a little ragged, a little secretive in the way they blocked the view. On spring afternoons the air smelled of grass and horses, and honeysuckle banked against the stone walls. In the distance were the Blue Ridge Mountains, where freshets ran down and fed into the creek, which ran to the Rappahannock, all the way to the Chesapeake Bay.

It was then, in the midst of this summoning, that a girl stepped into the room. Tall and slender, with clear blue eyes, and thick blond hair held back with bobby pins. She hesitated near the picnic table, like a visitor not yet arrived but already visible because she has been so long anticipated. Perhaps it was the picnic table itself that allowed for her, with its suggestion of guests and conditional gatherings.

A girl who had found her way alone across Europe. One of those children sent away during the war, one of the lucky ones, escaped into strange but mostly fortunate circumstances. No longer by the picnic table now, but at a railroad station, out in the country, on her way at last to rejoin her family. On the train, on a mild bright fall afternoon.

She sits by the window in the dining car, a cup of coffee on the white tablecloth in front of her. The people she's been with had wrapped up a parcel of rolls for her, a small pat of butter. She is dressed in a brown wool jacket and skirt, clumsily cut, but her hair has been carefully brushed and pinned behind her ears. She is fifteen, sixteen, with the luminous skin some girls have at that age, the ones who haven't yet tried out their powers, who are just coming into themselves.

Through the window beside her, she watches trees pass by, marshland, canals, a bright stretch of fields. Now a factory with a smokestack, warehouses, roads. The outskirts of a city. For a few minutes narrow streets flick by, and the backs of brick buildings, people's washing strung on lines hung between porch posts, their white underwear fluttering, their socks and shirts.

The rocking of the train is soothing. She sips her coffee. From the parcel, she takes a soft brown roll. She is pleased to have this roll and the pat of butter, pleased to have a cup of coffee, grateful for her seat on a train. She's not ready yet to think about her family, from whom she has so long been separated. For now she's content to look out the window and watch the fields spreading out, gulls reeling in the sky as late afternoon turns toward evening.

Fir trees. Then a river, widening. She is passing once more into the country, this girl who wasn't, but who might have been.

Lorna leaned closer to the window. Now the western half of the sky filled with gold and all that had just been brightening, trees, islands, grasses, birds flying across the water, darkened again under that radiance. In a few minutes, it would be over, the golden light, the dark interruptions, yet for now the lake held it all.

ACKNOWLEDGMENTS

I AM PROFOUNDLY GRATEFUL to the many friends who have listened to me talk about this novel as I worked on it, and whose lively attention and encouragement has meant so much to me. Some have read drafts, as well, and made invaluable comments and suggestions. I am forever indebted to Joan Wickersham, Maxine Rodburg, Phil Press, and Tracy Daugherty, and to Marjorie Sandor for her luminous friendship, and also to Juliet Annan, whose long support has been such a gift.

My editor, Marysue Rucci, read draft after draft of this novel, asked vital questions, offered critical insights and clarifications, and patiently waited for the story to emerge—I truly cannot thank her enough for such dedication. I would also like to thank Zachary Knoll, whose editorial advice was so helpful, Jiaming Tang, for his kind assistance, and Sonya Mead, for last-minute translations and for inviting me to Amsterdam so long ago. I am very grateful as well to my agent, Colleen Mohyde, who has seen me through every one of my books with humor and grace. Finally, thank you to my family for keeping me company always, especially my husband, Ken, who lived through every day of this story with me and insisted that he always found it interesting.

ABOUT THE AUTHOR

SUZANNE BERNE is the author of four previous novels, including *The Dogs of Littlefield* and *A Crime in the Neighborhood*, which won Great Britain's Orange Prize, now the Women's Prize for Fiction. She lives outside of Boston.